BLACK LIES

By
Alessandra Torre

Black Lies Copyright © 2014 by Alessandra Torre
All rights reserved.

No part of this book may be reproduced or transmitted in any form or by any means, electronic or mechanical, including photocopying, recording, or by information storage and retrieval system, without written permission of the Publisher, except where permitted by law.

This book is a work of fiction. Names, places, characters, and incidents are the product of the author's imagination or are used fictitiously. Any resemblance to events, locales, or persons living or dead, is coincidental.

ISBN-13: 978-1500847234
ISBN-10: 1500847232

Editing: Madison Seidler
Cover Image: Perrywinkle Photography Utah
Cover Design: SK Hartley
Interior Design: Bob Houston eBook Formatting

BLACK LIES

By
Alessandra Torre

This book is dedicated to:
Wendy Metz
SueBee ♦Bring me an Alpha!♦
Keelie Chatfield
Karen Lawson
Marion Archer

You have been with this book since it was half-done and frisky as hell. Thank you for the late night calls. The picking and pulling at these pages. Thank you for pointing out its weaknesses and obsessing over its strengths. This book would not be the same without you.

Prologue

I watched Molly's apartment, a Mediterranean-style orange townhome with window boxes full of hot pink hibiscus. His jeep sat there, a mud-spattered box of American masculinity in a sea of foreign cars. It'd been twenty-two minutes since he walked in, his hands dipped into jean pockets, his head down, steps walking without thought, as if he had walked the path a hundred times.

I tapped my nude nails against the gearshift. Closed my eyes briefly and let the air conditioner breeze wash over me. I had a massage scheduled in an hour, so this situation needed to resolve itself soon or I'd be late for my date with Roberta's hands.

Movement, upper right apartment. Hers. A door flew open, Lee's head moving quickly down the open hall, a blonde head close behind, tugging on his shirt, arms gesturing wildly. I could imagine the words flying out of her mouth. *Lee, don't go. Lee, it isn't what you think!* I wondered if the word 'love' left her mouth, if their relationship had progressed to that point.

He disappeared into the stairwell. I leaned forward, wished I had a drink, something to crack open and enjoy while my hard work came to fruition. This had to work; this had to happen. She couldn't have him; he was mine.

His head bobbed between the cars, his face coming into view as he walked up to his jeep. Face set, features hard, a look I hadn't seen on his face before but knew well. Resolute. Decisive. I clenched my hands in excitement, watching as her face came into view, blotchy and wide-eyed, her mouth moving rapidly, giant breasts heaving as she yelled something and grabbed at his shoulders. I wanted to roll my window down, just a peek, enough to hear this exchange, enough to savor this moment just a little bit longer.

That's right. Turn and walk your pretty self away from this man. He will no longer touch your face. He will no longer make love to your body. He is mine. I will take your place.

I watched him get in, the door slamming hard enough to make her jump. And then, with the screech of tires—the best sound in the world, better than my fantasies—a sound of finality that left her standing in the empty parking spot, black mascara tears staining her cheeks, her scream loud enough to pass through my tinted windows.

Victory is mine. I grinned, giving myself a virtual high five, and put my Mercedes into drive. Pulling onto the street, I headed south. Maybe after my massage I'd swing by my boyfriend's office. Drop off a sandwich for him. Celebrate my victory with the other man in my life.

Go ahead. Judge me. You have no idea what my love entails.
I love two men. I fuck two men.
If you think you've heard this story before, you haven't.

PART 1

This is a love story, but not one that is easy to read.

Chapter 1

My life has always had a plan. I think my parents, pre-conception, sat down and planned it out. Drilled into me with constant reminders and a follow-by-example regimen. I was a child of wealth, expected to do nothing but everything. A 4.0 was required, though I would never hold a job. Ivy League was mandatory, but only because that was where I would meet my husband. I would not carry any additional weight, as that would be an embarrassment, but could not show off my figure, as that would be classless.

The plan was simple. Earn a respectable degree while being molded into the perfect wife. Marry quickly. Support my husband while pursuing my other interests, such as charity work and running my home.

I never liked the plan. Foiled it in as many passive aggressive ways as possible. Learned at an early age to hide treachery behind a sweet smile and innocent façade. In my parents' eyes, I was behaving. Thriving. Turning into the woman their DNA deserved. In actuality, I was lying in wait, getting my perfect black ducks in a row and ready for the day that mattered: my twenty-fifth birthday.

***

8 YEARS AGO

Twenty-five candles. It was ridiculous that I was getting a birthday cake; the tradition should stop in the teenage years. Yet, here it was, carried by my mother's reedy arms. Mother, the perfect image of my future, should my future include Botox and fillers, pinched lips and over-plucked brows. I smiled because it was expected. I let her sing the song, my father's voice falling off after the first few words, his attention caught by the ring of his phone. I smiled for the photo and blew out the candles, missing three on purpose, seeing Mother's eyes flicker, her smile remaining fixed.

She cut the cake, the scent of Chanel No. 5 drifting over the table as she served me the smallest possible piece, a center cut, away from the decadence of an end piece. Then we ate, three of us scattered over a twelve-seat table, the scrape of silver against china the only sound in the room. Father stood first, leaving his plate, and kissed my head. "Happy birthday, sweetie."

Then there was only Mother and I, and the interrogation began.

"Are you dating anyone?" She set down her fork. Pushed her barely touched slice of cake forward and eyed mine pointedly.

"No." I smiled as I had been taught. Always smile. Smiles hid feelings.

"Why not? You're twenty-five. You only have a few good years left."

"I'm happy, Mother. I will find someone soon."

"I think you should reconsider Jeff Rochester. You dated him for almost two years." Four months. Four months that we spun into a two-year relationship to keep my parents appeased and his gay lifestyle a secret.

"I've heard that Jeff is seeing someone. And we really didn't have any chemistry." I took another bite of cake, enjoying the pain in her eyes when I swallowed it.

"Chemistry isn't important. He's from a good family—will provide for you."

My trust fund would provide for me. I didn't need a relationship without chemistry, a prison sentence that would paint a smile on my madness and lead me into an early case of depression and pharmaceutical drug use. But I didn't want to mention the trust. Not when I was an hour away from finishing this party and heading straight to the bank.

"Janice Wilkins told me she saw you working downtown. Please tell me that's not true."

I smiled. "I have a degree in quantitative science. It's not unreasonable for me to consider using it. I am doing consulting for a medical firm. Overseeing some FDA trials."

"Please don't. Work causes stress, which will prematurely age you. And you only have—"

"A few good years left." I finished her sentence, keeping my voice light. Took another bite of cake. Scraped every bit of icing off the plate and slid the fork into my mouth. Sucked on the tings. Killed a little of my mother's soul.

"We've worked so hard for you to have a good life."

"And I do. You've done a wonderful job, and I'm very happy."

"What about Ned Wimble? I heard he and that Avon heir ended things."

I set down my fork, squeezed my hands together underneath the table, and smiled.

I left my parents' house a few hours later, a bag of gifts in the trunk of my car. Cashmere cardigan. Sapphire earrings from my father. A JD Robb paperback from Becky, the maid who probably knew more about me than both of my parents combined. She was the one who cleaned up my puke in the bathroom when my drunken teenage self didn't make it through the night. She'd thrown away condoms, birth control packets, and vodka bottles. Held me at fifteen, when I suffered my first broken heart, courtesy of Mitch Brokeretch—who didn't deserve my virginity, much less my tears.

My real gift wasn't in the trunk. It was in the date, the trust paperwork that had been completed before my first birthday. Twelve million dollars waited for me in a joint account that I had watched from afar for over a decade. With that date, with the papers I was about to sign, I would be free from my parents, from their expectations and requirement that have held this money above my head for the last twenty years. I drove to the attorney's office, and, thirty minutes later, was a free woman. I allowed a small smile—a real one—upon my exit from Jackson & Scottsdale. Allowed a full beam once I visited the bank and transferred the funds into a money market account that was solely in my name.

Then, freedom. It felt damn good. I put down my convertible's top and screamed into the wind. Celebrated the evening with one of my building's valets—a twenty-one-year-old kid who only made it five pumps, but brought some good weed and laughed at my jokes.

It was a sad start to my new life.

Chapter 2

3 YEARS AGO

I spent my first two decades planning, holding out for the moment when I could desert this culture. Throw off my cardigan and manners and rush headfirst into life. Dance in the moonlight. Smoke a cigar. Ride a motorcycle and fall in love for a reason other than social standing. I had romantic notions of waiting tables, hitchhiking across America, kissing a strange boy, feeling a rush of unknown possibilities. I hated every stitch of my surroundings and craved escape. Wanted to leave the dinner parties, the ingrained disdain of others, and raised brows of judgment. I wanted the happily-ever-after of movies. Where my family would share their day while eating at a round table. Wanted to visit life in a world where mothers hugged daughters with bruises and consoled them after first dates went awry. My dream had legs, fully developed fantasies, my future as clear as my past. The day of my twenty-fifth birthday, I had felt free. Filled with hope and possibilities. The first day of the rest of my life.

    Yet, five years later, I was still stuck. I'd had a few wild nights. Fucked some strangers with calluses on their hands. Visited a 7-Eleven and bought a hot dog. Went to Tijuana long enough to realize I would never go back. Then ... like a migrating bird, I drifted home to this world. Settled back in without even realizing it. Five years later and I was still surrounded by the people from my youth. The friends who weren't friends. The parties in which everyone smiled but no one had fun. Where life was a constant race to one-up each other, and the prom queen was still the bitch no one liked but everyone flocked to like maggots to meat. I needed to escape this life, I needed to find something different, I needed to make my own path, but it was hard to escape the only world I had ever known.

The man appeared in the doorway behind me, his chauffeur hat in hand, and met my eyes in the mirror. "I'll be out front, whenever you are ready to leave for the event, Ms. Fairmont."

"Thank you. I'll be out shortly."

He nodded, turning to leave, my eyes returning to the mirror. Brown eyes lightly outlined in mint chocolate. Enough makeup to hide flaws, but no more. *Classy, not trashy.* My mother had trained me well. I stared into my eyes and tried to find the person in them. The mirror showed the woman I had been raised to be. Designer gown that was subtle yet sophisticated. A polished exterior, from my hair to my heels. I stared at my shell and wondered why I couldn't break from it. Tonight was the primary fundraising gala for an organization close to my heart. An important event that shouldn't be missed. Maybe tomorrow I could turn over a new leaf. Try again to leave the nest and live a genuine and happy life. I applied a coat of clear gloss over my lipstick and avoided my eyes in the mirror.

***

"Brant Sharp."

"Layana Fairmont."

"I like your hair."

"I'm not a prostitute."

His mouth didn't change, but his eyes warmed. "I can overlook that fact."

The five lines of our meeting, uttered two hours into the fundraising gala. Unromantic. I blamed my bold response on alcohol, two glasses of wine already downed, my self-loathing slightly pacified by merlot.

I accepted the hand he extended, shaking it firmly as I studied the man, his name instantly recognized as soon as it had floated off his gorgeous lips. I had—on some minor level—stalked this man ever since I got involved with the Homeless Youth of America.

Brant Sharp. Genius. Billionaire. Philanthropist.

He was even better looking than I imagined, the tiny thumbnail image used in press releases barely showing his features. Certainly not doing this man any justice, his looks worthy of a *GQ* cover. But his intensity, that was what really surprised me. He peered at me as if I was a problem, and he searched my soul for a solution. He also seemed inordinately pleased by my hair, his eyes frequently leaving mine to stare at their erratic strands.

I can overlook that fact. I laughed at the response, the sound one he seemed to enjoy, his own mouth twitching a bit. Not a smile, but close. For me, one for whom a smile meant masked emotion, it was a refreshing change.

"It's a pleasure to meet you. I'm a big fan of your work with HYA." Homeless Youth of America was the only holdover from my mother's painful rearing—a charity she pushed me into at a young age, one that ended up gripping my heart and not letting go.

Any hint of a smile dropped. "I wouldn't call it work. My office cuts a check. Nothing else is done."

"The funds mean a great deal." *Funds* was putting his contribution lightly. Last year I personally donated half a million dollars, six percent of the annual donations. His check covered ninety-two percent. It was enough to make him the honorary Chairman of the Board, though he'd never shown his face at the facility or the board meetings. We had heard, discussed freely over coffee and stale donuts, the rumors surrounding our chairman. Beth Horton, a sharp-tongued mother of seven, whose face carried a permanently dour expression, unless sharing an exciting piece of gossip, had brought up the escorts to me.

"There's been hundreds," she confided at last year's board meeting, wedging an entire powdered donut into her mouth as I watched closely, as interested at the prospect of her choking as I was the discussion of Sharp's sex life. "My driver's brother is a doorman at his downtown condo and said the girls show up all hours. Beautiful girls, but clearly prostitutes. He never leaves with them, and they only stay for a few hours." I nod, half-believing the words. It would explain why he'd never been photographed with a woman. The man appeared to not date, a fact that drove the women of San Francisco mad and had sparked occasional rumors of homosexuality. The rumors never went too far ... too many women who had met the man, worked for the man, dissuaded them. I liked the idea of prostitutes, of the man unleashing holy hell on a woman of the night in the privacy of his home.

The funds mean a great deal. He didn't respond to the comment, and it hung between us. I took a sip of champagne. "I'm surprised to see you here."

"Why is that?" The laser focus of this man was unnerving. When he stared at you, there was no wavering, no doubt that he would listen to your words and process them accordingly. I tried to relax, the pressure of an intelligent response high, the knowledge that I was in the presence of brilliance a heavy concept. I'd never been a woman to find intelligence sexy, four years in the nerd-fest that was Stanford curing any woman of that misconception. But this man ... maybe it wasn't his intelligence. Maybe it was the combination of that intelligence with confidence and intrigue, mixed in a martini glass of striking looks.

I shrugged. Took another sip of liquid courage. Wished for something stronger than champagne. Noticing that he had moved closer, I had the unnatural urge to lean into him and sniff. Test the waters by placing my hands on his tux's lapels and tugging. Would he hold the eye contact? Would he step back? Or would he drag me somewhere private and fuck me senseless? My reckless confidence of earlier wavered in the presence of this man.

I swallowed. Tried to bring my mind back to the conversation. "You've never come by the campus. Or attended a board meeting. I just assumed that the spring fundraiser would also be skipped."

"Thomas Yand is on the guest list. I'm hoping to speak with him. He's been avoiding my calls."

"Ahhh..." I stepped closer. Lowered my voice. "So this is an ambush."

"That was the plan. A conspirator would help." He playfully raised his eyebrows at me, and every feminine bone in my body came to attention.

Yeah, definitely not gay. I could understand why his female employees rushed to this man's defense. I'd spent two minutes in his presence and my body had had about nine spikes of arousal. I swallowed. Painted an offhand expression on my face. "What do you have in mind?"

***

He didn't need a conspirator. He was one of the wealthiest men in the world. As powerful as Bill Gates in terms of the tech community. But we played our roles well. Flirted over cheese trays and whispered over champagne. Celebrated with conspiratorial smiles when Yand was cornered—me on one side, Brant on the other. I let their conversation take off, then stepped away. Retreated to the other side of the room, where Anne Waters, a bleach-blonde with double D's, accosted me, licking crab cake off her fingers and diving into a long tale of her spring shopping in the city. I nodded politely while my mind wandered, my resolution to live a different life strengthened with every unladylike lick of her fingers. I snuck a glance at Brant, saw deep focus as he nodded at Yand.

Inside me, there was a flicker of want, a pull that surprised me. I had certainly expected to respect the man—it'd be impossible not to respect a man whose IQ level doubled mine, whose annual donations were the blood that kept half of the city's charities' hearts beating—but my expectations, had I ever envisioned meeting the reclusive man, were that I would dislike him.

Reason #1: He was impossibly wealthy, had lived that lifestyle since he was a teen, been waited on and fawned over every day of his adult life. It was a tried-and-tested recipe for an asshole.

Reason #2: He was impossibly intelligent. I would have expected the ego to match the brains, creating a pompous, arrogant nerd. One who expected submittal in the form of worship. One who'd spout off uninteresting facts while staring at my breasts.

What I didn't expect was everything that he was not. Quietly confident. Unassuming. Gorgeous. Intense interest that didn't play games.

He glanced away from Yand for a moment, his eyes pulling to mine, and everything stopped as our gazes held. His eyes broke contact, and I watched him extend a hand, perform a perfunctory shake and then move, dismissing Yand with a polite smile, his legs carrying him in my direction. Again, our eyes locked, and I wanted to look away but couldn't. Could only watch as he stalked across the room in smooth strides until he was before me, a smile entering his eyes as I tried my best not to swoon.

His presence halted the conversation. Realizing the silence, I glanced at Anne. "Excuse me, please," I murmured, taking advantage of the opportunity to flee. Brant pulled out my chair, nodding politely to my tablemates, whose watchful eyes followed every movement, a circle of vultures ready for their next meal. Together, his hand leading the way, we escaped toward the rear doors.

"Thank you for your help with Yand," he said softly, his head lowered slightly to me.

"Thank you for saving me from those women," I whispered back, smiling politely as I passed Nora Bishop, a woman I was fairly certain had spent most of the nineties on her back beneath my father.

It took twelve steps to reach the doors. Twelve steps during which I realized how much I wanted this man. I thought of the stories—the prostitutes—then the heat of his hand moved, from my back to my elbow, gentle but pressing. He controlled with courtesy. And I wanted more. Needed more. Then our bodies were outside and alone on the balcony, the warm summer night bringing a balmy breeze that smelled of ocean and summer. There, his hand left my elbow, and I was able to have a moment of clear thought.

I rested my elbows on the rough balcony ledge, the cut of concrete comforting against the finery of ridiculous wealth. All of this a show. We spent all year fundraising for children who would cry over the prospect of new sneakers, then shelled out a hundred thousand dollars on a party. I turned and looked back at the full-length windows that rose three stories and showcased the entire production in all of its false glory. Then I glanced at Brant, handsome elegance cased in tuxedo black, a picture that belonged to this world combined with a man I felt was above it. "Was it worth it?" I nodded at the party and glanced over at him, his profile strong, his eyes on the horizon, the flickering glow of exterior torches lighting the dramatic shadows of his face. "Dealing with these vultures for a chance at Yand?"

"It was worth it as soon as I saw you." Soft words. Dramatic impact.

I smiled, stepped up on the thin ledge, one that allowed me to lean over the balcony and put my face fully into the wind. "You don't know me Brant." *I don't even know myself.*

"No, I don't." He said the words mildly, as if the concept was unimportant.

I turned and watched him. Saw the calm set of his features. He was poised, undeterred. As if my attraction to him was unimportant, either due to confidence or because he didn't care if we ever saw each other again. The path of confidence was the option I preferred; the other was a problem. I was unaccustomed to denial, to losing, the thought of being discarded difficult to comprehend. I didn't know who I was, what I wanted, but I knew I was want-able. Had nothing if not self-assurance. I swallowed a foreign seed of insecurity. "Let's get out of here."

That turned his head. Hands in his pockets, he moved closer, enough for me to smell his cologne, an expensive scent that made me think of yachts and cigars. "Where do you want to go?"

I faced forward, closed my eyes against the ocean breeze, and exhaled. "Out of here."

Chapter 3

We hopped the balcony fence on the far end, where there was a staircase that was closed off for the party, the tiny act of rebellion perfect in its ridiculousness. I removed my heels, our dash down the stairs almost Cinderella-like in its execution, his strong hand pulling mine, our fingers interlocking when we reached the bottom. I tried to gather the bulk of my dress, the expensive fabric ruined at the bottom, Versace making an ironclad appointment with my dry cleaner. Giving up, I looked for my driver, the sea of black cars in the lot signifying the upper classes' lack of ability to diversify in any way. The silver Rolls moved, seeing me first, a bellman's white glove appearing and opening the door for me. "Ms. Fairmont," the young man said stiffly, extending a hand to help me into the car.

I half-expected Brant to touch me in the car, his hand to steal onto my leg, his prostitute-loving self to put those beautiful lips on my body in some way. He did nothing, just settled into the seat beside me, his fingers drumming a pattern on the armrest as he stared out the window.

"My house, Mark." My family's driver, a man who has been in my life for over a decade, nodded, his eyes never flicking to the review mirror. My use of him was rare, reserved for situations like this, events where I expected to imbibe. Despite my mother's scrawl on his paychecks, I had his loyalty. Who knew what secrets he kept for my parents, but he kept a file cabinet's worth of mine. I turned my attention off him and to the mystery beside me.

I'd known plenty of geniuses. Stanford was stocked full, so I had experienced every make and model. And, for the most part, there were known types. The ones who genetics had blessed with intelligence but no social skills. Then there were the pompous, insecure men who feigned confidence by vomiting knowledge tidbits at every opportunity. Then the kind who made me the most nervous: the quiet types who watched you while notating every nuance of your character for analysis at a later moment. The type I shared a car with at that moment in time.

He took his eyes off the view and turned to me. Studied me with open intensity, his eyes scraping open every damaged pore on my psyche.

"Stop." The words came out before I could stop them.

His mouth twitched. "Why?"

"Don't think. Your brain could probably use a rest." I smiled.

"Worried about what I will come up with?"

"No." *Yes.*

"Why'd you leave with me?" Open curiosity in his eyes. Like any woman needed to explain running off with a billionaire.

"I figured you should have one night you didn't have to pay for."

His eyes smiled. "I like paying."

"Why?" Now I was the curious one. About every piece of this man. He was fascinating, the most interesting piece being his utter lack of concern about my opinion of his actions.

"It's less messy. I can dictate the night. No emotions involved."

"Emotions can make it hotter."

"And more painful."

"You been hurt?"

"Not yet." He stared at me so steadily, an odd emphasis placed on the words, as if he was giving his heart to me with both hands, certain that it would lead to his demise.

I suddenly didn't *want* it. Didn't want the weight and pressure of expectation. Didn't want to do anything but bring the light back into this man's eyes.

The car slowed, and I saw the gates before us, moving slowly as we waited for entrance. I reached over, unclicked his belt, his eyes following my hand, his brows raising slightly.

"We're here."

***

Mark dropped us before the front doors, my hand pushing on the knob, my hand stealing behind and pulling Brant into the dark house, his quiet steps following me straight through to the back. There, the silent slide of glass against rubber opened the back wall of my bedroom, the ocean stretching before us. It was an act I'd done before, the view impressive, the ocean air clearing the room of stiffness, the view suddenly embarrassing in front of a man who probably owned islands. I turned away from him, hid the sudden blush of my cheeks, and held up my hair. "Unzip me."

There was a moment of pause, a moment where I tilted my head, waited for the pressure on my zipper. Then it came, the slow drag, the fingers of his other hand following, four points dragging down my bare back as he took it the entire way, past the curve of my back, until he stopped, half of my backside bared, his breath changing in tempo, a few stuttering inhalations bringing a smile to my face. *So, he is human.* His hands slid up, hot points of contact, and skimmed the tops of my shoulders, shedding me of the dress as the material fell down my arms and off my body. I turned, naked, save my underwear, and cast a mischievous smile toward his clothes.

"Strip 'em."

"You do it." A challenge and order in the tone.

I shook my head. "I've got to break you of the habit of ordering women around."

He scowled, pulled at his bowtie, yanking it loose and working the buttons on the front of his shirt. "When's the last time you did what you were told?"

I shrugged. "Hard to think back that far." Then, as much as I wanted to stand there and watch him strip, I turned and stepped out of my dress, heard the thud of his dress shoe as it loosely hit the floor. I stepped toward the bed, reaching forward to pull at the duvet, and jumped a bit when I felt the heat of his hand turn me back into the hard surface of his chest. A full body press of skin against skin, hard planes meeting soft curves. *Nothing* between him and my...

"No underwear?" I murmured, our faces inches away, his lit by the glow of night.

"Seemed like a waste of time." He didn't kiss me, even though I lifted my chin, invited the touch. His hand stole under the line of my panties and cupped my ass.

"So what does that make mine?"

"A pretty distraction." He slid his hand higher and wrapped tighter around my waist, and I think I saw a peek of a smile before he pitched us both onto the bed.

A roll of naked skin, legs tangled. The crawl of me along him, our mouths met, first kiss formed. His mouth was hesitant, his hands confident, and I had the moment of wonder if he kissed the escorts before he fucked them. Then, the kiss deepened, our connection solidified, and I put the thought of prostitutes out of my head.

When he pulled back, sat away from me, his hand dragging over the curves of my skin, there was a pause. A pause filled with the soft sound of breath, a pause filled with a moment of decision when he looked into my eyes and his gaze held a question.

I didn't answer with my mouth. I rolled over 'til my legs left the bed and feet hit carpet. I stepped over to my dresser, opened a drawer and fished through panties and thongs until my hand hit foil. I pulled out a condom and walked back, my eyes taking an appreciative tour of his body as he lay on his back, exposed. His eyes smiled at me, his mouth only curving enough to highlight what might be a dimple, no move made to cover the impressive organ that lay against his thigh.

I didn't expect the confidence he carried—thought a computer nerd would be more bashful of his body, more arrogant of his mind. But he hadn't quoted a single fact, hadn't brought up his company or money in any way. He treated this the same way I did, as two adults looking for a good time. He held out a hand, took the condom, then set it behind him on the bedside table, his hand returning to grab mine. "Not yet. Come here." He pulled me alongside him, pressed forward until parts of us touched, and he was close enough to press a kiss against my lips, his fingers starting at my shoulders, softly working the muscles of my neck, gently probing as his touch ran down the lines of my frame. I closed my eyes, letting out a sigh as I relaxed against the pillow and he slid his hands lower, palms flat on the swell of my breasts, his touch gentle as he spread his hands and took me into them. "You are beautiful," he said, a whispered scratch in the tones. His body moved closer. "I'm sorry if I'm ... I'm not used to romance, Layana."

My eyes opened, my wandering hands stopping in their delicate exploration that was about to reach his cock. "I don't think I'm looking for it."

"I thought every woman was looking for it." He pulled me on my side, ran his hands around, until they cupped my ass and pulled me against him— hot air between us.

I looked up into his eyes, and finally found the moment when he lowered his mouth to mine. No. *This*. This was what every woman was looking for. A mouth that responded hungrily yet tenderly when kissed.

This. A firm drag of my body toward the end of the bed, eyes dominant, hands strong, the push of my inquisition down to the mattress.

This. My hands in his hair, clawing at his shoulders, my body bucking underneath his talented tongue between my legs.

This. Our bodies entwined in my sheets, his weight on my wrists, the moment of primal connection when he spread my legs and thrust himself inside, his cock moving with sure strokes, my cries of pleasure silenced by his kiss.

This. His body arced into mine, his hands pulling me hard against him, the bury of his cock when he finished, gasping my name, the shudder of his breath against my mouth as he rolled me over and gave one final thrust.

This. This was what I wanted, what my new self desired. The romance, it could wait.

Chapter 4

"You did what?" the shrill voice echoed in the large office, bouncing off antique desks and framed honors.

"I'm an adult, Jillian. I have every right to entertain whomever I wish."

"She's not a trailer park hussy, Brant. She's a respected member of society. Extremely intelligent, though you wouldn't know it from the life of leisure she lives."

"I would consider those marks in her favor. You're speaking as if you'd rather me date an uneducated redneck. I left her house last night and went home electrified. I worked all through the night and solved our issues with data recovery. The woman lit a fire in me."

The woman stood, pearls rustling, the fury in her eyes finding their mark and burning the skin they touched. "She's looking for a husband. A new last name, a finish line to the race of life that all of these debutantes live."

"I find it interesting for you to know so much about her intentions."

"You know me, Brant. I have nothing but your best interests in mind. Trust me when I say to let whatever happened last night be the end of it. You don't need a relationship, and would do best to stay away from this woman. Next time you want to get your rocks off, let me call the service."

With a foot on the desk leg, he leaned back. "You realize how ridiculous it is for you to order me whores. Most maternal figures would be beaming to see me taking out a respectable woman."

"Your mother would want this. Trust me."

He frowned, flicking a piece of trash toward the basket before looking up into her eyes. "I don't understand you half of the time."

She smiled at him, a hint of sadness in her face. "Trust me, Brant. I could say the same about you."

Chapter 5

I ran along the sand, my tennis shoes squeaking with salt water, the give of sand beneath my soles encouraging as I felt the muscles respond, my legs lifting and pulling, jumping to action as I pounded down the beach, increasing my speed as my house came into view, the finish line in sight. I was wheezing when I came to a stop, my hands wobbly on my thighs, the burn of my chest matching the scream of my muscles, the endorphin high making it all worthwhile. I forced myself to stand, to move forward, my muscles sighing in relief at the leisurely pace of my steps. My arms shaking out, the muscles loosened as I rolled my shoulders and my neck.

Two miles. Shorter than yesterday but faster. I glanced at my watch, at the frozen stopwatch there. 15:04. I cleared it, the time returning to the display, and started the uphill climb to my deck, where a bench and shower station waited. The woman standing at the gate stopped me short, her rigid posture bringing back the memory of every prep school headmistress I ever had. I paused, eyed her warily, ``and then continued my forward movement.

"Is there something I can help you with?" I opened the gate, entering the same space as her, wondering, as I glanced to the front of the lot, how she got back here. We were a lesson in contrast, my skin wet from ocean spray and sweat, a sports bra and spandex the only thing covering my frame. She wore at least two layers, nylons covered by a pants suit, a turtleneck peeking out from her jacket. My drops of sweat versus her pearl necklace. My wild brown ringlets barely contained by a headband and elastic, her coiffed updo barely shuddering in the strong wind. My chest still heaved while she stood, ramrod straight, with a look of cool disdain on her wrinkled features. I frowned at the expression. What the hell had I done to her?

"Jillian Sharp." She started to hold out a hand, her lips pursed, eyes sweeping over me, but then thought better of it, choosing to nod instead, as if she was the Queen of England, and I should curtsy.

"Layana Fairmont. Is there something I can help you with?" My mind was working in overdrive as I repeated the unanswered question. Jillian Sharp. CFO of BSX, Brant's digital conglomerate. She was the face before the face, the one conducting any news conferences, interviews, or board meetings. She was, best I was aware of, very intelligent, very business savvy, and very busy. Which begged the question of why she was standing on my deck at—I stole a look at my watch—1:12 PM on a Monday.

"I spoke to Brant this morning. He mentioned your little..." She sniffed in a way I took to be disapproving, her features pinching, an irritated look cast at a burst of wind, "*meeting* last night." *She probably wants to be invited inside.* It would be the polite thing to do, given the sun beating down on her, the salty air, which was no doubt ruining her Chanel suit. I let her stand there, my mind working over her words.

"And?"

"May I come in?" She huffed, as if annoyed with asking the question, and I contained the smile that wanted to come out and play.

"By all means." I smiled. "You're already on my property, might as well come inside my home." I sat on the beach by the back door. Worked the laces of my tennis shoes as slowly as I felt like, feeling her irritation build as I stripped my feet of shoes, then socks, then hosed down my bare feet and dried them. Had she not been here, I would have stripped. Stepped into the outside shower. Scrubbed the sweat off my body and enjoyed a half hour of hot water, pounding and massaging my tired muscles. Then would have wrapped myself in a towel and moved inside.

So there, the new Layana did retain some bit of manners. I toweled my feet completely dry and opened the door.

Two bottles of water, grabbed from the fridge, one slid over the island to Jillian, who inspected the bottle before setting it down. She said nothing as I stared at her, guzzled every drop from the bottle before wiping my mouth with the back of my hand.

Silence. I was damn sure not going to say anything. She was the surprise guest of the hour. The very busy, had things to do, important woman. I could stand there all week without being affected in the slightest.

She cleared her throat, the sound one that reeked of tea and crumpets but I knew her background. Read a feature article in *Glamour* magazine that touted her as one of the most powerful women in Silicon Valley. She wasn't a blue blood. Wasn't even properly educated. Attended a community college. Worked as a fourth-grade teacher until 1997, when her nephew, one aforementioned Brant Sharp, built a computer in his basement. A computer that made IBM's latest creation look like a bowl of Jell-O. A computer that made his parents drop every future plan and invest their savings in Team Brant. He was young. Eleven. Needed a chaperone. So Aunt Jillian quit her job and hitched her wagon to Brant. Lived off food stamps and her savings account in a spare bedroom at Brant's house for two years. Then she brokered their first deal and all of the Sharps moved their bank account decimals seven places to the right.

"I'd like you to stay away from Brant."

Wow. Not what I was expecting. I had half expected her to pull out an appointment book and pencil in our wedding date while the summer calendar was clear. I swallowed a mouthful of water before speaking. "Excuse me?"

"Brant doesn't need the distraction of a relationship right now." She remained in place, standing on my floor on an island of Jillian, back still straight, stick still firmly wedged somewhere up that ass.

Did the woman *know* he used whores? "That seems like a decision for Brant to make." I leaned on the counter, met her eyes steadily. *You're in my house. Step the fuck back.* "Last I checked he's not eleven years old anymore."

Her eyes flickered, as if the information I shared was secret, not something known by anyone ready to part with $3.99. Her jaw tightened. "Don't assume that you know him, or anything about me just because you did an Internet search. He is not built for a relationship, does not have time for you. I'm coming here, woman to woman, to ask you to stay away."

"And I'm telling *you*, woman to woman, that it's none of your business." Any interest I had had in Brant was quadrupling with every word out of this woman's mouth. I had smiled and obeyed for twenty-five years. I wasn't about to be put in my place by this schoolmarm.

She moved, dug in her purse, a cream Hermes that I had in green. A laugh bubbled in my throat when I saw what her hand pulled out.

"You're going to try and *bribe* me to stay away from him?" Her hand froze at my laugh, hard eyes swinging to me mid-click of her pen. "We spent one night together. He's not preparing to propose."

"It's better to be safe than sorry," the woman said stiffly. "Plus, at this point, there are no emotions involved. Walking away should be, in your case, a breeze. You are a smart girl. I'm sure you'll make an intelligent decision." She signed her name to a check she had already filled out, ripping it from the deck with the subtlety of a hyena, then thrust it out, as if it might burn her fingers if kept any longer in her touch.

I didn't look at it; I held my gaze on her face until she looked up in exasperation, our eyes meeting over the granite island. "I appreciate the visit, but I think it's time for you to leave."

"It's for your own good, sweetheart. You don't want Brant. He's damaged goods." The acidic words were said with a dash of affection, the nicety not minimizing the truth in her eyes. She believed it. She set down the check. Pushed it forward with her pen.

"I don't need your money."

"A million dollars never hurt anyone, dear."

I dropped my eyes to the check, surprised to see her name across the top. *One million dollars.* To me, it meant an extra vacation home. Maybe a condo in Colorado. Nothing that would change my life. But it was still a significant amount of money. Especially to be written off her personal account. "It's worth a million dollars to you for him to stay single? Or is it me that you have such personal disdain for?"

That flicker of gray again. A tropical storm of emotions in this small woman. "Trust me. I want what's best for Brant. And, for you."

I pushed back the check. "No thanks. And it has nothing to do with Brant. I'm not going to be bought off from anything."

She chuckled, the sound anything but jovial. Instead, it scraped long, dead fingernails down my spine, reducing me, in one squeeze of her vocal chords, to a misbehaving child. "Oh, how easy it is for a child of wealth to take the moral high ground. I imagine, had you had to work a day in your life, that you would react differently. If it were your money that built this house. That purchased your ocean-front view."

I stared at her, bit back words of retort that didn't really hold any substance. She was right. Didn't mean I was going to let her stand here, in my damn house, and make me feel guilty for it. I watched as she ripped the check in half. Let the pieces of it scatter to the counter.

"Fine. You don't want my money? What about HYA?"

My fingers tightened on the counter, everything changing in the kitchen in that one moment. She wouldn't. She couldn't. "What *about* it?"

"Last year BSX donated..." She moved her gaze around the kitchen, as if there was complex math being done in some corner of her mind.

"Seven and a half million dollars." I found my voice—it moved out of my throat without invitation. *She wouldn't.*

"Seven point six," she corrected me, her voice hard. "I head our charitable contributions team, along with twelve other departments at BSX. Step away, or I'll pull this year's donation."

My world grew a little smaller. Donations were due next month. We were asking BSX for eight million, which would, in addition to normal expenditures, pay off the existing debt on three new homes we put under construction during the last year. Without that donation, the organization would have to cover both mortgages for a full year. An impossible task. And, honestly, my fundraising skills ... I couldn't make up that deficit. No way. I could barely raise the two million dollars I had pulled in last year. I swallowed. Stared at this evil woman who suddenly held a full house in her deck. A full house of homeless kids.

"Get the fuck out of my house."

And so my relationship with Jillian began.

Chapter 6

I didn't react well when being told what to do. I was also selfish. Both of those arrows pointed in the direction of calling Brant. Planting myself front and center in his life in any way I could.

But I couldn't ignore the kids. The ones I spent Tuesdays and Thursdays with, the one break from my superficial life, the peek I got into a lonely, sad existence that HYA brightened in a few small ways. Important ways. The old woman was right about one thing. There were no emotions attached at this point, no reason why I couldn't just walk away from the man. Walk away and allow thousands of children to have a little brightness in their lives this year. Would I take that away from them just to spite Jillian Sharp?

Yeah. Probably. I never claimed to be a saint. Manipulation should never win. Plus, I should never lose. My new mantra was to do as I wished, not as society expected or wanted. On that note, I was almost obligated to give her the proverbial middle finger.

I dumped a liberal amount of Kahlua in my coffee, sat down on my sofa, and stewed over the decision. Stewed over why Jillian was so dead set against a possibility that hadn't even become a possibility yet. Was it me? Some hatred of a stranger she'd never met? Or any woman who might interrupt the flow of Brant's life? How many kitchens had she stood in? Checks had she written? Foes had she faced?

Three cups of coffee later, I slumped low in the couch, the pillow imprinting expensive designs in the side of my face, when my phone rang. I jerked to life, wind-milling my hands and feet for a brief moment as I found my way to my feet and regained my bearings.

I stood there for a brief moment, my bare feet on bamboo floors, blinked, and tried to find the source of my awakening. The shrill sound of my ringtone reminded me, my bleary eyes finding the cell on the kitchen counter, my weak legs bringing me closer.

BRANT displayed on the screen. I silenced it, stumbled back to the couch, and collapsed facedown.

Think of the children.

***

My second nap ended sometime after lunch, the irritated growl of my stomach punching through any alcohol-induced slumber. I made it through half the steps involved in a chicken salad sandwich before I was reminded of Brant's call, mayonnaise fingers plucking my phone and dialing my voicemail.

One new message. Received at 11:07 AM.

"Layana. This is Brant Sharp. I enjoyed last night, sorry to skip out without saying goodbye. I'd like to take you to dinner tonight to make up for it. Let me know if you are free."

No goodbye salutation. Just an ending of the call, my recorded voice informing me of my options in regards to his message. I pressed 4, saved it, ended the call, and tossed down the cell. I finished fixing my sandwich, a frown pinching my features.

***

He called two more times that week. Left two voicemails.

The next week nothing.

The next week nothing.

The fourth week he sent a large arrangement of orchids. The card simply said, "Call me."

Day thirty-four: BSX wired their annual donation, meeting our request, eight million dollars.

On day thirty-five, I called him back.

"Hey." Total silence in the background. No hum of machinery, no busy San Francisco street.

"I'm sorry."

"Trust me, I won't leave in the middle of the night again. I learned my lesson."

I laughed. His wry tone made me smile. "It wasn't that. Truly. I just needed to get some things in order before I saw you again."

His next sentence was a grumble in words. "Clear the bench?"

More like wait out a contract. "Something like that."

"So ... your bench is available?"

I laughed. "As unsexy as that sounds, yes."
"Good. I'd like to take you to dinner tonight."
I smiled. "Pick me up at seven."

**

Jillian must have had a direct line to this man's brain. She called within three hours. The number unfamiliar, I answered it while folding laundry, whites laid out across my sofa like flags of surrender.

"I didn't expect you to be a woman who would renege on a deal." No polite words of greeting, no introduction before diving into the meat of the issue. I recognized her voice instantly, my smile widening as I got a month's worth of pleasure in the sound of the irritation in her voice.

"All's fair in love and war, Jillian. We have a year before BSX's next donation to HYA. That should give us both enough time to sort this matter out."

"I don't expect to remember your name in a year."

I clicked my tongue at her. "Word of advice, Jillian? Don't push back. It'll only cause me to pursue him more."

"Word of advice, *sweetie*?" She dunked the last word in poison, drawing it out in a manner that made my brow arch with admiration. "Realize when someone is trying to do you a favor."

I didn't have a witty comeback for that one. Didn't really understand it enough to respond. I swallowed, folded the white tank top over twice in my hands and added it to the pile. "Don't worry about Brant. I won't hurt him."

"That isn't really what concerns me." She hesitated; I could hear the catch in her breath before she spoke again. "Call me when you find out what does."

I didn't talk to her again for nine months. I called her the night I discovered his secret.

Chapter 7

Wealthy men were a breed I knew well; a wealthy man raised me, my impressions of him stolen during brief moments of notability during my first eighteen years. I had dated the young versions, ones who had been born into the world of trust funds, Harvard legacies, and country clubs. Their sense of entitlement had been seconded only by their undeserved egos. Then, I graduated college and moved into the world of men, older versions who reminded me too much of my father, men who took rather than asked, and who expected subservience from anyone with breasts.

Wealthy men had their benefits: the limos, vacation homes, private jets, and exorbitant gifts. They also had their shortfalls: arrogance, unfaithfulness, an impossible schedule, and, more often than not, an opinion of women that left much to be desired. But hey—that was the rare thing I'd had in common with most of my dates, a mutual lack of respect. And probably the reason why I'd never had a relationship bloom to fruition.

Brant was completely different than every other wealthy man I'd ever met. He listened when I spoke. Looked into my eyes and not at my breasts. Asked my opinions, valued my intellect. He approached our new relationship in the cautious way that a cat approached food, pushing delicately before gaining footing, his steps as new and explorative as my own. We danced around each other, our moves becoming stronger, more sure-footed with each passing day. Together, we created and explored our roles; sex the only area of our life where no practice was needed.

The man ... was an animal. I sipped my coffee and shifted in my seat, the sore ache of my body reminding me of a few nights before, his skillful manipulation of my body that had brought me to orgasm four, five ... then six times. I twisted slightly, watching Brant as he stepped into the coffee shop, his eyes finding me as he walked over, brushing a kiss against my lips.

"Been waiting long?"

"Five minutes. Here." I pushed across his coffee. "Straight black, you unexciting man."

He settled into the seat, picking it up with a dignified scowl. "It's manly. Puts hair on my chest."

I laughed into my cup. "I don't want hair on your chest. I prefer it as is, perfectly manicured by your team of beauticians."

That earned me a real scowl. "I don't have beauticians. They're..." My eloquent man seemed suddenly at a loss for words. I laughed, pushing gently on his wrist until his coffee was out of reach, then leaned across the table and stole another kiss. He grabbed the back of my neck, pulled my mouth harder to his, asserted his masculinity in a rough moment of passion. I pulled off, blushing as I sat back down, a passing woman glaring at me as if we've just screwed on coffee shop's floor.

"I'm sorry about yesterday." The joviality was gone from Brant's voice.

I shrugged. "It's not a big deal. I shopped. Ran some errands while downtown."

"I've been fighting a deadline on this wireframe overhaul ... sometimes I get in a zone working and lose track of time."

"It's *fine*. I was just worried. I'm not mad—just hated bothering Jillian about it." Hated bothering Jillian was a mild way of putting it. Brant and I'd set dinner plans: 6 PM at Alexander's. I'd waited at our table for a half hour before leaving, my calls to Brant going unanswered. I had hesitated to text Jillian, my fingers finally moving across the screen purely out of concern—in case something had happened, in case he was missing. I half-expected a snarky response, something that referenced how unimportant I must be to him. But she had responded quickly and professionally.

HE'S HERE AT THE OFFICE. WILL PROBABLY WORK LATE. NO DOUBT LOST TRACK OF TIME. I'M SORRY.

The fact that she had been civil in her response only irritated me more, tipped the scales a bit in her favor, setting precedence for an act of similar civility on my part. I broke off a piece of muffin.

"Let me make it up to you."

I watched him while chewing, blueberries mixing with sugar and flour to make a delicious combination in my mouth. "Go ahead," I mumbled.

"Today, I'll blow off work. Be all yours."

I swallowed the bite. "But you're under deadline. You've been working for three weeks to make—"

"I don't care." He reached over the table and gripped my hand. "You are more important, and I have set aside a full day of groveling to make up for last night."

I raised an eyebrow. "A full day? That's a hefty commitment, Mr. Sharp."

He met my eyes. "One I'm ready to make."

I leaned over, lowered my voice. "And what do you have planned in this day full of groveling?"

He tugged my hand up to his lips. "I thought I'd start by us dropping by my condo. I have some ideas of ways to make it up to you."

"Sexy ways?" I whispered playfully.

He leaned forward, a gentle hand pulling on the back of my neck until his mouth was against my ear. "Ways that will make your legs tremble around my neck. Ways that have me so hard and ready that I may not make it all the way there. Ways that will have you screaming my name and—"

"Let's go." I jerked to standing, the legs of my chair squeaking as they slid across the floor. Pulling on his hand, I bee-lined for the door.

Chapter 8

Brant's downtown condo was his sex den, the place where high-class hookers had entertained my man and satisfied every carnal desire he'd had over the last two decades. Yes, I was now standing in a room where other women had moaned his name, serviced his cock. I couldn't care less. Because the man standing before me, his eyes dark, body clenched, fingers stripping the clothes from my body? I could see into his soul. He didn't have eyes for anyone else in the world. He wasn't thinking, picturing, wanting, anything but what I had. He lifted me, setting me on the bar top, his hands sliding my shorts off my legs, removing my sandals, caressing the skin as his hands journeyed back. He knelt on the floor, looked up into my eyes, and pushed on the inside of my knees, spreading my legs until I was open, his eyes dropping, the new height of him at a perfect level.

"Brant," I moaned, the exposure too much, the open stance causing air to hit places that were typically hidden.

"Be quiet, baby." He slid his hands up my inner thighs, my hands finding their way to his full head of hair the same time his right hand brushed over me. I inhaled, opening my legs further, and he groaned slightly as he ran a finger over the lips of my sex, outlining the folds with a whisper soft touch, the teasing brush causing my body to react, to cry for him in the only way it knew, moisture collecting, his breath hissing as he pushed a finger partially in. He looked up, his head moving beneath my hand, his eyes coming up to mine, the eye contact held as he pulled his finger out and tasted my juices, his eyes closing briefly. "God, you taste so sweet. I want to bury my face in you, Lana." He reestablished eye contact, his finger returning, teasing the outside of me, soft strokes breaking me apart as he caressed every bit of me, the pad of his fingers exploring, testing, circling, and pushing, my back arching, mouth dropping as I stared at him, unable to pull my eyes from the scene of his touch.

I pulled at his head when I couldn't take it anymore, pulled his mouth to my sex, my body starting when the hot touch enveloped me, his tongue dipping inside me before covering my clit and starting a wet suction of stimulation that had me gasping into the air, my hands frantic on his head, my eyes catching in the faint reflection of us in the window, the picture it showed one of desperate need. I clutched the counter and pushed at his head, unable to ... I bucked underneath his mouth ... "Brant—I" ... then I screamed, unable to stop myself, my hips grinding a frantic pace against his mouth, his hands gripping my hips, pinning me down, holding me to him as I broke apart.

He relaxed his mouth as I came down, his tongue keeping the movement but softening it, the orgasm stretched out beneath his tongue, my breath coming hard, and my arms giving out. I collapsed on the bar, my legs going limp, his hands finally letting my legs close. I opened my eyes when he lifted me up.

***

He carried me to the bedroom, my limbs struggling to reawaken, his deposit on the bed gentle, his hands moving my arms and legs into place, the drop of his pants revealing how ready he was. "Wow." My arms worked enough to prop me up, my eyes flicking from his arousal to his eyes, catching on the half smile that tugged at his lips.

"You are so beautiful right now," he said, ripping open a condom and sliding it over his shaft, the bob of his sheathed cock tempting, the level of his erection mouth-watering. I bent my knees and spread my legs, giving him the carnal view I knew he wanted, a low swear emitting from his mouth as he kneeled on the bed, running his hands along my legs before preparing himself for entrance. "Tell me if it hurts," he murmured, moving forward, the head of him pushing inside, the girth causing a sigh to slip from my lips, my eyes dropping to drink in the gorgeous sight of my pussy's lips wrapped around his cock.

He was thick. Cut. Groomed. Beautiful. He pushed slightly in, then out, several more inches left, the condom wet with my arousal, the sparse hair of my cunt wet and matted, framing his cock as he took his time, letting me adjust, the slow drag of him so ... everything. I lost intelligent thought, broke from my view of us and looked up to him, his eyes on mine, and the look on his face so vulnerable, so raw. He stared down at me as if I was his world, as if our month-long courtship was so much more, as if I already had his heart and he had mine. He worshipped my face with his stare, and the only movement was the rise and fall of his face as he thrust and pulled at my self-composure. The moment when he fully pushed, when he broke past the sweet and moved to the painful, the moment when my body fully adjusted to his length and girth, the need as great as the satisfaction ... I saw it. We said it through our eyes, the words unnecessary, our bond completed as he lowered his mouth to mine and stole a piece of my soul.

I was falling for him.

Chapter 9

I rolled against his chest, my touch finding its way over his stomach, the lines of his body, his abs jumping beneath my fingers as he exhaled. My hand moved lower, sliding under the sheet, a growl coming from his throat as I closed my hand around him, the thick muscle awakening underneath my touch. "Don't start unless you want more."

"Of that?" I teased. "I'll always want more." I gave him a final squeeze and then released, dragging my hand back up to his chest, wanting a few more minutes of this. Brant was relaxed, his intensity subdued to a level that was adorable, his eyes currently closed against the pillow, the only movement the rise and fall of his chest underneath my hand.

We lay there in silence for a bit, after-sex pleasures still shooting the occasional synapsis in my limbs. I closed my eyes and replayed the sex. I didn't enter this relationship a virgin. I'd had my share of lovers, seven or eight if I had to guess. I'd had orgasms. A few freaky nights where I'd walked on the wilder side of the sheets. But I'd never had the sex I'd had with Brant. A full session with a man where the focus was on one thing: my pleasure. His orgasm came, it was always included, the final act, but it was a side effect, not the goal. Brant's goal, each and every time, was to leave me sated, every possible orgasm pulled, tugged, and yanked from my body with his greedy hands, mouth, and cock.

I wrapped my leg around him, pulled tighter. Felt his hand squeeze me in response. "Tell me about the escorts." I didn't know where that came from; it jumped from my lips without warning. Beneath me, I felt Brant's body tighten a bit, his hand stopping the lazy exploration of my skin that it had started.

"What have you heard?"

"Hundreds. That they came here, not your home."

"This is closer to the office. And ... I have too many valuables at home, my work, my privacy. This worked better."

I propped my chin on his chest and watched his face, his blue eyes coming to mine. "Hundreds?" I asked.

He frowned. "No. Over the last twenty years..." He shrugged. "There have probably been fifteen."

I digested the number. On one hand, it was more than mine. On the other, it was less than I had expected. "And ... why prostitutes?"

He blushed, something I had never seen from him. "Pleasing a woman ... it's important to me. I wanted to be taught, by a professional."

"Taught?"

He moved a curl of hair from my cheek. Wrapped it around his finger before tucking it behind my ear. "I was young the first time. Seventeen. Had never even kissed a girl before, my whole world pretty much confined to the basement. I wanted to date, my hormones were going nuts, but Jillian and my parents didn't want me running around town flagging down the first girl I saw."

"So they ordered you a prostitute?" I pushed up off his chest, the motion causing my breasts to move, his eyes dropping to them, a deep exhale easing from his chest as he took a moment, his hands sliding up my back and curving forward, cupping my breasts with reverence. "Brant," I said, trying to focus as he shifted total concentration to my chest. "Brant," I repeated. "Your parents got you a prostitute?"

"No," he mumbled, trying to pull me higher, his mouth coming up, kissing my neck and trying to make its way lower. "Jillian got me Bridget McCullen, an eighteen-year-old girl straight off the pages of my fantasies."

"A prostitute," I repeated, sliding lower, moving my breasts farther away, the new position letting me feel exactly how much my body affected him. I grinned despite myself.

He finally looked up. "Well, I didn't know she was a prostitute. Jillian had her knock on the door one day when I was home alone. The girl pretty much dragged me from the basement to my room. Gave me my first blow job and made me forget all about computers for a good three minutes."

"Isn't that ... illegal? You were seventeen. She's your aunt! That's creepy in so many different ways I can't even name them all."

He laughed. "It was the best thing they could do for me at the time. And I didn't want to leave the house, didn't want..." He looked down, busying himself by pulling our sheet higher. "I understood them keeping me close. Protecting me. I didn't know she was a prostitute. I thought she liked me, and had just moved in nearby. She hung around for two years. Took me from a boy to a man. Then ... she was gone."

"What happened?"

He shrugged. "Moved away, got a boyfriend? I don't know. I was heartbroken. Was certain we were meant to be, 'til Jillian had a heart-to-heart and told me everything. How the girl was interested in payment, nothing more. How I should concentrate on the good, what I had gotten from the relationship. I was pissed. Didn't talk to her for a few days. I'd moved out by then, was living here. A few days passed, then she sent over a new girl. I understood the test. I couldn't be pissed at her for giving me something I wanted. So I could turn away the girl, knowing she was a prostitute, or take her and accept the screwed up reality that was my life." He looked at me. "So I fucked her. And it was different than with Bridget. I understood the dynamic, and I could control the situation. So I focused on what I wanted—the ability to please a woman. And I figured, one day, I would have a woman worth using that ability on."

I stared at him. Blinked. Stared some more. "You realize," I said slowly, "that you shouldn't be sharing all of this with me. This is the stuff that you're supposed to keep secret. The skeletons that show your vulnerability."

He laughed, his arms wrapping around me, rolling us over until he was on top, and his cock was still there, still begging for attention. "Then there you have it. All of my skeletons. Will you still have me?" He nibbled a path along my neck, and I giggled beneath him, reaching a hand down and gripping the part of him I couldn't get enough of. "Skeletons?" I mused. "Well, I do like a good bone."

He groaned into my neck, thrusting into my hand. "That was so cheesy."

I laughed. "Good cheesy?"

He shook his head against my curls. "Bad cheesy."

"I like bad," I whispered, my voice dropping, my hand tightening, his hips fucking his cock into my grip.

"God, woman." He reached forward, stretching across my body and yanking at the handle of the bedside table, his hands knocking over items in his haste. "I don't know what to do with you."

"Really?" I teased. "You don't know what to do with me?"

"Correct that," he rumbled, lifting off me just long enough to cover his cock, his hands slightly shaking in his urgency. "I know exactly what to do with you."

Then he was back above me, and his cock was inside of me, and he showed me exactly what his plans entailed.

Chapter 10

Jillian and I engaged in a silent battle, one where she pushed in every passive-aggressive way she could, campaigning with all her strength against the relationship that Brant and I were forming. A battle without words, but through the man she loved and I had fallen for.

I walked into the next roadblock on a Tuesday morning, my day dedicated to HYA. Pulling through the gates, I was greeted by a shiny new male specimen, complete with a genuine six-pack, blinding white smile, and rugged good looks that a Hilfiger model scout would trip over herself to snag. He jogged across the grass, lines of dirt smeared across the ripped muscles of his chest, a trio of kids tailing him, their arms fighting for the football he carried. I watched him run toward me and wondered who he was and what he was doing inside the sanctuary that was this property.

Employees and volunteers at HYA were carefully vetted. Background checks, drug tests, and references were required. We'd had the same staff, give or take, for the six years I'd been involved. A new face wasn't often seen. I watched him, his head coming up as my convertible came to a halt, his hand raised in greeting.

I put the car in park, my mouth curving at the view of the kids, detaching from the stranger to run toward my car. Opening the door, I was accosted with hugs, greedy hands pulling at my clothes, and one helpful boy closing my door with solemn responsibility.

"Thanks Lucas." I wrapped a casual arm around his shoulders and hugged him briefly.

"They like you." The stranger stood before me, legs slightly parted, the football jumping a lazy trip between his two hands.

"They like everyone." I smiled, extending a hand. "Layana Fairmont."

"Billy," he said, giving my hand a firm shake, then holding the grip a bit longer than necessary.

I pulled at my hand, turning to the children to disguise the motion. Reaching out, I snagged the closest body and pulled her to me, tickling the little girl briefly before turning toward the main house and sprinting forward. "Race you guys to HQ!"

My tennis shoes hit the damp grass, the squeal of voices behind me causing me to increase my speed. I glanced over my shoulder, seeing the new guy—Billy—staying close behind me, his eyes leaving my legs to come up to my face, a flirtatious grin shot at me.

I ignored the look, turning back and focusing on the hill before me, my legs pumping up the embankment as I slowed my stride a bit to give the kids a fighting chance. Reggie, a seventh-grader who'd come to us three years ago, his arms already covered with gang ink, passed me, his long legs eating up the distance. I let him go, casting a quick glance around me to find the other kids. I slowed a little more, then let out a yell of mock frustration when the race ended.

I bent over, breathing dramatically, my back patted consolingly by Hannah, my personal favorite at the HYA compound. I turned to smile at her, my eyes catching on Billy, who watched me closely, an interested grin on his face. I looked away.

***

"How long have you been a volunteer here?" The question came from the other end of the main house's kitchen. I didn't stop my PB&J production, didn't turn, knew the source of it without looking, the manly drawl a dead giveaway.

"Five or six years. I'm only here twice a week." I unscrewed the lid to the jelly, avoided looking at the man who I was pretty sure just moved closer.

"I'm new." *Duh.* "Just a volunteer."

"How'd you find out about HYA?"

"Who?"

I paused my jelly application. Glanced over to see the man's eyes darting around. "HYA ... Homeless Youths of America..." Something was wrong with this picture, and I tried to pinpoint it. The man was nervous.

"Oh." He let out a short laugh. "Umm ... I think I read about it online."

Nope. We were a privately funded organization, run by donations. We stayed, for the most part, fairly discreet.

"Who was your referral?" I had abandoned the sandwiches, had set down the knife and was leaning against the counter, any attempt to avoid staring at his abs somewhat successful.

"My referral?" Fascinated, I watched the points of sweat dot his forehead and wondered what the hell this man was hiding.

"New volunteers require a personal referral from someone inside the organization." I crossed my arms and watched his face.

His eyes darted like ping-pong balls. I knew he'd had a referral. Had to have. Wouldn't have gotten in the gates, wouldn't have the official nametag, which his shirtless self had stuck to the front of his workout shorts.

"Umm..." He looked around, as if for rescue. I stepped closer, tilted my head and pinned him in place, my eyes not wavering from his. I couldn't figure out what he was so worked up about, my innocent question one that had never caused anyone a moment's pause. He swallowed, the bulge of his Adam's apple moving painfully in the tight stretch of his neck. By the time his mouth worked, I was ready to crawl into his throat and pull the words out. "Jillian Sharp."

I should have known, should have expected the name. A handsome stranger at HYA, tripping over himself to make my acquaintance, every firm muscle on full display for my eyes. I smiled. "Jillian," I drawled. "What a pleasant surprise." I tilted my head and studied his face, a handsome canvas that looked as if he might vomit in the closest trashcan. "You seem like a nice guy, Billy. You and I will probably get along best if we just stay away from each other."

He swallowed. "Stay away from each other?"

I smiled. "Yep. Sound good?"

His brow knitted. "Forever?"

I chuckled. "If she keeps you on the payroll that long." I moved around him, stepping toward the main house. One final thought came to mind and I spun, pointing a finger at him. "Oh, and Billy?"

"Yes?" A dread-laced response.

"Don't hurt these kids. They fall in love easily. I don't give a damn if you stay or go, but don't hurt them." I stared him down until he nodded, a movement filled with hesitancy. I held the eye contact until I was sure he understood, then I continued up the hill.

Chapter 11

2 YEARS, 8 MONTHS AGO

I didn't understand. I ran my hands lightly through Brant's hair, his deep breathing indicating a better level of sleep than I would get that night. He was beautiful at rest. The thick brush of his lashes. The bones of his face that created the perfect canvas. Brilliance and beauty all rolled into one.

I didn't understand why I was his first relationship. Why, once he completed his journey into manhood, he had continued to use escorts for sex. Why he had no real friends, no real ties to anyone other than his parents and Jillian. Why, when he seemed custom built for a relationship.

He wasn't perfect. I'd found some flaws. He got distracted, didn't always listen to conversations, or plans, had a memory that would probably qualify him for pharmaceutical help. He missed another date. Hadn't shown up at all, his cell phone going unanswered until the next morning, when he provided a weak excuse about falling asleep at his desk. A different man, I might have suspected of cheating. But Brant made it clear early on where his focus lied. Work and me. Nothing else, no one else. The man's dedication was impressive, might have even been alarming, had I not been gunning for a relationship with both throttles wide open. There were no other men waiting in my wings. Any casual flings had ended when I met the intensity of this man. Every tool in his shed was superior by two to any other suitor. And my interest had been heightened by the fact that his aunt would pay a million dollars just to keep me away.

I loved that he was different than the men of my past. He didn't have the cloak of aristocracy, didn't care enough to be aloof, snooty, couldn't care less if we played by society's rules or wrote our own. We had created, in three months of togetherness, an igloo of sorts in San Francisco society. A haven of two, a place where I felt comfortable saying 'screw it,' even if I didn't actually wander too far outside any lines. It would come, my world was expanding, my boundaries blurring. I was moving in the right direction toward happiness. Brant, in his oblivion to anything but work, and us, was pulling me there.

Love? The word hadn't been verbalized yet, but it was coming. In our eyes, touches, in the affection. But both of us were cautious, guarding our virgin hearts with ineffective hands. I kept reminding myself that it had only been three months. Three months since I'd finally returned his call and we both dove into this relationship. I rolled forward, breaking the view of his beautiful profile and turned, fitting my body into the curve of his own, his arm lifting then tightening around me as he sighed into my neck, my name a whisper off his lips.

It didn't make sense. He was too perfect. How was I the first woman to tie him down?

In five hours, we would drive two hours, and I would meet his parents. Maybe *they* were the reason my perfect boyfriend was still a bachelor. Maybe they were satanic, or would ask for a sample of my skin. Maybe they were doomsday preppers, who would teach me to can vegetables and show me their collection of guns. Brant didn't say much about them, his primary point of contact being Jillian. The Internet provided even less. But maybe they were the reason for his single-dom. I slid down in the bed, pressed a soft kiss to Brant's forearm, and tried to go to sleep.

***

"Would you care for more lemonade?" The delicate lilt of Gloria Sharp caused me to lift my eyes.

"No, thank you." I took a sip of the still full glass, wondering if her question was a muted attempt to get me to drink the tepid lemon water. I set the glass down, trading glassware for silverware, cutting a small piece of chicken and placing it in my mouth.

Food. The excuse we all have to not talk, chewing providing a convenient break from the polite conversation we had all endured. The Sharps seemed unaccustomed to company. They stared at me, as if I was a new species, on display at a museum, asking few questions, content to look, from me to Brant to me to Brant, as if trying to put the pieces together in a puzzle that didn't match.

Brant stood, his plate in hand, leaning over and kissing the top of my head. "Excuse me for a moment."

I looked up with a smile, begged him with my eyes to stay, but he nodded his head back. "Restroom," he explained. I watched him leave, heading through the dining room, my eyes pulling on his red polo shirt to no avail. I turned back to the Sharp's finding two sets of eyes on me. No chewing, just staring. I swallowed. "I love your home. The fact that this is where Brant—"

"Ms. Fairmont," Brant's father spoke, the voice of a man older than his years. Strained. Thick with unuse.

I paused in my progression of the conversation. Smoothed my napkin in my lap and waited for him to continued. Smiled. God, I hated using that smile. "Yes, Mr. Sharp?"

"You should probably know that we don't think it is a good idea for Brant to be in a relationship. You seem like a very nice girl, but you should probably think about moving on."

Smile. I'd mastered the action. Learned to keep my eyes relaxed, my face muscles loose. So the action looked natural, not forced or tight. You could tell so much about a person from the way they smiled. But not me. My smile gave away nothing of the curses of my soul. "Why is that, Mr. Sharp?" I looked at his wife. Her eyes down, hands nervous.

"Brant's done better in life when he hasn't had a girlfriend."

Brant's a grown man. I kept the smile in place. Brought it down a level so I didn't look deranged. "I care very much for your son. He's a brilliant man. You should very proud of where he is in life."

The man gave me an exasperated smile, as if he was ready for my bullshit to be over. "We'd just like it if you could keep your distance. Restrict your time with him to a minimum. Let him focus on work. He does best when he does that."

There was the sound of a door somewhere else in the house and I looked up, seeing Brant duck in, snagging a piece of meat off a skillet in the kitchen before continuing on, his eyes sheepishly meeting mine. I placed my fork down. "Dinner was delicious, Mrs. Sharp and thank you both for having me over. Brant, do you mind showing me the basement? I'd love to see your old workshop."

His mother's mouth twisted, the father's hardened, and they could both kiss my ass because Brant was an adult, one more intelligent than the rest of this house put together, myself included. The woman rose, the flop of her sandals against tile as she snagged my plate and headed to the kitchen, a glance at my half-eaten meal not going unnoticed. Brant breezed through the room, grabbing my hand on his way. One short hallway later, he swung open a door, and I stepped down a flight of stairs into the basement.

Roughly six hundred square feet of dimly lit space, the back wall illuminated by fluorescents— an unimpressive setting for impressive feats. He sat on a stool, spinning a little as he stretched out his arms and leaned back. "This is it. My home for almost a decade."

"Fancy." I walked slowly along the counter, a drag of my finger bringing up enough dust to choke a horsefly. I looked over the wall, a meticulous system of cubbies and cubes, no photos or mementos stuck to its hole-dotted surface. "Has this place changed since you lived here?"

He pulled open the closest drawer — got distracted for a moment, flipping through items before pushing it closed and leaning back. Looking over the room, he said. "Looks about the same." He ran his hand over the grid work of storage. "I put all of this in place. Looks like Dad hasn't touched it." Reaching out, he patted the worn wood counter. "This is where I built Sheila."

"Sheila?" I grinned at the fond look in his eyes and took a seat on the stool next to him. The room felt good. Lived in, despite its decades of loneliness.

"Sheila Anderson. The hottest chick in my third grade class. Jillian started homeschooling me in fourth grade. So Sheila Anderson's memory had to keep me alive. Focused. I thought building a computer would make me cool."

"Trying to impress her?"

He twisted his mouth, looked away. "Something like that."

I moved my chair closer. "Did it work?"

He wiped his hand over the surface as if memorizing the lines in the wood. "Don't know. Never saw her again." The stool squeaked as he rotated, faced me fully. Drug the stool until I was between his open legs.

I tilted my head and gave him a mock frown. "I'm a little jealous of this Sheila girl."

His hands reached forward, making small twists at the front of my shirt, unbuttoning one, then two, then the entire front of my shirt, the fabric gaping, a sigh coming from his mouth as he slid his hands inside. Cupping the lace that was my bra, my skin came to life underneath his hands. "You have nothing to be jealous *of anyone* about."

"I don't know..." I whispered. A small groan slipped out when his fingers pulled down the cups of my bra, my breasts falling out before him, hanging heavy with need, the brush of his hands over them bringing my nipples to full alert. "She did have a computer named after her..." I left my hands on my knees. Did nothing to stop him as he took his time with my skin, the brush of his lips soft as he leaned forward and tasted my neck. Played his tongue along the hollows of my throat as his hands gently pulled on my nipples, then moved to squeeze the weight of my breasts.

"That computer was a piece of junk," he whispered, moving his head back and taking my mouth with his. His kiss soft, his movements slow. He sucked on my bottom lip and teased my mouth. I gave up my grip on my knees and threaded my hands through his hair. Pulled him closer.

"How many girls have you kissed in here?" I asked against his mouth.

"Hmmm..." His lips moved, kissed a soft trail along my jaw, his hands taking liberties with my breasts that would make Sheila Anderson blush bright red. "Do you count?"

"No." I pulled his head by his hair. Guided it back to my mouth.

"Then none. Unless you count the Farah Fawcett poster I professed my love to."

"Shhh. You're ruining this with your talk of senior citizens."

He laughed, went for my belt. There was the creak of a door and I stiffened, pushing Brant back. Kept my back to the door as I heard the flip-flop of his mother's steps. "Brant? Dessert's ready."

Brant's eyes stayed on me, his mouth curving into a boyish smirk, his gaze dropping to my exposed chest, my shirt still gaping open. "All right Mom. We'll be up in a second."

No response from her. Just the retreat of footsteps and the click of a door. I clamped my hand over my mouth as a ridiculous giggle erupted from my mouth. He reached out, gave me one last grope before standing, pressing a kiss to the top of my head. "Button up my little minx. Let's get out of here before I have my way with you."

I shushed him, my hands fumbling, certain that my flushed cheeks and his smile would give away our actions. But a few minutes later, when we made our way through the house and back to the table, his parents seemed none the wiser.

Dessert, a lemon pie that would put Marie Callender to shame, was more pleasant, conversation moving at a steadier clip. If I had to guess, Brant's mother had given his father a stern warning during our basement time. The man seemed contrite, and Mrs. Sharp's eyes apologized with every contact. When silver scraped empty plates, I rose to help clear the table.

I followed her through a swinging door into a small kitchen, the yellow fridge and Formica countertops indicating the Sharp's lack of desire to spend their wealth. I scraped plates into the trash, the small space quiet with our sudden isolation from the men.

"I'm sorry," she blurted out, her voice soft. "For what Spencer said. About you not dating Brant."

"It's fine. Really." I didn't want to talk about it, didn't want to give the hundred nosy questions inside me an opening to spill out. My prying would only damage this fragile connection. I looked for a safe topic. "It's wonderful that you allowed Brant, at such a young age, to take off school to build Sheila."

"Sheila?" Mrs. Brant looked over from the sink, confusion clearing from her face when she understood my reference. "Oh – the computer. I'd almost forgotten; it's been so long since it was referred to as that. It was kind of a memorial thing … the name didn't stick. Apple didn't want the negative connotations attached to the project." She turned off the water, taking the dishes from my hand and sliding them into the soapy water.

"Negative connotations?"

She glanced over. "Oh – I forgot – you were too young. Sheila Anderson. The little girl who was murdered all those years ago. It was the summer Brant started working all the time. They never found her killer – or her body for that matter. Just…" Her voice faltered. "Just her clothes. Bloody. Not far from here. A few girls disappeared that summer, but she was the first. And … Brant had always had a crush on her. He took it hard. That was around the time … well." She stopped talking, glancing over my shoulder, the kitchen suddenly smaller as I felt Brant move up behind me, his hand wrapping around my waist and pulling me into his body.

"Mom putting you to work?" He planted a kiss on my head.

"Barely. She was just telling me about –"

"Old memories," she interrupted. "Thanks for bringing her by, Brant." Grabbing a hand towel, she wiped at her palms. "It was a pleasure to meet you, Layana."

I smiled. "Thank you. It was wonderful to meet you both."

"You leaving?" The large body of Brant's father closed off the doorway, and the space was suddenly claustrophobic.

"Yes. Thanks." Brant clapped his father on the back, and we squeezed our way out of the kitchen and made our exit.

I was quiet during the ride home, my mind walking me back through the evening. I wondered at the reasons behind Jillian and Mr. Sharp's aversion to our relationship. Wondered whether Mrs. Sharp had agreed with her husband, despite her apologies for his statement. Wondered about Sheila Anderson and why Brant didn't mention that she had died. I could have asked questions. But I didn't. I looked out the window and thought.

Chapter 12

2 YEARS, 6 MONTHS AGO

I stuck my head in Brant's office, his head popping up, hands furious on keys, un-pausing in cadence as he smiled. "This is a nice surprise."

"Don't get too excited yet," I teased, walking around the desk, his fingers keying at a rate faster than humanly possible, his eyes glued to me, his mind capable of more simultaneous action than mine. "I'm kidnapping you."

"Sounds..." He finished his typing, picking his hands up and swiveling his chair to face my approach, his hands reaching out and pulling me into his lap. "Interesting. Where are we going for this kidnapping?"

I shook my head. "Nope. I'm not telling you that. That'd ruin the fun. How much time do you need before we can go?" I glanced at his computer screens, three side-by-side monitors that each displayed file download progresses.

"I'm yours. Steal me away before Jillian reminds me about the budget meeting that starts in fourteen minutes."

"Shoot." I hopped off his lap, snagging my purse off the floor. "Then let me get you out of here."

"You make me so bad," he murmured, his eyes dark as he snagged me back for one last kiss.

"Oh yeah," I giggled. "Skipping budget meetings. You can get fitted for your leather vest now. Stick with me and you'll be going to bed without flossing. Getting really crazy."

I pulled him around the desk, peeking out of his door with an exaggerated gesture before turning back and putting a finger to my lips. "Run on three," I whispered. "One...two..." I opened the door and sprinted.

***

"Here?" Brant looked out the window at the homes before us, my car settling into a spot out front. "I've been here before."

"At the ribbon cutting. I know. I was there too. That didn't count. Get out." I opened my door and stepped out, taking a few steps back and snagging a stuffed unicorn off the lawn.

Brant's door shut and I looked over to see him, his posture awkward, his eyes sweeping over the compound, five brick homes, a fenced yard connecting them, three kids clustered in the shade of an oak, a dog sniffing the edge of the fence and eyeing us as if wondering whether to attack. Brown eyes hit me and his tail started to wag. I stepped toward the gate and flipped the latch. Squeezed through and squatted, running my hands over the collie. "Hey Buster." I ran him through his three tricks: sit, shake, and down, glancing over when Brant entered the yard and crouched to our level.

"Buster, huh?" He reached out a hand and tousled the collie's head.

"Yep. Meet the most loved dog in the Greater Bay area."

I heard the soft sound of steps seconds before a small body flung through the air, knocking my squatting self back into soft grass.

"Miz Lana!" Hannah, a six-year-old bundle of trouble, squealed as she squeezed my neck tightly enough to restrict air flow.

"Hey sweetie," I gasped. "Let me up a minute so I can introduce you to someone." I put a hand on the grass and hoisted us both to standing, flashing a smile at the two other kids, ones I'd never seen but would guess to be a few years older than Hannah, the close press of their bodies indicating a sibling familiarity verified by the twin shocks of red hair both possessed. I readjusted Hannah's weight until she rested on my hip. "Hannah, this is my friend Mr. Brant."

"Hi Mister Brant." She reached a solemn hand out, a hand Brant shook with equal seriousness.

"Nice to meet you Hannah." Brant's eyes flipped to mine. Dark and intelligent.

I turned to the others. "You guys must be new. I'm Lana, and this is my friend Brant."

"I told them all about you," Hannah said with importance, her dark arms tight around my neck.

"Well ... tell me about them then, since you know everything," I teased.

"This is Samuel and Ann. They're from Boatland."

"Oakland," the boy corrected, glancing at his sister.

I smiled. "Welcome to the house, guys. Which one are you staying in?" The houses were named after states, HYA's goal to have fifty in the next five years. At the moment, our three-acre estate contained five. We were looking at a lot in Sacramento for more homes, as well as spots in San Jose and Los Angeles.

"Georgia. Though they said we have to split up next month." Worried glances shot between two faces that were too young to have any concerns other than spilled milk.

"Don't worry about that." I readjusted Hannah on my hip, her weight tiring. "By next month you guys will have so many friends here you'll be begging for time away from each other. And the separation will only be at night. Days and meals are all free-for-alls between homes, so you guys will have lots of time together, should you want it." I glanced at Brant. "I've got to take Mr. Brant inside, but I'll see you guys again before we leave." I gently set Hannah down, giving each newbie a big smile before looping my hand through Brant's and pulling him toward the main house aka HQ, a six thousand square foot structure on the back of the property, where meals were served, sleepovers and movie nights held, and general bedlam occurred all day every day.

"This place is amazing," he said, glancing at the homes, the basketball court filled with moving bodies, a bevy of girls sprinting around the corner of a nearby house and flying past us.

"It is." I nodded. "All made possible by your donation."

"Maybe I should increase it."

I grinned. "That was, in part, my ulterior motive in bringing you here."

He paused, his firm hold on my hand bringing me to a stop. "You don't ever need motives, Lana. Anything you want, anything that makes you happy... just ask."

"I know." I tilted my head. "But I figure you might as well see the impact of your money." I pulled him forward. "Come on. I want to show you the main house."

***

We stopped on the third floor deck, an open area scattered with outdoor furniture, a group of girls sunbathing to our right. From its height, you could see the entire campus. "How many kids live in this house?" he asked.

"None. This is the social hub, where everyone eats, plays, and studies. The houses are set up for breakfast and sleeping, little else. That system seems to cut down on temper tantrums over who is in which house."

"I can't imagine that the kids would ever want to leave. This place is like summer camp."

I looked away. "Every kid wants love. To have parents whose focus is on their happiness. We can't do that for a hundred kids. We try, but we can't. They'd all leave this in a heartbeat for a chance to feel wanted. Loved."

"You weren't?"

I laughed, pushed on his arm. "I was talking about homeless kids, not my parents. My parents gave me everything I ever wanted."

"Money and presents don't equal love. I live in a huge house that doesn't hold a bit of love. I know what empty feels like. It's one of the reasons why I hate living alone."

"My parents loved me." I know the words must be true. Parents love their child. They just choose to show it in different ways. Mine chose to love by expectation.

"I love you." He stepped closer, his hands settling on my waist. "You, Layana Fairmont, are impossible not to love."

I scoffed. "You don't know me enough to love me." I've never been loved. Thirty years old and no man had ever uttered those words. A sad truth. Made possible by the dark lines of my ability to push away every man other than the one who stood before me, pulling me closer, his eyes owning me. This man I pulled closer, had turned over my heart somewhere along the place where I made the valiant effort to try and escape the artificial life plan that was ingrained in my blue blood.

"I love you. Every dark and light piece of you." He lowered his mouth, but I stopped his kiss, pressing a hand on his chest.

"There's no kissing on campus," I whispered. "HYA policy."

He frowned. "Don't I hold an office of some sort in this organization?"

"Board president."

He grinned. "I hereby, and for the next five minutes, strike that rule from the books." He pulled me closer and pressed his lips to mine, a soft sweet brush of commitment, one that changed, grew more passionate and possessive, his hand moving to cup the back of my head, his mouth sealing the deal, catching my heart as it jumped over the edge of forever.

I loved this man back. Done. My heart was officially toast. When the kiss ended, I told him as much, his mouth taking mine with a final touch that celebrated the occasion.

I heard a gasp from our right and broke our connection. Turned to see Hannah, her brown eyes big as saucers, alarm on her face at our flagrant breach of the rules. She pressed a firm finger to her lips, then made a zipper motion, doing a solemn and careful pantomime of locking her lips and throwing away the key.

Then, her face broke into a grin and she tore off into the house with a squeal.

Chapter 13

2 YEARS, 4 MONTHS AGO

I pulled up to his house, the entrance lights glowing, illuminated the path as my car pulled forward, sensing the presence of a vehicle, more lights coming on, palm trees and stone coming to life in an orchestration that must have set Brant back a few hundred thousand. I pressed the garage door opener, my bay opening, and I parked. Waited for the door to shut, to stop the cold wind from whooshing in.

I left my shoes just inside, Brant's level of clean OCD ridiculous. I walked through the silent house, waiting at the base of the stairs; my head tilted, and I listened. No sounds. He was probably downstairs.

I took the elevator, the doors quietly opening to an underground computer lab that rivaled Ironman's in size and capabilities. His back hunched, bare under the fluorescents, pajama pants the only thing on his tall frame. Straddling a stool, he worked over a pile of wires, a loop on his head, his hands moving quickly, tools lined up beside him in neat order. I settled into the leather chair in the corner of the room. Tugged the blanket off the back of it and wrapped it around my body. Watched him work.

"Hey baby." He didn't turn, the clink of tools the only sign of his activity.

"Hey love."

"I'll be done soon."

"Take your time. Mind if I put some music on?"

"Please. I adjusted the play tracks. Let me know what you think."

I picked up the Laya, Brant's latest prototype, a tablet that wouldn't hit markets for another year. Opening the music center, I was instantly impressed. He had done more than adjust play tracks. The layout of the music center was completely different. I chose my mood: lazy. Drawing an abstract sketch with my finger, a lazy swirl with an occasional dot or skip of interest, I clicked play. It knew my touch, recognized fingerprints with the speed of a blink. And, within seconds, it was playing the exact song desired—a song I didn't even know, but it was exactly what I wanted. Coldplay. The music flowed through speakers hidden along the walls, and I curled into the chair and watched the love of my life.

Love. It was no longer a strong word for our relationship. It was now the perfect word for our relationship. I loved this man. I could not imagine a life without him. He was the complement to my fears, a man firmly set into the trappings I desired, but with the independence and confidence to turn a blind eye to all of it. Together, we avoided the public life, had started a simple life of elegance, exploring the nuances of each other while enjoying the pleasures of which he had been gifted. With this man, I could see the possibility of a family. A genuine life. Married *and* happy, without myself in the dominance of a man who wanted a trophy wife.

"Do you approve?" He didn't turn, continued working.

"I approve," I said softly. "You are brilliant, baby."

"Thanks love."

I watched him, the flex of his back, the way his muscles yawned when he ran his hands through his hair. Listened to the soft mutter of his words as he spoke to himself. Smiled as the room went dark, crescendos played against my skin, and I fell asleep against the soft leather.

I was woken by kisses. The drag of his hands across my skin as he pulled me down in the chair, my legs nudged open, the burn of his skin as my bare knees bounced against the hard muscle of his thighs. He shouldn't be muscular. Shouldn't have tan skin, cut arms, a defined chest. He should be pale. Scrawny. He spent twelve hours a day under fluorescents, before computers. But I didn't question how God blessed him. Didn't question how or why, especially not in moments like this.

He pulled me farther, 'til my back was flat against the seat of the chair, my butt hanging off of it, his hands soft, probing, lifting my legs to the sky and pulling the soft silk of my shorts, the scratchy tease of my thong's lace coming along, moving up and then off my legs. And then I was bare before him, his hands pushing up the cotton of my tank, over my breasts, his body stilling when I was fully exposed before him.

"Perfect," he breathed. Ran his hands lightly, from breast to thigh, back and forth, side to side, just the skim of fingertips across skin, just light enough to make me arch into his touch, beg for more with my eyes. I waited. Breathed. Parted my legs before his eyes and lifted my knees, 'til my feet rested on the edge of the chair and I was open before him, nothing he couldn't see. His eyes dropped, focused on the place between my legs, a soft groan coming from his mouth, his fingertips dragging lower and running softly over the lips of my sex.

"Perfect," he repeated, his fingers brushing up and down over that spot, not pushing, not spreading, just a gentle caress that had me lifting my hips, his name whispering from my lips, wanting, needing more.

Then he pushed a finger inside and everything changed.

"God..." The curse, tumbling from his lips, as his mouth lowered to mine. Stretching his body forward, the hard muscles of his chest pressed against mine as he kissed me. I wrapped my legs around him, pinned his hand inside me, the gentle movement of that finger causing my breath to catch, mouth to freeze on his own.

"Yes, Brant. Oh my God, yes."

"I love you so much," he whispered, his mouth leaving mine, dropping to my neck, a hand pulling my legs apart as he moved down my body, his mouth soft on my skin, a delicious journey down as his finger continued its perfect tease inside my body. It's amazing what a finger can do. Such a small digit, but able to go exactly right *there*. My back came off the leather, my breath arrested as he touched some place that made my world go dark. "Don't stop," I whispered. "Oh my God, don't stop."

I couldn't keep my eyes open, but I wanted to. Wanted to see the look on his face, the dark intensity that stole over his face when he watched me. Wanted to see the moment he pulled out his cock, wanted to see the firm head of it, his hand wrapped around the base, the stroke of his fingers as he yanked at it.

This was his favorite moment—watching me come. It made the skin on his cock stretch as he hardened to a level past belief. It caused his eyes to darken, his breath to hitch. The muscles in his chest tightened, his hands quickened, my name a quick moan on his lips. And I knew what was coming. What would happen as the shudders ceased, as I tumbled down the delicious hill that was my orgasm. At that moment, the most perfect moment my body would ever know? That was when he would thrust. Remove his fingers and shove inside. Fill me to breaking before starting a rhythm that would trump whatever ecstasy I just experienced.

And the knowing, the expectation ... opening my eyes and seeing him prepare himself, his own excited anticipation at what was about to happen...

The heavy lids and pants of his breath as his finger continued its lazy brush inside of me. I bucked against his hand and came so hard I broke.

Waves upon waves, the sounds from my mouth senseless, unmeaning. I arched against his hand, humped it like an animal in heat, my body exploding around his finger, the perfect flick of his fingers making my feet kick, the glimpse of his face, dark intensity, his cock, hard and ready, and I couldn't stop it, it stretched, continued, beautiful insanity that turned my world into stars and my body into a constellation. And then, before I fell from the sky, at the moment when my breath began to catch and my eyes flicked open, he shoved inside of me and I lost it again.

Hard, fast. He fucked me as if he hated me, but the words spilling out were nothing but love. He bent over me, dug his hands into my hips and held me tightly in place. Pounded away, my name repeating on his tongue, the urgency in his movements carrying me higher, spurring my pleasure. This was for him, and that made it for me, knowing that the loss of his control was a gift, a rarity that I was one of the few to see. I wrapped my legs, dug my heels into him, and raked my nails across his skin.

When he came, it was Brant Sharp intense, one hand tight to my neck, the other squeezing the meat of my ass, pulling me tighter, as if he would never get enough — be deep enough, be one enough — of me. He thrust fully in, moaned my name, and shuddered through the final fucks of his orgasm.

"I love you so much," he whispered, lifting me, his hands tucking underneath my body, picking me up in a way that his cock stayed in, spinning with me until he was below and I was on top, stretched out over his body, my chest against his chest, the quick beat of our hearts off sync.

"I love you too, baby."

Outside, I heard the roll of thunder. A storm was coming.

Chapter 14

"When's the event?" Brant took a sip of ice water, his eyes catching the waiter's, the man scurrying to his side with the bill.

"Next Tuesday. I'll call you that afternoon and remind you." Jillian set down her fork, relaxing back in her chair, her hands smoothing the napkin on her lap.

"I'm not sixteen. I can remember a dinner. Though, if you let me have an assistant, you could stop worrying entirely. She could tie my shoes *and* get me to work on time."

The woman's eyes softened. "You know you're forgetful."

"You don't have time to keep me organized. You're a busy woman. The company needs you more than I do." He pulled a credit card from his wallet and dropped it on the bill, pushing it to the edge of the table before returning his stare to her.

"You're not busy enough to need an assistant. And I don't want some stranger thumbing through the details of our lives. You and I have looked after each other for twenty years. No need to change any of that now."

Brant watched her, his mind skipping, brought back to square one by her palm, hitting the linen tablecloth with enough force to cause him to jerk.

"Stay with me Brant," she said sharply. "You're getting distracted and I need to run. Dinner ... next Thursday. Be there."

"Layana will remember. Email her the details." Brant leaned back, watched her closely, saw the squirm in her seat against the chair. "You still hate her."

"No," she spoke sharply. "I never hated her. And don't now. She's fine. She's just not what you need."

"I don't know how you'd know what I need. You've never even seen us together. Come by, she's an incredible cook. You can join us for dinner."

The woman shook her head stubbornly, the glint of light reflecting in her diamonds. "No. I appreciate the offer, but no. Plus..." She smoothed her hands over the stack of papers before her, straightened the line of their edge. "I don't think she would particularly want me there."

He laughed. "Layana? See, you really *don't* know her. She doesn't have an unfriendly bone in her body." Another shift. His eyes narrowed. She was hiding something. But then again, he always got that sense from her. "What?"

"Nothing. Any plans for this week?"

"Layana's planned something. I'll need the jet."

Her frame stopped all movement. "For how long?" Skin around the mouth tight. Wrinkles emphasized. He looked at her and wondered. Why was she so attached to him? So afraid of his relationship with Layana. It wasn't natural. Wasn't normal. He shrugged. "We'll be back by Monday. Don't worry, the work won't suffer."

"It's a very busy time, Brant."

He tilted his head. "Not really. No irons in the fire. And you've done a good job of quieting any issues."

"The board meeting is Monday."

"And I'll be back for it," he repeated slowly, watching as she rose to her feet with a quick jerk.

"Please don't forget the Rosewood event. I'll have my assistant send her the details."

Her. He didn't think Jillian had ever muttered Layana's name. A small snub, but noteworthy. Jillian was more of a mother to him than his own. It was important to him that they got along.

Chapter 15

The woman didn't give up; I'll give her that. From the start, Jillian laid down battle lines before Brant and prepared for war. Every date had been a battle, his schedule often filled with emergency items stuck in on a day that should be free. Twice during the preceding months, he stood me up, Jillian texting with a bullshit excuse after repeated calls to his cell went unanswered. And he let her do it all. Dismissed her actions with a shrug of his shoulders.

"I don't understand why she hates me."

"She's protective," he explained. "And stubborn," he added, reaching over the table to spear an olive from my salad.

"Protective? Why?" I stared at him across the table, the Californian coastline perfectly framing his features. Wearing a loose white V-neck tee paired with designer jeans, the watch that glinted off of his wrist a thirty-fifth birthday present from yours truly. He looked every bit the California playboy, so many of who dotted this shoreline. What he didn't look like was a genius. Geniuses weren't supposed to come in perfect packages with straight teeth, gorgeous features and a strong build. They were supposed to come with pocket protectors and acne scars, horrible table manners and obnoxious egos.

The beautiful man before me shrugged. Took a sip of ice water. "She's always been worried about a woman going after me for the wrong reasons."

I nodded. "A reasonable concern." I didn't know a wealthy man who didn't share the same concern. But those same men ate up the benefits of their concern. Went through twenty-year-old cocktail waitresses like they were Kleenex. Brant... well everything Brant did was different. "Does that worry you?"

He stopped chewing, swallowed, and set down his fork. "Worry about you?" He sounded genuinely confused. "Dating me for my money?"

"Or your brain. Or that cock." I raised my eyebrows suggestively at him but his expression didn't change. Dead serious eyes stared back at me.

"It's never crossed my mind." He didn't say the sentence in a tone that indicated he needed to consider it. He said the sentence like the ludicrous idea was one that was beneath him. I reached out, ran my fingers over the top of his hand, the palm of it rolling under my touch and cradling my hand. He lifted, bringing my hand to his lips, and placed a gentle kiss on my fingers.

I smiled. "Thanks for the vouch of confidence."

"Thanks for sticking with me."

"But we're on for this weekend, right? You, me, and Belize?"

"Wouldn't miss it."

Our connection was broken by the wait staff, who brought our second course amid a flurry of trays and groveling and manners. We moved on to steak and salmon, and our conversation moved from Jillian the Difficult to Christmas and whose family would be blessed with our presence.

But it didn't leave my mind. I watched him cut his steak, look in my eyes and listen to me, take occasional sips of his beer. And I thought of Jillian. I understood protectiveness. I felt the emotion where Brant was concerned—a fierce need to protect what was mine. The problem for Jillian was that he was *mine*. Not hers. An aunt didn't have any property to protect, no claim over which to assert her dominance. And it was too late. I had him—had never been so sure of anything in my life.

I was a stupid, self-assuming girl. Sitting at that table? Smug in my confidence of my ownership? I'd never been so wrong. I didn't have him. I only owned half of him. The other half? It was a living a life I knew nothing about.

Chapter 16

BRANT

I have been with a hundred women, but never loved one until her. I could be with a thousand more and never find another Layana. She is beautiful, classy, but with a sharp edge that defines her personality, a thread of dark that complements all of her light. One that will cut you should you cross her. One that will fight for her wants, her needs, her opinions. She stares in my eyes and loves me with a vehemence all her own. A scary, passionate type of love. One that rips away all pretenses and allows us to love each other bare and without consequence.

I understand that my parents are scared. That Jillian fights against Layana with claws out, terrified that her involvement in my life will cause a repeat of the past. But I am stronger now. A man, not the boy of before. I've never felt so in control, so grounded. Maybe it's from the medication, maybe it's from maturity. But I'm not gonna risk it; I'll continue the medication until the day I die. It balances me. It keeps my relationship with Layana safe. With its help, she will never know.

True love makes a person reckless, makes them take risks and make sacrifices. True love tests the boundaries of our person, makes us yearn to be better and fight for the ground we stand on. I will fight for this love. Lie for it. Steal for it. It is worthy of that. On paper, we are a horrible match. I have no light; she brims with it. I am serious; she is fun. But off paper, that is where our magic occurs. I want to be more like her. I want to listen to her laugh and have had something to do with it.

I love her completely. She returns the love wildly. This love is worth the unsaid truths. The hidden lies.

Chapter 17

I knew the moment his cell rang, it's rattle against granite, that it brought trouble. I stepped to the island, flipped it over, and saw JILLIAN on the screen. Silencing the call, I returned to my Cheerios, and listened to the static of Brant's shower. My bags sat by the door. Brant's were being packed as I chewed, the task handled by two girls who seem well versed in all things travel. I needed to borrow them for the next trip. Hell, with their level of efficiency, I should just move them into the guesthouse. They'd solve half of my organizational issues in a month.

I chewed cereal, heard zippers sound and doors open, then the two women wheeled a single suitcase by, polite smiles nodding my way. I let them out, returned to my breakfast, and heard the tone of a voicemail sound against the counter.

The damn woman called back within ten minutes, at the inconvenient moment when Brant stood in the kitchen, leaning against the counter, an apple in hand. He stepped forward, flipping the phone over. "Hey L."

His eyes caught mine and he pulled the phone away from his ear, pressed a button and the speakerphone came on, Jillian's reedy voice filling the kitchen.

"...maintenance crew has it now. They might need to order a part; they're running diagnostic tests now. But there's no way it is flight-worthy."

Bullshit. My eyes flicked to Brant's. He said nothing, rubbed his neck as he stared at the phone.

Her sigh crackled through the phone. "I'm sorry, Brant. I hate that this ruins your trip. The plane should be back in order in a few weeks. Maybe you guys can reschedule after Vision 5's launch."

"It's fine. Nothing you can do about it. I'm glad you caught us before we headed to the airport." He reached forward, took the phone off speakerphone, and ended the call with a few short words. Then he tossed the phone on the counter, glancing at me with a wry look. "Sorry babe."

I shrugged, squatting down to unzip my bag and unpack any liquid contents in excess of three ounces. "No big deal. I'll grab my laptop. See what flights are open."

He frowned, squinted his eyes. "Flights?"

I straightened. "Yeah. Commercial flights."

"I ... don't fly commercial."

I laughed, rising to my feet and staring at him. "What do you mean you don't fly commercial? Your body doesn't physically have the capabilities?"

His eyes hardened. "We'll just go another time."

"No." I stared him down. "You'll push it off and we'll never go. I've already set everything up for this trip. You and I have never gone away together. Something always comes up. We're going."

"Commercial." He said the word like it physically tasted bad on its way out of his mouth.

"Yes. First class. Toughen up." This was interesting. Five minutes earlier, I would have said Brant didn't have a snobby bone in his body. Didn't need any of the trappings of wealth and luxury that he spent all day ignoring. Maybe I was wrong. Maybe he gripped all of this as tightly as I did. Maybe he'd also be lost in a world that didn't include massages and concierges and enough money to last the rest of our lives. I opened my laptop and turned my back to Brant. Brought up flights to Belize while cursing Jillian's hand in this. It takes a meddler to know a meddler, and I'd bet ten thousand bucks that there was nothing wrong with the BSX jet.

***

"This is bullshit."

"This is normal. Welcome to life." I stared at the back of a Hawaiian shirt, the tourist before us having misunderstood San Francisco weather when making his travel plans, anticipating a sunny climate in which sandals and short sleeves would be appropriate in April. I knew this information from his wife, a scrawny woman with sharp elbows and a voice that carried, a voice that had lectured him on his packing choices for the last twenty minutes. Twenty minutes in which we had moved approximately halfway to the point in which our first class tickets would make a difference in our security clearance wait time. Twenty more minutes behind this couple. The flare of Brant's nostrils warned me he wasn't gonna make it.

He wasn't handling this well. Had balked at the long-term lot we left his Aston in, not liking the looks of the parking attendants. Had been less crazy about wheeling his bag the half-mile stretch to the terminal. Didn't understand, upon our arrival at the Delta counter, that the line of bodies stretching through the space all belonged to people ahead of us in line.

I was sick of his bitching. Hell, maybe this was the reason Jillian didn't expect us to last. Maybe *this* was the deep, dark secret I had anticipated for the last nine months.

Brant was a public transportation pussy.

My brain winced at the crudeness of my inner thoughts, glancing around casually to make sure my obscenity wasn't telegraphed.

Nope, all clear. The line ahead of us shifted and we stepped one beautiful step forward. I glanced at my watch, worried about the time. Too late, I yanked my wrist down. Tried to hide the motion with an elaborate yawn.

"We late?"

Brant had become obsessed with the time. He was certain we were going to miss the flight. Had checked his watch and calculated our rate of airport progression so many times that I took away his watch. Stuffed in into one of the nine zippered compartments of my Michael Kors bag.

"Nope," I lied. "We're good."

"I don't think we are. There are 121 people between the first security checkpoint and us. They seem to be processing individuals at a rate of fifteen to twenty seconds per interaction. If you take an average of eighteen seconds per person, then we are looking at almost twenty-two hundred seconds. Thirty-six minutes. Given that I can't see the next stage of the process, we can only guess at the duration of that wait. But our tickets indicate that boarding ends fifteen minutes before departure. So unless your clock has a time of ten twelve or later, which would allow us a tight window of twenty minutes for the next stage of the security process, we will miss the plane." He stared at my wrist as if the power of his stare alone could force the bones in my wrist to turn. I tucked my hands in my pockets out of pure stubbornness. Why couldn't he be normal? The type of boyfriend who glanced at a watch and stated some unfounded prediction that we might miss our plane? I didn't need intelligent foundations for my worries. I just wanted to move obliviously toward my demise. I noticed that the chatterbox in front of us had stopped talking about clothes and had moved into our space, gawking at Brant like he was an informational display, her pokey elbows jabbing into the girth of her husband. She stepped toward Brant, her head cocked, and I stifled a laugh at the alarm that crossed his face.

"Looks like you'll have to recalculate," I whispered, nodding my head toward a new line that opened to the right, the action catching the attention of our entire section, heads snapping, feet scurrying, as everyone did a jerky dance where they tried to decide to embark on a new path or stay in the soon-to-be-shorter current location. "Do we move?"

He watched the traffic, his eyes bouncing, then shook his head. "No."

I stayed in place, stepping forward as our line thinned considerably. "I'm not sure you were right," I said shortly, watching the speedy pace of the new line.

"About what?" He seemed calmer, the clench of his jaw less noticeable.

"This line being faster."

"It's not."

I looked up at him, my hands pausing in their search for a mint. "What?"

"This line's not faster. It's gonna take an extra five to seven minutes in this line."

I whipped my head right, looking in exasperation at the other line, Hawaiian shirt guy and his loud wife a good eight people closer to security than us. "Then why'd you tell me to stay here?" I couldn't help it. I looked at my watch.

"I watched her." He pointed to the wife of Hawaii. "Then decided on the opposite course of action." He met my glare head on. The corner of his mouth crooked a little.

I couldn't stop the laugh; it bubbled out with enough force that I had to sit, my ass on the edge of my suitcase, every ounce of the day's stress leaving in that one moment. And suddenly, it didn't matter if we made the plane or not. If the weekend was a disaster, or saved. All that mattered was that I was with him. I shook my head. Tilted my head back when he leaned down, tugging a soft hand on my ponytail as he kissed me. "I really do love you," I whispered against his mouth.

"You have no idea how happy that makes me," he replied, taking the time for an extra kiss. Behind us, an exasperated sigh sounded, the irritated tap of a feminine shoe making our holdup of the line known. He offered me his hand and hefted me to my feet, his other hand scooping up my suitcase and moving us a few steps closer to takeoff.

***

I might have gone years without discovering his secret. He certainly hid it well enough, Jillian a primary aid in that deception, a large part of her world dedicated to ruse control. I wasn't the only clueless one. It was something the media, a force that loved Brant, had no clue about. Something his company executives were unaware of. And me, someone who saw the man once or twice a week, had his hands on my skin, his mouth in my ear, his eyes on my own... it took nine months for me to discover the secret. It could have taken even longer. I look back now and see very little clues.

But the closer we grew, the more time in each other's presence... it was only a matter of time. I now understood Jillian's fight, her battle to keep us apart, the minor things she did to place obstacles in our way.

As it was, I discovered his secret on our first night in paradise.

Chapter 18

There was the flap of curtains in pitch-blackness when I woke up. The crash of waves put me in my bedroom but the air was wrong. Not the icy Californian chill, but a balmy caress, warm enough to comfort, cool enough to kiss my skin. I sat up, my eyes adjusting, the white linen curtains billowing in the wind, the glow of the moon becoming visible. I relaxed back against the sheets, rolled, stretched out my arms, feeling nothing but emptiness beside me. Stilling, I listened, lifting my head when I didn't hear anything. "Brant?"

Dead silence. No one in our suite but me. I slid off of the bed, my bare feet slapping across the floor as I made my way to the bathroom. Found my purse and pulled out my cell. Powered it on.

This resort didn't believe in electronics; they were of the mindset that you couldn't relax unless you 'Got Away From It All!' and 'Returned To Nature!' It was one of those concepts that seemed like a good idea until we got here. Within two hours we realized our attachment to air conditioning and Internet, our technology withdrawals peaking at the moment when we failed to find in-room electrical outlets to charge our cells. I flipped on the bathroom light and watched my Samsung go through its opening scripts, the time finally displaying. 1:22 AM. *Late.*

I called Brant's cell, realizing, as it went to voicemail, that his cell was off, its battery-saving mission more important than my own. I stepped to his suitcase, unzipping its top and digging through it, looking for the brick of his cell. What I wasn't looking for, when my hand shoved aside underwear and swim trunks, was the ring box.

Oh no. My hand froze, as I stared at the black velvet box. *No. No. No.* A woman got proposed to only once, assuming she picked wisely. It should be handled perfectly, the correct amount of delighted surprise filling her eyes. This discovery, at this moment in time, might ruin my reaction. I reached forward, brushing my fingers over its surface, and fought the urge to pull it out. Flip it open. Take a little peek.

I didn't. I pulled back. Zipped the suitcase closed. Stared at it. I would still be surprised. I hadn't seen the ring. I'd just practice my shocked face. Make sure it wasn't grotesque or too exaggerated. I saw his phone, the bulge of it sticking from a side pocket and grabbed it.

I set both phones on the entrance table and took a chance, walking to the back balcony and stepping out. As I scanned my eyes over the beach, moonlight reflected off waves, the sand pristine, unmarred. No billionaire walked along its surface. Nothing but nature. Yeah, it was pretty. Big deal. I would have traded it all for a television with HBO.

A ring. A proposal. This was the perfect place for it. Mrs. Layana Sharp. The name alone put goosebumps on my skin. Was it what I wanted? Absolutely. No question. My biggest complaint with our relationship was that I wanted more of it. More time with Brant. More insight into the beauty that was his mind, the pieces of him hidden behind his slight smile. I wanted a partnership, wanted children with the man, wanted to move in and fill up a home with memories. Be his wife. Grow up and have a purpose. And tomorrow, it seemed, I would have it.

I scanned the beach one last time and turned, stepping back into the room and closing the doors, the sound of the ocean muted. I glanced back at the bed. Took a moment and contemplated a return to it.

I was used to waking up alone. The few nights I had spent at Brant's he often got up during the night. Headed down to the basement to work or drove to the office. It didn't bother me; I wasn't someone who needed a full night's bed commitment to feel secure. But here, in this resort, with no work in sight, where was he? And why didn't he leave a note? The questions tugged at me. Kept me from moving toward the bed. I moved to the closet instead. Tugged a robe over my silk pajamas, loosely tied the belt, and worked my feet into slippers. Grabbed both of our phones, my room key, and a handful of cash. Schooled the goofy smile on my face into a more appropriate one. Then I stepped out, tugging the door shut behind me. And went to find my future husband.

It didn't take long. It was a small resort—another issue that ensured the Sharp party of two would not be making a return visit. There just wasn't enough to do here. Not for a couple who didn't want to hike nature trails or watch sports. Especially not for a man who got his kicks off on things that beeped and lit up. Ten minutes later, I walked into the place I should have started at—the hotel bar. Even though Brant didn't really drink, didn't seek out social mingling or groups of people. But, at almost 2 AM, it was one of the only places open inside the gates. I walked through the doors, eyed the scant crowd, and saw him, his back to me, hand resting on the bar, in a cluster of people I didn't recognize.

I smiled, relief washing through me. I didn't know what I expected, what the tight grip of my back muscles had anticipated, but the tension left when I saw him. I made my way through the bar, my pajamas out of place, a few women giving me looks that deserved a sharp word, but I continued. Fished his phone out of my pocket as I moved, powering it on. I'd give him his phone, kiss him goodnight, and then make my way back upstairs. I didn't need to stay down there; I wanted to go back to our bed, would have my cell if he got drunk and needed help finding his way back to the room. I smiled at the absurd thought of a drunk Brant and moved closer.

A few steps away. Bodies moved aside, gave me a better view of him.

Closer. My slippers caught on the tile and I tripped slightly. Caught myself, my face heating.

Heard the murmur of his voice. Reached out. Placed my hand on his shoulder and pulled gently.

The smooth rotation of his torso, the over the shoulder glance that came full circle and looked down at me ...

In the next few minutes, everything about our relationship changed.

I had fallen for him. Planned our future, already mentally accepted his proposal.

It turned out I didn't even know him.

Chapter 19

TWO YEARS, THREE MONTHS AGO
BRANT:

I had intended to propose in Belize. Cancelled that plan when the jet was nixed. Reestablished that plan when Lana bullied us into commercial. Then our trip had a hiccup; she got sick and the moment never happened.

Tonight. The second attempt. I shake a pill out, place it under my tongue and try to relax. Swig ice water and stare at the back wall of my office, a stainless steel surface broken by glass views of the hills.

Everything exact. Everything perfect. She deserves nothing less. This will be the moment that solidifies our future. A story we will tell our children's children. She is already a loose cannon, will no doubt foil tonight's plans in some impulsive way, and everything is in place to minimize the impact. All that matters, at the end of the night, is that I have the ring and can articulate a question. The rest will sort itself out.

She will say yes. It is a given. We love each other, crossed that hurdle months ago. The bond between us is unquestionable. My personality had needed a quantitative analysis to make my decision; she won't need anything other than her emotions. The fire that makes her throw her arms around me and kiss my neck. The grins I watch stretch across her face. The smolder that sits in her eyes when we make contact across a crowded room. She is committed. We are in love. Marriage is the next step to forever. I pocket the ring and stand, striding out of the office, my eyes catching the clock and reaffirming that I am on schedule. Three hours to forever.

***

Two hours to forever. I watch her fasten her earrings, the stance before the mirror one of casual elegance, yet sexual all the same. Slightly spread legs, her hip cocked, head tilted, all of her curves present before me. I step closer, settling in behind her, our eyes meeting in the mirror as I pull her an inch back, the press of her fitting into me perfectly.

She is nervous. I can see a darkness in her eyes, a tremor in her hand as she pushes the diamond stud through her earlobe. Something is off—from the deep inhale of her breath to the smile she gives me. Tighter, less free. It's not the false front she serves out to others, but it isn't the smile I know. It is a distracted mix of the two. Something is on her mind. Something her eyes say she isn't ready to talk about. I bend forward, inhale the rich scent of her as I place a soft kiss on her collarbone. "Would you rather stay in? We don't have to go out." A question whose answer can ruin tonight's plans but I don't want a reluctant companion. Not tonight, at the official start of our life together as one.

Another smile that is not her smile. "No. We should go. I want to." Her breathing is off. Quicker than usual. I suddenly want to pull her into the bedroom. Slide up her dress and connect with her. Lose both of our senses in the hard press of our bodies. Put our center back, reassure me that she is mine and she is here and she is happy.

I don't. Instead, I hold open her coat, let it fall over her shoulders and open the front door for my future wife. Pull it shut and pray to God that she says yes. Suddenly, everything I know seems up in the air.

Maybe not tonight. Maybe I wait until this funk passes. Until she smiles and the light reaches her eyes. I watch her move down the steps and follow.

***

One hour to forever. She doesn't question the helicopter, or that night's unorthodox use of the Rolls and my driver. Tucked under my arm, her head turns to the window, the lights of San Francisco tiny against the shoreline as the chopper moves steadily through the sky. She doesn't ask questions. Just settles into my arm and watches the reflection of a low sun as it shines off the peaks of rocky waves.

"I love you," she says softly.

My arm tightens around her, embracing the feel of her. She loves to be held, a part of her anxious for the physical confirmation of our bond. "I love you too."

She tilts her chin up and meets my eyes. "Forever," she says firmly.

"Forever," I repeat, leaning down and pressing a kiss against her exposed forehead. The copter shifts and I tighten my grip. "Buckle up. We're landing."

Forever. It had sounded ominous on her lips.

Chapter 20

Despite the strong wind, the helicopter sets down easily on Farallon Island. We open the door to two tuxedos, waiting with outstretched arms to help us out of the chopper and along the irregular ground. We duck and run, Lana's bare feet nimble on the uneven surface, her heels in her hand, a true laugh spilling from her lips as she grips my arm tightly and climbs over the small hill of rocks before us, the slick surface of my dress shoes making the journey treacherous. Just what I need. I can picture the headline: COUPLE STUMBLES TO UNTIMELY DEATH JUST MOMENTS BEFORE PROPOSAL. Not that there has ever been a timely death.

It is all worth it when her head clears the rocks and I hear the catch in her voice. Her eyes had found the table set on a flat rock, white linen, candles, and champagne present. The height elevates us on a ledge with nothing but rock and ocean and sunset on all sides, the jagged skyline of San Francisco twenty-seven miles to the east. The suit to our right holds out a floor-length coat that I help her into before shrugging into my own, the buffering wind giving the evening a chill. Sitting, we accept flutes of champagne as the setting sun paints a landscape of beauty on all sides. It is perfect. Just as I imagined, the small island a private sanctuary for this moment.

"You went all out." She meets my eyes over the table. Direct. Nothing else between us right now.

"All out would have coordinated whales. Their union wouldn't agree to demands, but I'm hoping we see some tonight." I nod to the waves. "I was told this is the spot to see them breach."

A moment of silence falls over us as she wraps her coat tighter and glances out at the water. I wish for a whale, for nature to prove its support of our union with one dramatic show of grace. In my right pocket, folded and unfolded a hundred times, my speech. I don't need the paper; I know the words. Had recited them perfectly while shaving. Tried a different take, a different tone, while driving to the office. Have changed the format ten times, the wording twenty. The weight of the paper has been comforting all day, yet suddenly seems wrong. I throw away the plan and reach for her hand. "You know I love you."

Her eyes move to our hands. "I know."

No. I need to see her eyes. To have that connection, to read her. The Layana I know doesn't hide. I don't understand it, yet forged onward. "You know that I will do anything for you. To make you happy."

She looks back up. *Finally.* "I know."

Standing, I move next to her chair and kneel, pulling out the box that holds our future. "I love you with every piece of my heart. Will spend my life making you smile. Please do me the honor of spending the rest of your life as my wife." I crack open the box, the top opening easily, the darkening sky making the blue diamond no less impressive. I hold it out, realizing—before my arm finishes the action, my eyes glued on her—all of the things wrong with this situation.

The flush of her face.

Panic in her eyes.

A bite of her cheek.

Regret in her stare.

Wetness on the edge of her mascara.

She closes her eyes tightly and a lone dark tear drips down its side. I stare at that tear, and feel every piece of my carefully constructed world break.

***

She doesn't give me a reason. Doesn't do anything but cry as I stare, examining every line of her as she covers her face. Eventually, there is a stiff shake of her head and I close the lid, putting the ring box back into my pocket, a place that has already grown cold in the last few minutes, the scrape of my knuckles against the cashmere of my coat a sickening texture. Something is wrong. Something has happened and broken the perfection of us.

I need to find out what has happened. We are fixable. Nothing will change that.

I will wait until the day I die for her. For me, there isn't, and will never be, anyone else.

Chapter 21

LAYANA

Our relationship had been perfect. A gorgeous, brilliant man. One who loved me with every spare inch of his heart. Spoiled me. Listened to me. Valued me. One who I loved passionately in return. I had gone ahead and made plans for us. Big plans sucking up large parts of my heart. Plans involving a house full of children, growing old as one, a joining of our lives that would never end.

Then, I found out his secret. And on that night, my world imploded. Every fantasy I had of happily ever after, of children and marriage: gone. I was faced with a hole of deceit and had to decide if I wanted to jump in or walk away. I could have ended everything. Broke it off and continued on—tried to find another love, a different happy ending. Instead, I stood at the rabbit hole of hell and looked down. Toed the line of indecision, even while turning down his proposal. I waffled, I moped, and I drowned my sorrows in chardonnay. And then ... finally? I squared my shoulders and stayed. Didn't let on that I knew his secret. But that day, when my fairy tale died? I lost my trust in him, in our relationship. And a few months later, I met Lee.

PART 2

Lies. A mountain of them between us.

Chapter 22

TWO YEARS AGO

A few months after Belize, I was in a convenience store, examining colorful lines of candy, trying to decide which one was worth my change, when he walked in. Out of my normal neighborhood, I had driven down to Palo Alto to visit Brant at work. Stopped in an area I shouldn't be in because my Mercedes needed gas and my bladder wouldn't shut up.

I felt him before I saw him, a presence behind me, uncomfortably close, and I turned my head and caught his eyes. Staring right at me. Not evasive, not ashamed. Looked at me in the same way a baby does, innocent and direct, so direct you wanted to break contact but I didn't. His stare was so unlike Brant's that I mentally stuttered, caught in this moment in time where we both stared and then he smiled.

Wow. Cocky. Confident. Sexual. So different from Brant's. Brant's fixed expression was intensity, his face still and stoic. Brant was a man who listened, then reacted, impulse not in a trait in his wheelhouse. Neither was carefree, playful, or flirtatious. This man's smile was all three, and I was drawn to it, my own smile curving in response.

"Hard decision," he said, nodding his chin to the shelves.

"Yeah." I nodded, my smile still on. Like I was a marionette doll, the goofy expression painted in place. *I should turn back. Move away.* Instead I kept the eye contact, my damaged relationship at the type of fragile place where decision-making abilities should be revoked.

"I know you..." he said slowly, squinting slightly, his smile a little more guarded, recognition dawning in his eyes. Actual recognition, no 'Don't I know you?' flirtation to follow.

I stopped breathing, my smile still in place, dreading yet curious about whatever words would come next.

An 'aha' moment when he made the connection. "Aren't you Brant Sharp's girlfriend?" He whirled away from me, his head tilting as he scanned the magazine rack behind us, his hand skimming over and grabbing a magazine. A groan slipped through my clenched jaw.

Wired Magazine: the go-to for geeks worldwide—had just proclaimed me Tech Hottie of the Year, an honor that should have been bestowed on someone actually in the electronics industry, not just a girlfriend of this century's brainchild. Yet there I was, on the glossy cover, covered in nothing but wires, the confident grin on my face making this their bestselling issue so far. Geeks apparently liked nudity, no matter who wore it. And there, in giant letters across my midsection, my appearance's validation: "Lucky Layana: where Brant Sharp gets his creative inspiration."

I stopped smiling, reached out and snatched the magazine from his hands, took four steps to the side and stuffed it behind a few issues of *Martha Stewart Living*.

"Well now, that just answered my question," he said with a smile, putting a hand on the rack and leaning in, just enough that I could smell the scent of fresh grass coming off him.

God, that's a good smell. I stole a discreet sniff and then stepped back. So...the gorgeous man *didn't* know me. Had just recognized me from the magazine, either the *Wired* cover or another one. Over the last few months, Brant's media machine had gone into overdrive, put me on seven of them, the PR campaign headlined by Jillian, a woman who had jumped fully into Team Layana. She and I had talked, the night I found out the Secret. Mended fences in our new common goal to Keep The Secret. The stiffness was still there, but with an objective now shared between us, she had moved bleachers, her energy moving onto things other than ending our union. Her most recent efforts centered on pushing me into the spotlight. I knew what she was doing. She wanted the focus off him, his privacy left intact while the vultures feasted on my flesh instead. It'd been working. I'd done five interviews that month.

The media machine coined me Lucky Layana, due to my supposed inspiration for Brant's last creation: the Laya. The Laya was single-handedly responsible for increasing BSX's bottom line by an extra eight figures that quarter. A shining star. All thanks, in the media's mind, to me. Ridiculous.

"So are you?"

My return to the candy quandary was looking like a lost cause. "Am I what?"

"Lucky." His voice low, it grated of intentions, desire, and Iwannafuckyourighhere sex.

I looked up, meeting his gaze and was taken aback by the sizzle of chemistry between us. This was nothing like how it was with Brant. This was electricity and danger and raw want, a combination that pushed my feminine buttons and made me reckless. "Why don't you try me and find out?"

He chuckled, stepped back, the yellow suede of his work boots creaking on the linoleum floor. "You're not that kind of girl."

I kept the eye contact, swallowed the apprehension sitting in my throat. This was wrong. This was bad. I should run home, wait for Brant, and forget this ever happened. My voice disobeyed, coming out cool, confident. Exactly as I'd always wished a flirtation to sound, yet *this* time was when I finally nailed it. "Not that kind of girl? Then you really *don't* know me."

"Anybody can talk big in public." His eyes dared me, his cocky smile returning, and he glanced at the hidden magazine, then back at me.

"Then take me somewhere private." The challenge was in my tone, even as my conscience screamed a long, silent death somewhere in my bones.

Private turned out to be the back of the store, a gravel lot enclosed on both sides with privacy fence and junk cars, an abandoned bucket and empty packs of cigarettes littering the ground that our feet kicked through. He shoved me against the wall, his hands pulling at my Vince sleeveless tank, sliding it down over my shoulders, the neckline popping as it stretched beyond its means, his strong hands ripping further until the pale top of my breasts were exposed, peeking out of the lace of my bra. "Nice," he murmured, dropping his head, pulling down with greedy hands until the cups of my bra were pulled aside and my breasts hung free, out of the cloth, his hands cupping and squeezing them as his body pressed against me. Inside me, my conscience battled with need, every brush, grip and grope of his hand like fire across my skin, lighting my arousal till it was at the point of madness. I struggled with my emotions, unable to keep a clear head as I gasped for breath, his head lifting until we were staring at each other and everything paused.

A long freeze in time, both of us caught until he broke the moment with the long scrape of a chuckle. "What are you doing Lucky? Aren't you late for afternoon tea?"

I growled at him, leaning forward and biting into his neck, the taste of his skin one of sweat and salt, heat and man. Dirt and want. A far cry from the cologne and dignity of which I was accustomed. "I thought you were a man of action. You nervous? Worried you can't compete?"

He pulled my mouth from his neck. Twisted my face with his hand until I was staring full force into him. Dominant eyes, the playfulness gone. Nothing but gorgeous alpha male, competitive forces at play in their depths. I'd seen the look in Brant's eyes before. When he was attacking a problem. Going after a competitor. But never when he'd stared at me.

"I'm worried I'll fuck you so well I'll ruin you for life."

God, I know it was wrong. But in the face of recent events, I closed my eyes to reason.

I liked it. I wanted it. I wanted it to fuck me.

And it did. Right there in that overgrown parking lot. An employee's car watching us pulse and moan against dirty brick. Heaven above cursing my soul while I spread my legs and let his cock take me hard. A cheap gas station condom on his cock. Hard and clean and hotter than I've ever gotten it before. Including from Brant. He fucked me to use me, his focus on his pleasure, his attraction to me not masked in any way. It should have felt wrong, it shouldn't have been hot, but it was, dirty and desperate, and I came hard, my hands gripping the rough brick, my legs shaking, the pleasure ripping a forbidden path through my body.

He finished a minute later with a roar, not attempting to censor his speech, his cry whipped by the wind, my own moan loud against his neck, his hands tight on my ass, pulling me into him, the gasps and pants letting me know how long and how good his finish was.

"Fuck," he swore, pushing off the building, his cock dropping out of me, one of his hands hard against my shoulder, keeping me pinned to the wall as he stripped off the condom and tucked his cock back into his pants. Zipped up ripped jeans with one hand while his heavy breaths and wild eyes traveled up my body. "So that's what the other half gets."

"Fuck you," I shot back, with as much challenge as I could, given that my linen shorts were stretched tight around my ankles, my shirt up, tits out. A strong breeze gusted, and my nipples responded, the skin tightening, my cunt heavy and wet with my arousal.

He squatted before me. Gripped the top of my shorts and worked them up, my legs sliding together to aid him, the scuff of jeweled sandals against gravel as the heat of his fingers drug up my legs, his eyes never moving from mine, their directness more of an invasion than his cock.

At my navel, I felt the turn of his hands as he fastened the button, then he slid his knuckles higher. The rough skin of them brushed over my stomach, then the curve of my breasts, my breath hitching as he rolled his hands over and squeezed possessively. Hard enough to almost hurt, he used the grip to pull himself up, and I had to look up as he rose to his full height.

Another squeeze. I felt every single finger as they spread across my chest. He alternated the pressure and I would have laughed except that I was on the thin verge of asking him for round two.

His hand released. He pulled up my bra and down my shirt so quickly that I got distracted from whatever I was about to say. And ... with clothes in between us, we suddenly had less in common.

"Get back to his mansion, Lucky. I'm sure he's waiting."

"He's not."

He grinned again, this one less playful, harder, cynical. "You always fuck strangers within five minutes of meeting them?"

"Did they leave that fact out of the article?"

"I guess high class bitches like cock just like any other."

"I guess low lives don't know how to take a girl on a date."

A catch in those eyes. A slow nod, the corners of his mouth turned up a tad, a dimple breaking through. Brant had a dimple, though I hadn't seen it in months.

"Then let me take you to lunch."

I glanced at my watch, the Tag sparkling brilliantly against the afternoon sun, framed by California-kissed skin. "A little late for lunch."

"Then beers. Unless that's too lowbrow for you."

I shrugged. "I can fuck in a parking lot; I think I can down some dollar wells."

His face darkened, and I had already seen more emotion from him in thirty minutes than in the last month with Brant. Ever since my rejection of his proposal, there'd been a gap of sorts. Maybe it was me, maybe he had withdrawn, maybe it was a little of both. Whatever the reason, this man's passion, his attitude… it was a refreshing change.

We got in his vehicle, a jeep, one that pulled a trailer full of mowers and tools, my eyes skipping over the contents, inventorying everything, his eyes catching the movement. "Sorry. Left my Ferrari at home."

I sat on a broken vinyl seat, my fingers itching to pull open the glove box and check the registration, put a name and some bit of understanding to the man who sat beside me. The jeep hitched, then jerked, throwing me against the steering wheel as he tore out of the parking lot, my white Mercedes still parked in front, the candy bar craving still present as I let him drive away.

"What's with the tools?" I had to yell over the music, some country song about broken hearts and Texas, his hand leaving the shaky shifter to turn the dial down, the easy way his hand returned to the shift knob sexual in its dominance.

"I do landscaping. Cut, trim, edge, plant. Work with my hands." He glanced over. "That work for you?"

"It doesn't need to work for me." I gripped the seatbelt. Hoped his next tight turn didn't tumble us into the ditch. Whoever decided on pulling the doors off these vehicles needed to be shot. I wondered about the vehicle's safety rating.

"You always such a bitch?"

I laughed. Shook my head. "No." Brant would never call me a bitch. Didn't use words like that. Thought of them as unintelligent, a waste of syllables when there was so many more appropriate terms.

"So I'm just lucky?"

"You're ... different," I mused, unsure how to say all of the things I didn't need to say.

"I'm just ordinary, Lucky. That's not necessarily a bad thing."

No. I thought a piece of us all yearned to be ordinary. I'd like to escape into it myself sometime.

He pulled up to a bar I had never seen, in a part of town I have never visited. The In Between—sandwiched between two larger bars that probably served food and had wait staff and a sanitation rating above a D. But we walked into the In Between, the bartender looking up with a familiar smile and greeting him by name. *Lee.* Wouldn't have guessed that. Lee fit strange on him, would take some adjustment of my mind. Guess we missed introductions in our romantic rush to the parking lot.

The first stool I sat on wobbled badly, my discard of it and attempt at stool #2 also a failure. I accepted the failure, hooking my feet on the rungs and looking up, into the bored face of the bartender.

"Whatcha want?"

"What do you have?"

"Millers, Bud, and Pabsts."

Super classy. "Miller Lite please. Bottle."

I got a draft two minutes later, the glass looking less than clean, a Solo cup more welcome, had one been available. I took a strong chug of the beer, happy to find it cold, then set it down, feeling his eyes on me. I turned my head, catching a glimpse of his smile, the glass pausing on its way back to my mouth.

His smile was my kryptonite. It was shy in the way that only a confident man can work, the slow drawl of a mouth that asked you for permission to step inside and fuck your mind.

I took another sip of beer and he watched my mouth. And even when his smile stopped, it continued in his eyes. He fucked me with those eyes. I felt them pull off my clothes and push me back, climb on top of me and make me his. I couldn't look away; I couldn't help but smile back. I should be confident, I should hold the cards, but instead I blushed and lost track of thought. This man, he could be the death of me. I knew that , but feared I could not stay away. It was worth losing the war for time in the battle with him.

He wiped his mouth with the back of his hand. "Anyone ever tell you you're weird?"

"In what way?"

He laughed. "Every way." He took a heavy sip of his own, reached over, and grabbed my stool, in between my legs, his hand brushing against the crotch of my shorts as he gripped the wood and pulled it, my hands gripping the bar top for balance as he drug the stool and me toward him, stopping when I was in between his legs, his hand on my bare thigh, sliding confidently up the muscle until he reached the hem of my shorts.

"You're pretty weird yourself."

"You don't know me yet."

He was right about that. This man was a complete mystery to me. "I have a pretty good idea."

"I'm glad one of us does."

I stared at him, fascinated. By the way his fingers dipped under the line of my shorts, by how he was sexual and frank, yet secretive. Cocky, but with a hint of vulnerability. He showed distain and attraction for me all at one time, and acted as if it was completely normal. But most fascinating, most tempting: all of the ways he was different from Brant. In the loose gesture of his hand, as he tipped back his head and empties his glass. The manliness in every movement, the smell of him, one of earth and grass and sweat. Masculinity personified, and proved legitimate in how he had fucked me against the wall. Hard, invasive. For his own need more than mine. Greedy, animalistic. Marking me with his cock. He was the type of man I had always run from, but might just be the type I had always needed.

He swung back on his stool to me, looped a hand around my back and slid me to the edge of the mine, taking a moment to lift one leg, then the other, until I was all but straddling him, the push of his jeans against mine maddeningly stimulating.

"Kiss me." He pulled the glass from my hand. Set it on the counter and faced me fully. Cupped my face and stared into my eyes. Waited. I closed my eyes, exhaled. Turned my face to his.

Nothing. I cracked an eye open to see his smile, the slight shake of an oncoming laugh.

"I didn't say, 'be kissed'. I said, *'kiss me.'*"

Anger made me yank his shirt, fisting the fabric and pulling him close, my butt working its way off the stool and onto his lap. I attacked his mouth, surprised at their meeting, surprised at how soft and supple his response was, his hands curving down my bare back and pulling me tighter to him. I loved my mouth in his, the flex of his tongue under mine. We did not feel like strangers; our mouths instinctively knew each other.

He turned in his stool, taking me with him, pinning my back against the bar as his hands kept me glued to his lap, his mouth breaking from me long enough to speak.

"You want more?" he whispered. "Cause I want to feel the inside of your mouth before I send you back to him."

"I want more," I gasped.

Two minutes later, we were in the bathroom.

I didn't think places like this, bars smaller than my walk-in closet, had bathrooms. But this one did. A tiny cube, a pedestal sink screwed to the wall, condom dispenser on the wall, a drain beneath my feet. Thirty square feet, max.

The door slammed shut as my back pushed it closed, his hands forcing the action, the taste of beer on his tongue as we kissed. His hands, pulling at my shirt, yanking it over my head. A quick flip of his hands freed my bra, his hands skimming the straps off my shoulders. Our kiss hot and fevered, I pushed any rational thought from my head and enjoyed the moment, enjoyed the touch of a man who could not get enough.

He took a break from my mouth, dropping his head and staring, like he had never seen breasts before, a heavy sigh tumbling from him as he scooped them into his hands, his hold tender, his gorgeous mouth—when he dropped it to their surface—not. "God, these are beautiful." He nibbled the delicate skin, inhaled deeply as his tongue circled my nipple, sucked one into his mouth, and devoured each in turn as my head dropped back against the door. I heard the metal of his belt, the ting of it against tile as his jeans dropped, my own hands helping to skim his shirt off his torso until he was naked before me, his head coming off my chest, his eyes, when they met mine, showing the breaking point of his control. And God, he was hard. I could see it in my peripheral vision, felt it as it bumped against me.

"Get on your knees," he rasped.

I had no interest in getting on that floor. I'm pretty sure it hadn't seen the scrub of a mop in months. But I had every interest in taking him in my mouth. Every interest in making his look of raw lust continue. I snagged his pants, created a pillow for my knees, and knelt down before him.

God bless. Even though I'd done this a hundred times, it felt different. Opening my mouth, wrapping my hand around the complete stiffness that was his cock, licking my lips and hearing him inhale ... I had never been this wet. Never wanted this so much. Never desired a hard hand on the back of my head, an impatient shove, to look up in a man's eyes and see disrespect and desire all rolled into one heated stare. I dove down on his cock, pumped my hand, inhaled through my nose, and took as much of him as I could, gagging at times, my mouth finding a rhythm, sucking and withdrawing, sucking and withdrawing, the groans from his mouth letting me know I was doing it well.

I sucked him until my jaw hurt and his hands yanked me up. Ripped down my shorts, the button flying somewhere, my body naked before him, his hands spinning me until we both faced the dirty mirror, our eyes wide, chests panting. Something outside bumped against the door, reminding me of our location. "Bend over," he growled, and I did, moving my legs back until I was leaning against the sink, staring at our reflection as he looked down, wrapped his cock, tested my pussy, and then shoved inside.

I gripped the sink and tried not to scream, but ohmygod I was addicted.

Chapter 23

We returned to the bar, two warm beers waiting, the bar twice as full as when we left, meaning that six bodies now dotted the tiny landscape. He picked up the glass, downed the drink, then pushed the empty glass forward. "Thanks for the beer."

I raised my eyebrows. Ignored my own. Dug my cell out from my pocket and checked for missed calls. Zero. "Thank *you* for the beer."

He waved to the bartender, a man in a tight shirt, one who gave me a smile that I was pretty sure was mocking me for our bathroom playtime. "Naw. I'm pretty sure your drinking and fucking budget is bigger than mine. I'll be in the truck." He swung by me, shaking a few hands and slapping backs on his way out, his stride relaxed, confident.

I looked back at the bartender, who wiped down the counter and gave me an expectant look. "He got a tab?"

"Not one he's paid recently." The man reached for our glasses, raised an eyebrow at my full one before dumping them both in the sink.

"Figures." I dug in my pocket, coming up with a twenty, and smacked it down on the counter. "Thanks."

"No problem. Always great to see one of Lee's girls."

I paused in my exit, turning around to glare at him. "I'm not one of his *girls*."

The man snorted back a laugh, shrugging as he plucked up the cash, stuffing it in his front pocket. "Whatever."

One of Lee's girls. I wish I'd driven. Wished I could get back into my car and return to luxury. Instead, I crawled up into his jeep. Suffered the ten-minute car ride back to the convenience store, the wind whipping my hair as his speakers crackled through the bass beats of Florida Georgia Line.

He came to an abrupt stop behind my car, his eyes sweeping over the clean lines that had put Brant back six figures. "I assume this is you, Lucky."

"It's Layana." I grabbed my purse and unclipped the seatbelt, stopping when he flipped open the ashtray and fished out a business card, the edges worn and bent. "Lana to my friends."

"I'm not crazy about that name."

"I'm not crazy about Lee."

"Whatever. Call me if you ever want thirds." He grinned at me. Revved his engine as if he was ready for me to get out.

I stared at the card. Wanted to crumple it up but didn't. *He has a business card.* The fact was both ridiculous and endearing.

I got out having no idea what to do with the card. Watched as his jeep pulled off, the trailer behind it sending a cloud of parking lot dust into my face. I got into my car, my skin dirty, my pussy taken, half of my clothes stretched out or ruined.

I pulled over three exits before home and parked in a Lowe's lot—locked my doors, lowered my face to the steering wheel, and cried.

Chapter 24

I walked into my house, stripping as soon as I entered the bedroom, needing the shower yet not wanting to wash off his scent. I smelled like him. Like oil and grass and dirt and sex. It was out of place in my world, in my bedroom, in my life. And I knew it didn't make sense, but I wanted more of it and loved Brant even more after that afternoon.

He'd been so different from Brant, so outside our box. I liked the different. I wanted more of it and hated myself for it. Wanted more than I could get from Brant, more sides, more than the man who held my hand and listened to my words and proposed to me in moonlight.

I turned on the water and dreaded stepping into the shower. I put my leg up on the tub and pushed my fingers inside. Closed my eyes against the sore need there. Wanted him. If I erased him, I would need him again. I opened the door and stepped into the stream of water. Cried again as I washed every part of the day off my body.

I was slow to turn of the water, but felt the urgency. I had to get dressed. I was having dinner with Brant that night.

***

Lies. A mountain of them between us, the linen tablecloth too pure and small to hold them all. They tumbled down the sides, spilled around and crowded the filets before us, the melted butter catching some of them in its flame.

I had many; he had few. I was fully aware of my deceit, and I could only guess at his. We'd talked for hours in this relationship, but had said little that wasn't, in some part, a lie.

"I heard that you're honoring your parents at the Xavier Event."

He nodded. Speared a piece of mushroom. "I've decided to name the new building in their honor." A building. A hundred million dollar investment, their names displayed proudly on the top. A kind gesture, if it wasn't the tenth building he'd built this decade. Three of them on BSX's campus already bear my name, the challenge of a new employee finding his way to the right one becoming to a hazing practice among veterans. Other boyfriends gave roses; Brant gave buildings. Literally gave them. My name was on the property deeds, his companies paying me a handsome sum of rent each month.

I sipped my wine. Held the taste in my mouth for a moment before swallowing. 1961 La Mission Haut-Brion. A lingering finish on my tongue. Success went down smooth. "Are you giving the building to their foundation?"

He nodded without answering. Cut a piece of steak. "Tomorrow, can you get with Jillian? Look over the foundations endowments this year. See if you agree with where they are going."

Jillian. I hid my disdain of the suggestion behind a polite smile. Though, in the scheme of Activities To Perform With Jillian, earmarking BSX's millions sounded like an enjoyable activity. "Sure. I can prepare you a summary of the organizations and the impact—"

He waved off the offer before taking a sip of wine. "That's not necessary. As long as you're happy, I'll be happy. What'd you do today?"

An abrupt change of conversation. Typical of Brant, yet I felt thrown in the spotlight, on the chopping block for execution. "Ran errands. Slept." I read in an article once that liars elaborate. I believed it. My tongue was itching to get creative.

He reached over. Gently touched the top of my arm, a habitual gesture, one I loved. A mini-connection in our love life. "Sounds nice."

"Maybe you can take off tomorrow. Spend the day in bed with me."

An abrupt head shake. "Not a chance. I'm close to breaking the battery capabilities of Onyx down to a fifth of current levels. Which could mean—"

"That you're brilliant," I interrupted with a smile.

He looked up. "That I'm lucky."

I shot him a wry look, and reached across the table, spearing a piece of his meat and bringing it to his lips. "Promise me that after you crack the battery issue that you'll celebrate with me. Give me two days of Brant, wherever I want to take you."

"I promise." He took the food offering, pulling it into his mouth and chewing, settling back in his chair as the tuxedoed waiter approached.

A month later, he created a battery slimmer than the closest competitor by half, one that would run for nine days without charging. I planned the vacation. Booked the house. But we didn't go. And I understood.

***

I was not a normal individual. I knew that. I used to be quirky. It used to be cute. I now think, when I brush my hair in the morning ... when I take the time to confront my reflection and stare into my eyes ... I think I was just lonely. Lonely and desperate and wanting to be held and loved and desired. Maybe that was normal. Maybe it was the ways in which I moved towards that goal what made me odd.

I sat on Lee's card for a week. Tucked it into the frame of my mirror. Eyed it while applying mascara and lipstick. Stared at it as I brushed my teeth and flossed.

When I closed my eyes at night, I thought of him. When my hand stole underneath the covers and pressed hard against the ache between my legs, I thought of him. I watched the sunrise over my lawn as I sipped coffee and thought about hiring him to cut it. Then thought of all of the ways this would crash to the ground.

I shouldn't call. But I couldn't *not* call. I couldn't stay away. You don't understand.

But when I did call, he didn't answer. And had no voicemail. I waited a week. Called again. The third week, his phone was disconnected. I grew frantic, then grateful over the obstacle, then frantic. I wanted him; I needed him. I wasn't ready to say goodbye. I needed another fill of his cock. I grew obsessed, yet could find no hint of him. The harder I looked, the less I found.

So I took some time off. Forced my mind off the search for Lee and focused my attention on Brant. Planned vacations, spent more time at his house. We went to New Zealand. Bought a house in Hawaii. Shelled our own oysters in Key West. I tried to forget Lee. Tried to find parts of him in Brant. Failed miserably at both.

Called him again and this time his phone rang. Week seven or eight. Still no voicemail. I listened to the phone ring until it died. Then I gave stalking a try instead.

Four months after our first meeting, I found him.

Chapter 25

ONE YEAR, 8 MONTHS AGO

"What are you doing here?" He came to a stop beside his truck, flipped his keys slowly in his hand as his eyes held mine. The man was not afraid of eye contact. Brant's eyes were constantly on the move, following his mind. This man's eyes glued and rooted me in place, his focus unnerving.

"I saw your truck. Thought I'd say hi."

"Just driving by?" His eyes flicked over the street. Found my car, then returned to my face. "Doesn't seem like your neighborhood."

It wasn't my neighborhood. But it was less than a mile from where we met. Two blocks from bar where he fucked me in the bathroom. I shrugged. "Visiting a friend." *Stalking you.*

"Still that rich dick's bitch?" His eyes didn't leave my face when he said the crude words. They rolled off his tongue like fucking marbles, smooth and glib, the heat of his gaze making my pussy pant in anticipation. God, I wanted him. His stance, legs slightly spread, full masculinity on display, the strength of his body showcased in the tight shirt and worn jeans, work boots on his feet.

"Yep." I stepped closer, my heels crunching on the gravel, and his dominant stare finally left my eyes, dropping to my feet and dragging up the length of my legs, a smirk coming over his mouth. "Still want to fuck the rich dick's bitch?"

His smile stopped and he jerked a hand forward, hooked his large palm around my waist and pulled me forward, my feet stumbling, but then I was flush against him, his back against the truck, his mouth hard as he kissed me deeply enough for me to taste beer on his tongue. My hands tangled in his shirt, prodding, feeling, his mouth hissing against my tongue when I ran my hands down and gripped the crotch of his jeans. "God, you are one fucked up woman." He pushed a hand over mine, let me feel his erection, the push against his jeans, my fingers outlining it, and I squeezed, savoring the feel of him.

"Step back," he muttered, pulling his mouth off mine, his head dropping back as he pulled my hand away, dropped it, and suddenly, the connection was broken. "Fuck," he swore, rubbing a hand over his mouth, looking up at me over his hand, those eyes tugging at my soul with one wary glance. I stepped back, feeling his desire for separation, unsure of what was causing the change. "Fuck," he repeated. "You are crazy."

I met his gaze. Said nothing. My body was still crying out for more. More. More. It wasn't like this with Brant. I didn't know why it is so different, didn't understand it, but regardless of the reason, my sexual connection with this man was so much stronger. He had to feel it. His eyes said he did. His eyes were steady as he chewed on his thumb. Thought.

"I have a girlfriend," he said the words as if they were dirty, and dropped his hand, rose to his full height and lifted his chin. "Is that a problem?"

Yeah. A big fucking one. I tried not to let my face show the war of emotions that were throwing a panic party in the front living room of my head. "No," I whispered the words. Any louder and he'd hear the lie in them.

He yanked open the door to his truck. Stood there for a minute, his body blocking the entrance to the cab, my mind playing catch-up, desperately wanting to know what was about to occur. "It's a problem for me. See ya *Lucky*." He sneered the last word, as if I was anything but, the tone a slap in my face. I was still standing there, heels askew on gravel, my face red, panties damp, when he floored the gas and left me there, in the hardware store parking lot. Alone. His head didn't turn, didn't look at me when he drove past. He just left. Probably to go to her. My hands curled into fists.

***

Brant didn't come home that night. I used my key to let myself in his house, telling myself I was staying there to surprise him with breakfast, not because I wanted him to hold me all night and reassure me that I was loved. Instead, I spent the night alone in his bed, hugging a body pillow and trying not to let my mind wander. Lee dominated my thoughts. He had a girlfriend. One he had left me in the parking lot for. One that he probably fucked half the night. I closed my eyes, pulled the blanket tighter, and wished it was Brant's arm. I fell asleep in his empty bed and didn't wake until noon.

Chapter 26

BRANT

When you really love someone, you cannot walk away. No matter what they do. No matter the lies from their mouth, or the actions from their bodies, you tie yourself tightly to their sail and vow to be there through thick and thin. Let the wind blow you where it may. Even if that place is a crash. Even if that place tears you apart and kills anything good.

Chapter 27

"The girl's name is Molly Jenkins. She's a med student at UCLA. Dean's List there, was a scholarship athlete until she damaged her ACL."

"What sport?" I flipped through the folder, image after image of buoyant blonde making me grit my teeth. The girl was prettier than me. Younger. Perkier. With what appeared to be D cups. Was *this* what Lee liked?

"Tennis."

I closed the folder, not needing to see any more perfection. Tennis. *Ugh.* "What's wrong with her?"

"I beg your pardon?" The wiry man before me shifted in his seat. Adjusted his glasses.

"I don't want her strengths. I want her weaknesses. Does she do drugs? Have a kid? Bang trailer trash on the weekends?"

Big dumb blinks behind wire-rimmed glass. I hired the best company in town and this is what I got. "Umm... my report was very comprehensive..."

"And left anything negative out." I tossed the folder onto his desk. "Where's the dirt?"

"I didn't find anything like that..." He wet his lips. Nervously tapped his hands in some odd drumming pantomime on his legs. I stared at his hands until they stopped.

"Where does she work?"

His face relaxed slightly. "Olive Garden. The one in Stonestown."

"Get me a copy of her schedule. What days this week she's working."

He nodded, short and nervously, the downward tilt of his head revealing the plugs that dot the landscape of his forehead. "Anything else?"

"No." I tapped my fingers against my lips. "Not yet."

I pulled out my desk drawer. Grabbed a checkbook and printed his name on the front. Completed it with a generous enough amount to properly incentivize the man. Then I ripped off the check and stood, holding it out.

"Call me when you know more."

He grinned, revealing a row of stained teeth, their tips pointing in more directions than a pencil holder. "Yes, Ms. Fairmont."

I gave him a polite smile and picked up my cell. Waited until I heard the door close behind him, then completed my call.

***

I'd never taken down a girl before. Didn't have prep school archenemies, the bitchy girls of television who killed hopes and dreams while modeling couture. My high school friends were civilized, structured. Women at Stanford were more focused on grades and futures over petty rivalries, no spare effort available to be wasted.

So I was entering this game a virgin. But, in my own estimations, a well-equipped one. Financed. Intelligent. And ... as a small point to my side ... I had fucked her boyfriend ... twice in three hours. I had some inkling of what he liked, wanted. Had enough confidence in his attraction to me, despite the fact that she was absolutely gorgeous and looked nothing like me. It was as if he had flipped open an encyclopedia, scrolled to the section of 'Opposite of Layana' and selected her photo. Go figure.

Also on my side: the element of surprise. I was a party of one. Alone in this battle, with no one aware of my scheming, no defenses raised. I would be attacking a sleeping kitten. An innocent, fragile kitten. Ripping her away from Lee and severing any chance of their reconnection.

I should have felt guilty, should have had compassion, but I didn't. Love is war and Lee was, or would be, mine.

***

The text came while I was in the shower. I discovered it while toweling off, my damp finger dysfunctional on the phone's screen, a few attempts needed before I could unlock the screen and view the alert.

** 1 NEW TEXT MESSAGE **

I opened it. Short and sweet, from my ever-helpful private investigator.

** HE'S WITH MOLLY JENKINS NOW. PANERA ON 43RD STREET **

I texted back.

** LET ME KNOW IF THEY LEAVE **

Glanced at my watch. 11:12 AM. I was supposed to be having lunch with Brant at noon. I set down the phone and hurried to my dresser, yanking out a pair of dark jeans and tossing them on the bed.

***

I pulled into the shopping center lot at the same time that Lee's jeep pulled out, my eyes catching the dark green body, two heads inside, as it careened out into traffic. My phone buzzed.

** THEY'RE LEAVING. I'M FOLLOWING. **

Thanks a lot. I called him, letting him know I was there, dismissing him for the day as soon as my car caught up to Lee's. I shouldn't be there. Shouldn't be stalking a man who didn't know enough to have any interest in me. My phone dinged again. This time, Jillian.

** BRANT WON'T MAKE LUNCH. MY APOLOGIES. **

Shocker. I shoved my phone in my purse, wave at the PI's car and earned a passing nod in return. Two individuals, two different motivations, united with a common goal. I pressed on the accelerator, wove through traffic, and caught up to Lee's jeep.

He drove like a maniac, his head turning often in her direction, her smile visible from my place behind them, every burst of her smile a knife in my heart. At one stoplight he reached over. Rested a hand on her headrest and leaned in, their mouths meeting for one heart-wrenching moment before my hand misbehaved and hit the horn. His head pulled off, looking toward the light, which changed at that moment. Then he looked into the review mirror, his eyes too far to read, but I'm certain there was irritation in them, his jeep jerking forward, our connection lost as he floored the gas. My mouth curved behind the tint of my windows. Sorry babe.

A few miles later they stopped at a park, Lee waiting as she got out, his manners unchanging in his ignorance of door-opening protocol. I watched as he held out a hand, hers fitting into it, and they walked, a blanket tucked under her arm, a bag slug over a shoulder that spent too much time in the sun. I parked my car in the shade, hidden between a moving truck and suburbia. Pulled out the binoculars I'd stolen from Brant's house, I adjusted them, honing in on the couple.

Hello stalking, I am Layana. Pleased to make your acquaintance.

***

When she ran she beamed, and he chased her.

When she napped in the sun, he played a hand gently through her hair.

When he pulled off his shirt and stretched out to enjoy rare San Francisco sun, I saw sex in her eyes.

I sat and watched. Focused in and spied. Growled into a stale handful of nuts as I saw pieces of what might be love. I guzzled warm water and he pulled her over. Had her straddle him as his cocky mouth turned up, his pelvis rocking beneath her, the view of her shriek visible as clearly as if I could hear the damn sound. They kissed, they stood, and they hurried, packing up her bag and blanket and racing to the car.

I didn't follow the jeep when it pulled out. I knew what foreplay looked like. I didn't need to watch them enter a home to know more. I didn't want to sit in a car and know they were fucking. I had the sudden recognition of a feeling, the surge of emotion at the back of my throat, one that receded tears, and I swallowed instead, yanked my car into drive, and headed home.

I needed a plan. I had seen enough. What I needed to figure out was how to destroy them.

Chapter 28

ONE YEAR, 7 MONTHS AGO

"I was thinking about us heading to the island for a week."

I blinked at Brant across a table full of brunch. He never brought up travel. Was normally so buried in work that I had to drag him away for fun. "When?"

"Maybe Saturday. We just finished the design phase of the photo frames. It'll take the tech team a week or so to get me initial mockups."

I swallowed a mixture of salmon and cream cheese. Dabbed my mouth with a napkin while I thought.

A week. Smack dab in the middle of Operation Kill Tennis Barbie.

A week. With the man I loved. Twenty-four hours a day of Brant, and any bit of personality that I could coax out to play. We needed this. He needed this. It'd been three or four months since we had gone anywhere, his psyche focused on the latest development, then the next, then the next. He lived to build. To improve. And this week's project was apparently us.

The island he was referring to was our Hawaiian home. It wasn't really on an island, unless you counted Honolulu, the large mass where our private peninsula jutted off. Our property held a twenty thousand square foot vacation home, complemented by a private pool, gym, spa. Chefs, masseuses, butlers, and maids. It would be good to get away. Hop from one paradise to the next.

I smiled at him. "Sure. I'll coordinate with Jillian. Get the details set up."

He stood, leaving his plate and walked over. Put a hand on the table and leaned over. Swept his lips over mine and smiled. "I love you."

I sat back in my seat, looked up, felt the brush of his hand as he cradled my chin. "I love you too."

"When will you let me be your husband?" A husk in the words. Need behind the question. I stared into the eyes of my love. A man who, in some ways, was still a lonely little boy who played in his basement while every other kid was outside.

"One day." My answer that was not an answer, yet the response I had provided for a year.

"A man might get tired of waiting." The curve of his mouth belied his words.

I reached up, gripped his shirt and pulled myself to my feet. Wrapped my arms around his neck and pressed against him. "Well, then maybe I should give you another reason to stay."

He took my kiss. Deepened it. Didn't object when my hands pulled his shirt loose from his pants. Let me drag him into the living room and straddle him. And there, with Sunday sun streaming through French doors, our clothes still mostly on, I distracted him from thoughts of marriage and reassured him of my love in the way I knew best.

Chapter 29

Newest fact about Molly Jenkins: she liked to drink. I looked at the PI's report, page 9 including an inventory of her trash can, photos next to an inventory list. I scanned it, my fingers tapping alongside the items as I moved down the page.

    12 empty bottles: Smirnoff Ice
    4 empty cans: Bud Light
    Tags from an article of clothing: Gap. $24.99
    Dry Cleaning receipt: One Price Cleaners
    Empty bottle: Kahlua
    Empty bottle: Absolut Vanilla Vodka
    Thank you card and envelope from 'Mom': see photo
    Monthly statement from Capital One credit card: see photo
    Empty Bag of Nacho Cheesier Doritos

I called him, musing over the list as the phone rang.
"Yes, Ms. Fairmont."
"Is this normal? All the alcohol?"
"It's the first bag we've inventoried. It's from last week. I left off all of the food items, but if you'd like we can also include those."
"Food items?"
"You know, banana peels, coffee grounds, leftovers, egg shells—"
"No," I interrupted. "I don't need all that. Just items like this. When will you have the rest of the bags done?"
"I can put someone on it today, if you think it'd be important."
"Yes. Please send me all of the reports as they are done. As soon as possible."
"I'll pull people off other projects. Get it to you quickly."

"Thank you." I hung up the phone, looked at the list again. Opened up the image with her credit card statement. Learned everything about her activities that month with one scroll down the bill. It was ridiculously invasive, this one aspect of the report. So much of her life broken down into simple facts by her trash. I spun in my chair. Looked at the silver can that sat feet away. Wondered how much of my life would be told through its contents. I placed a second call.

"John, this is Layana. From now on, have the housekeepers burn my trash. And buy me a shredder please. Something big and industrial." I hung up, interrupting his response, certain that the request was simple enough for him to complete without further instruction. Then I returned to the list. Stared at the items and tried to find an opening.

***

I got four more emails that afternoon, each with a new list of trash. Each list dated, covering the latest month of Molly Jenkins's life.

More alcohol. I counted six bottles and five 6-packs. Not enough to be an alcoholic, but the girl liked to party. She was also in college, so maybe that just made her normal. I got another nugget of information in her bank account statement. Put it side by side with her credit card one and compared notes. Learned a few things.

She frequented The Ginger Break. Had been there five times in the last month, four times on a Wednesday, once on a Friday. A Google search told me it was a bar a block from her apartment. Another search told me Wednesday is $5 Martini night.

I clicked my pen, examined my calendar. Wednesday was three days off. Doable. I leaned back in my chair and stared at the ceiling. Pulled scattered thoughts together in a semblance of a plan.

First step. Find bait.

Second step. Sequester Lee.

Third step. Watch and enjoy.

Chapter 30

"Why are you doing this?"

I glanced over a pomegranate martini into deep blue eyes. I had chosen well. His brow furrowed in a way that was gorgeously masculine. His eyes looked intelligent, but compassionate. As if he rescued kittens from trees before listening to your problems. His mouth was full. Twitched when he smiled. As if after he listened to your problems, he'd take you to bed and fuck away any concerns.

"Doing what, exactly?"

"Here." He set down his beer. Leaned across the table and lowered his voice. "Playing games with some adolescent." He tilted his head to Molly, a girl we had been eyeing from above for fifteen minutes. We were in the Ginger's version of a VIP room. Situated above the bar, with tinted windows that provided privacy, we had a full view of down below. The section didn't open for another three hours, but two hundred bucks got us a seat, a high-top by the windows, my knees bumping Marcus's if I leaned in too deep.

I met his gaze. Direct. It ate holes in the dark parts of my soul. "Let's go back over the plan."

He sighed, leaned back and stretched his arms out, regarding me with a bored stare. "I know that plan. You go down there, I go down there. We drink; you leave. More drinks; we leave. I take her home, fuck her eight ways to Sunday, then head on my merry little way."

I shifted. "Yes."

He leaned forward again, his knee bumping mine, his hand reaching out and gently touching the top of my hand. "You have nothing to worry about with her."

I moved my hand. "In what way?"

"You are a beautiful, sexy woman. She..." He glanced down, at the blonde head that all of this was about. "She's a girl. She can't compete." He leaned closer, and I sat back. Glared at him with the frostiest look I had.

"I didn't hire you to fuck *me*, Marcus. I'm in a relationship. Taken."

He laughed softly. "Forgive me, Layana, but you are here. You don't look taken to me."

I drained the martini and stood, yanking my hand from underneath his. "Save the sexy shit for her. I'm well-taken care of." I picked up my purse. "I'll see you downstairs in twenty." Then I tossed down a handful of bills and headed for the ladies room.

***

I took a deep breath and stared into the mirror. Adjusted the wig on my head. A thousand bucks and the thing still felt like something I bought at a dime store. Itchy. Hot. But at least it disguised me. I hoped to never see her again, but I couldn't be too careful. And heaven forbid she recognized me from a magazine cover.

I tucked a fake strand of strawberry blond behind my ear and smiled into the mirror. Tried to look friendly. Tried to wipe the look of possessive hatred out of my eyes. Sort of succeeded. I opened the door, stepped back into the club and headed for Molly.

***

The next stool over was open and I grabbed it, avoiding looking at her as I caught the bartender's eye. "Flirtini, please."

I felt the soft touch of a hand, gentle on my arm. "Flirtini? Sounds good."

Wow. That was easy. I turned casually, as if I was uninterested, gave a small smile as I noticed everything missing from the PI's report. Her blue eyes sparkled. They were open, genuine, the smile that flooded her face wasn't forced or fake. Her tan was natural, her breasts looked real, and I could literally smell sexuality coming off her. I had a brief glimpse in my head of her and Lee fucking, and blinked it away. "It is. It has champagne in it." I nodded to the bartender. "Here, let me get you one."

"Get me one? Oh no, you don't have to do that."

"I don't mind." I shook off her expression. "Please. I could use the company." The bartender slid two glasses our way and I pushed one in front of Molly. "Here." I held up my drink, lifting it to her. "To taking opportunities."

She giggled. "To taking opportunities."

We sipped, then I set down my drink and offered my hand. "I'm Britney."

"Molly."

"You here alone?" I asked, looking around.

She shrugged with a shy smile. "Yeah. I like to get here early on Ladies Night. Otherwise it gets too crazy."

"I can understand that. I like the quieter scene." I watched her sip the drink, the widening of her blue eyes. "Wow! This is great."

Drink up, baby. Drink up.

Molly was a friendly drinker. Twenty minutes and two drinks down, and I was finding out more than I ever needed to know. I steered the conversation toward Lee.

"Any hot guys come in here?"

She blushed. Shook her head. "Not really."

I winced. "Ugh. I hate being single. You?"

She laughed. "No, I'm taken." She smiled, as if the thought of my man was one that appealed to her. I ground my teeth.

"Where's your man tonight?"

She shrugged. "He's kind of flaky. Doesn't always show up ... sometimes he's a little MIA."

I bet. Though, his absence tonight had been carefully calculated. I had a team of three keeping him away from this side of town. I sipped my martini. Kept my voice mild. "That sucks. But you know men and their work... " I grinned. "He's probably slaving away to spoil you rotten."

I saw the flicker of a frown that crossed her face. Then, Marcus entered the bar, our eyes meeting over the crowd, and I leaned forward, gripping Molly's arm with false urgency. "Oh my God," I hissed. "My ex just walked in."

Her head snapped up, female bonding in full force, and craned her neck. "Where?"

"Tall, blond, and gorgeous." I kept my face forward, hand gripped on her wrists until her eyes stopped moving and locked on one place. "Do you see him?"

"Sex in a suit?"

I groaned, fighting a smile at the unwavering lock of her stare. "Yes. Please tell me he isn't headed this way."

"Not yet." She pulled her eyes off him. "What was wrong with *him*?"

"Him? Nothing. His residency was in San Diego, and I might have strayed a little during the time apart." I groaned again for good measure, feeling the flex of her arm when she stopped moving.

"Residency?" she whispered.

"Yeah. He's a cardiologist. Plus, an absolute freak of nature in bed." I hopped to my feet, ducking my head and sliding two hundred bucks across the bar. "I'm gonna run before I ruin my self-respect and drool all over him."

"You're leaving?" She shot me a wide-eyed look. "You don't want to talk to him?"

"So I can pine over the worst mistake I ever made?" I shook my head. Waved to the bartender and pointed to the cash, and then Molly. "No ... I've beat myself up over that already." I shot a glance over my shoulder, then held out my arms and went in for a hug. "It was really nice meeting you," I whispered in her ear.

"You too. Maybe we'll see each other again. Oh, and thanks for the drinks."

I held the hug. Made sure the knife was firmly in her back, then let go. Smiled regretfully, then made my way through the thickening crowd. Winked at Marcus over the space. *Go get her.*

He would succeed. She was drunk. Prepped. He was charming and sexy and—as far as she knew—a doctor with the sex skills of a porn star. I nodded to another member of this team, a man whose Google glass, in combination with my condo's security cams, would properly document the entire evening.

I exited the bar and headed for my car, a genuine smile lighting up my face.

Maybe she loved Lee. Maybe he loved her. But he was mine, whether he knew it or not.

Chapter 31

I was ready for the call when it came. Feet cocooned in a moisture wrap, propped on my coffee table, a Hulu-binge in full effect, my phone rang. I glanced at the clock, and answered Marcus's call. "Give me good news."

"She didn't do it." He sounded defeated, as if he had lost a million dollar sports bet. Given that I had promised him a ten thousand dollar bonus for closing the deal, I understood the attitude.

"What?" I sat forward, my feet coming off the table. "Why not?"

"I don't know. She just didn't. I didn't push it, stopped when she said no."

I realized my mouth was open and shut it before I lost all composure. "How far did you get?"

"She came back to the condo. We kissed ... her shirt came off. Not much else."

"I thought your skills were better than that."

"You should have tested them out." The playful lilt of his sentence pushed me over the edge of poise.

"Fuck you, Marcus. It's ridiculous you couldn't close a teenage girl."

"She's committed. She started crying, saying she was making a mistake. What was I supposed to do, unzip and pull my cock out?"

"Whatever. Let me know if she calls you. I'm gonna check the camera footage. I'm sticking to the original plan, unless the footage is useless. So, unless I say otherwise, carry on."

"Will do." He paused. "Either this guy's one in a million or you're a psychotic bitch."

I smile. "Or both."

"Yeah. Or both." There was a pause where we didn't know what to say. Then, "Night."

"Night."

***

I logged into the security program of my downtown condo, a three thousand square foot palace I rarely set foot into. Started the download of the evening's files while I called Don, the PI who had trailed the couple all evening.

He answered with a yawn. "I'm downloading the images now."

"Got anything good?"

"A few you'll like. I'll email them to you within the hour."

"The sooner the better."

I ended the call, clicked on the downloaded security cam file, and sat down to watch Marcus's failure.

He had tried, that was for sure. Done everything right. Hadn't chased, had let her come to him. Been aloof, yet sexual. Hadn't bragged about the condo, let her ooh and ahh over the place. When she had crawled onto his lap he had fisted her hair in his hands, ground her hips into him enough to let her see his arousal and show her his equipment. They had kissed ... she had wanted ... they had been close. I could see the moment he lost. The moment her brain and guilt had kicked into action. The pull away, the shaking head, a hand pushing against his chest. Then, her movement into a chair. Crying. Hugging her body and rocking and all sorts of ohmygodwhathaveIdone drama. Marcus had stood awkwardly, at one point glancing toward a ceiling cam with a grimace. Then he sat next to her. Pulled her into his arms and smoothed the top of her hair. Let her cry into his chest until she calmed.

Ugh. Why couldn't she have been a normal twenty-one-year-old drunk girl who succumbed to the sexy doctor with the big cock and fancy home? She was dating a yard boy for heaven's sake, one who was flighty and irresponsible and MIA half the time. This should have been easy; I should have won. Good thing I didn't need her mistake. I only needed the illusion of one.

I restarted the footage and watched again, taking screenshots of the moments that mattered. Then, I reviewed them all, confidence feeding through me. Yes. I had enough. And that was without even seeing Don's images.

I sent an email to my graphic designer, attaching the images. Don's email popped up and I forwarded that also. The designer would know what to do, which ones to pick. Would have a proof ready for me by Saturday morning. The same morning Brant and I would leave for Hawaii. I'd review the proof, then fly to the island. Give the boys a week to work and have everything set up by the time I returned. I closed my laptop and waddled to the bathroom. Unwrapped my feet and rinsed off the moisture mask.

Then I crawled into bed with a content heart and feet that smelled of cucumber.

Soon. Soon, everything would be fixed. Soon, Lee would be fully mine.

***

The weapon of my plan — the newspaper proof — was beautiful. I scrolled down the long image, checking the title, date, side copy that framed either side of our deceit. All legitimate. All accurate. Should she feel the need to check on the publication, she'd find what she should. What I've placed in easy reach for her hands. The center of the page, the main event, right under the headline, that was the beauty of the proof. In giant letters across the top:

AREA SURGEON'S WIFE FILES FOR DIVORCE AMID CHEATING SCANDAL

Photos. Crisp black and whites, one a respectable newspaper wouldn't print but in this lie, spoke louder than any words ever could:

Molly and Marcus. At the Ginger. His hand on her leg, his mouth to her ear, a smile I'd seen her use with Lee screaming from the page, her features easily recognizable.

Molly and Marcus. In his car, her mouth on his, the press of her hand silhouetted in the window.

Molly and Marcus. In my living room. On my couch. The zoomed-in photo only showed her bare back, leaning over him, his eyes burning up at her.

Molly and Marcus. My favorite. His hands digging into her back, her mouth at his neck, his head back, eyes closed. The crop made it look like he was inside her, getting the ride of his life, no person would believe anything differently.

The copy was short, beneath the photos, a paragraph that no eyes would ever see except for the ones that mattered.

One of our city's most respected cardiologists received divorce papers today in what could be the ending of a five-year union. The good doctor, whose wife has had him under surveillance after past incidents of cheating, was captured in the following incriminating photos with an unidentified young woman. No word yet on how long their dalliance has been going on. The majority of the photos received were inappropriate to print. For questions and comments, please email Don Insit at don@newseagleprint.com or call 213-323-9811.

    The page looked stunning, the photos leapt from it in a manner that you couldn't help but stare. He would stare. She would stare. He would accuse. She would object or confess. And either way, they would be done. I replied to the email, approving the work, then called Don. Gushed my thanks and verified the plan. He'd print two copies of the full-length newspaper spread. Next week I'd replace the day's cover sheet with this one. Stick it on her front step with a nasty note, in a place that Lee would be sure to see it. Let them both pour over the photos together. Then stand back, and reap the rewards of my labor.

    Flawless. Intelligent. I gave myself an awkward pat on the back and hung up with Don. Then I moved, yanking out a bag, and pulling open drawers. Wheels up in two hours, but I didn't need to pack much. Our Hawaiian closets were full, the bathrooms and kitchens stocked by a staff expecting our arrival. My toothbrush and laptop, not much else was needed. I threw a few paperbacks in my bag, along with a new lingerie set Brant hadn't yet seen. I texted Jillian to make sure Brant was around and ready, then I headed for the shower.

Chapter 32

I feasted on Brant with an urgency that surprised us both, dropping to my knees in the plane, his mouth dropping when I yanked at his zipper and pulled out his cock. "Here?" he whispered, the sound sinking into a groan when I took him soft in my mouth. Hardening. Against my tongue, the push of blood vessels expanding the size of him, filling fast, the gag of my throat as I had to pull off to accommodate him. The push of his hands on the back of my head, stopping me, needing me. I gripped his suited thighs and sucked him. Harder, needier, than I ever had. God, I loved this man. God, I wanted him. All of him. I wanted him to look at me and see no other woman. I wanted to be his wife and have his babies, and for none of them, or us, or him to be broken. I wanted the impossible, and I took this instant instead.

He whispered my name, his legs shuddered beneath my hands, and his hands guided my head. Urgently, the thrust of him in my mouth. "Don't stop." The beg on his mouth. "Yes baby." The sign that he was close.

And then.

Breakdown. His hand tangling in my hair, the hard thrust up and up, into my throat, one hand fumbling for and grabbing onto the armrest as he moaned my name and shot down my throat, my mouth working, sucking the cum from him, up and down and up and down, and then he pulled me off. Drug me by my hair until I was in his lap, his cock out against my thigh, still twitching, still wet from me. He held me in his arms, kissed the taste of me from his mouth, and whispered his love against the top of my head.

I loved this man.

With my whole heart.

I needed him.

He completed me.

I closed my eyes, curled into his chest, and felt the wrap of his arms around me.

***

I lay in our bed, the whip of the fan above me, and stared at the ring. Nestled in a dark blue box, the glint of its diamond brilliant, even in the dark. He had pulled it out hours before. As we ate on the roof deck, the wash of the ocean our backdrop to dinner, champagne cooling the heat of our food. He did the whole thing again, getting down on one knee and presenting the ring.

"You won't give up," I scolded him.

"I'll never give up on us."

"Me neither," I promised him, leaning forward and pressing my lips against his head. "Me neither."

I wanted the ring. Wanted the title. Wanted the forever. I gently worked the ring loose and held it, setting the box on the nightstand. Rolling the platinum setting in my fingers, the unique diamond stone glinting at me. Blue, a color I had never seen on a diamond. Not too large. Two to three perfect, unmarred carats. Flawless. It would be the only thing in our union unflawed and honest, with nothing to hide. It didn't deserve us. It deserved an innocent bride marrying a man with nothing in his eyes but love. But maybe those were the couples who got the imperfect, thousand-dollar Zales specials. Maybe the perfect, priceless diamonds were reserved for trophy wives and cheating husbands. Trust fund babies with mistresses on the side. People like me. And Brant. Maybe this diamond evened out our deficiencies with a few carats of retaliating perfection. I slid the diamond on, the fit perfect, the glow of it warm against my skin. I rolled, ran my hand along the back of Brant, his tan skin the perfect backdrop to the diamond I would never wear. Then I leaned forward, kissed his skin, and curled up against his warmth, the weight of the ring comforting. I closed my eyes and dreamt of perfection.

At some point, in the dusk of morning, before the sun fully exposed our room, I pulled off the ring and carefully returned it. Set it back in his suitcase, its spot nestled between sunscreen and a rolled socks. Then I crawled back into bed. Mourned its loss. And wondered, for a brief moment, if Molly had called Marcus. It was a black thought in a perfect day, but Lee wouldn't leave my head. He stalked my dreams. Dominated my imagination. Pulled on me with insistent hands whenever my mind had an uncontrolled moment. I should have forgotten him. I should have left him and Molly to their life of apparent bliss. But I couldn't. Instead, I was moving closer.

Intertwining my life with his until I couldn't tell when mine with Brant ended, and mine with his began.

A dangerous game. One that was fixing to get worse. Much worse.

Chapter 33

I ran along sand, my stride used to the give, my speed even as I dug through deep places and pounded wet footprints through receding surf. The beach was smoother than home, less rocks, more picturesque. At this time of morning, I was alone. A few towel boys, setting up chairs, nothing else. Solitude. The wash of water cleansing my thoughts.

I was lost. It was official. Turned around to the point where I didn't know if I was climbing uphill or down. My obsession, my game with Lee? It was a losing, impossible direction. I knew that. I knew that the smartest thing, the safest thing to do, would be to ignore him. Let him live his life. And stay on my side of town. With Brant. I didn't love Lee. I loved Brant. Lee was ... a distraction. A distraction that fucked me as if he was created to do it. A distraction that gave me another side of life, away from the finery, a side of life filled with impulse and fun. A distraction that I needed to keep the seesaw of my relationship with Brant level.

I pushed harder, my breath ragged as I took out my frustration on my muscles. Pumped my arms and gasped as I took my run faster, slipping in the sand at times, my calves burning as I sprinted through the sand.

Faster. Faster. I ran until my heart hurt and my lungs broke. Until I sank in the sand, my knees hitting the wet suck, my chest heaving as I flopped on my back. Closed my eyes and wished for California sand underneath my back.

It didn't work. I stayed in that place until my heart rate calmed, my chest stilled. Then I rolled over, tried my best to brush the sand from my back, and headed home. To Brant. To the life I should be living.

***

"Would you live here?"

I glanced up and shot Brant a quizzical look.

He shrugged. Sat back in his chair, the Hawaiian coastline painting an impressive backdrop behind him. "I was just thinking, maybe we should spend a few months here. Maybe half the year, spend the winters here."

"What about the company?"

He shrugged. "I could work from here. Convert the garage into a workshop. Maybe hire a few locals to help during project times."

I grinned. "A few locals? It took you five years to find Frank." Frank, the only BSX tech who had survived Brant's temper tantrums long enough to learn how to not piss him off.

"Then we could bring Frank." He smirked, reached over and grabbed my hand. "I like vacation Layana."

I rolled my eyes. Let him pull my hand to his lips. "What is vacation Layana like?"

He pursed his lips. Tilted his head as if to think. "Carefree."

"Carefree? What am I, a Teletubby?" I threw the remaining piece of my muffin in his direction.

"Fine. Not carefree. Less uptight." He raised his eyebrows at me.

"Everyone's less uptight on an island. Or maybe it's the fact that I'm a thousand miles from Jillian." I stuck out my tongue at him.

"Oooh ... easy now. She's probably got this place wired." He looked at the closest plant as if it might harbor a bomb.

I stood, wiping my hand on a napkin and tossed it down. Sauntered over and pushed at the arms of his chair, separating him from the table. Straddled his body and ran my hands through his hair. "In that case," I whispered, nipping his ear playfully. "We should put on a show."

"I'm in," he growled, peeling off my robe and taking any more words out of my mouth with his kiss.

There, under the glow of the morning sun, we thoroughly ruined the moral compass of anyone who might be listening in.

The jet takeoff was smooth, a thousand parts of machinery working in perfect synchronization to bring Brant and I back home. I moved to the back of the plane, to the bedroom, and pulled back the sheets. Fluffed pillows and called Brant back.

"What do you want to watch?" I flipped through the options on the touch screen, jumping when Brant's hand snaked through the open door and pulled me back, dragging us both toward the bed, his foot kicking the door somewhat closed.

"I want to watch you come," he whispered, grabbing the tablet and tossing it aside, his fingers pulling at my pants and dragging the material over my hips.

"Fine," I scoffed, pushing at his shoulders, until his mouth skimmed the line of my hip, my head dropping back when hot wet heat closed over my skin. "Go do what you do best."

A half hour later, we turned down the lights, Brant's fingers rolling my lazy body over until we both laid sideways, his body cupped around mine, and watched Gene Hackman and John Cusack battle it out on the big screen. By the time the end credits rolled, Brant was asleep, heavy breathing regular against my neck.

I reached up. Fumbled around the bedside table until my hand hit my cell. I turned it on and sent a short email to Don:

ON WAY BACK FROM HAWAII. PLEASE MAKE SURE FINAL COPY IS READY FOR PICKUP.

Then I rolled over, into his body, and closed my eyes. Tried to sleep. Tried to appreciate this moment with him. I lay there, my eyes closed, breath matching rhythm with his, but sleep wouldn't come.

In a few hours, I'd be home. Would swing by the printers, pick up the papers and make sure they were perfect. Then hit the sack and catch up on sleep. Tomorrow would be a big day. A relationship-ending one.

Chapter 34

I was a person of plans. Always had been. I liked order. Refinement. Intellectual thought that put objects into motion. Controlled their outcome.

Molly had been my problem.

This paper, this setup: my solution.

Carefully crafted steps to ensure a positive outcome.

Lose Molly. Gain Lee. Carry on.

Winning would give me a sense of accomplishment. A righting of one wrong. But still, a bigger problem loomed. Once I had both of them, then what?

How would this story end?

The best-laid plans still deserved a purpose. I needed to find mine.

For now, this one seemed foolproof. I swiped a hand over the newspaper. Our false cover wrapped around thirty-two pages of legitimacy. I couldn't tell the difference. They floated seamlessly. Our articles matched the inside pages, the paper weight, color, and consistency the same, the phone numbers and emails listed all sending Molly directly to Don. It was a work of art. I flipped through, flipped back. Ran my hands over the glaring photos that screamed sex. They made an impression all right. I took out a red Sharpie. Wrote WHORE in big red angry letters across the front. Set it down and looked at it from the angle Lee would. Perfect. He wouldn't miss it. Then I grabbed my cell, snapping a picture of the writing and texting it to Don with instructions. Then I called him.

"It's perfect. I just sent you a text with a touch to add."

Don wasn't confused. Knew what I was referring to. "Okay. You approve the copy?"

"It looks great. You got a guy to sit at her place?"

"Yep. And I'm on your boy. As soon as he heads her way I'll have him put a paper in place."

"I don't know when he'll go there. It might take a few days. Or even weeks. Just print a fresh paper each day with the correct date."

"I know, you told me. We'll stay on top of it." His voice was calm, competent.

I released a bit of anxiety. "And call me when your investigators see him head that way. I want to be there."

"You're the boss."

"Thanks." I slid the paper into a paper bag, carefully closed it. Ended the call and walked to the pantry. Put the evidence of our deceit into the trash compactor, then headed to the shower.

***

A week later, I watched Molly's apartment, a Mediterranean-style orange townhome with window boxes full of hot pink hibiscus. His jeep sat there, a mud-spattered box of American masculinity in a sea of foreign cars. It'd been twenty-two minutes since he walked in, his hands dipped into jean pockets, his head down, steps walking without thought, as if he had walked the path a hundred times.

I tapped my nude nails against the gearshift. Closed my eyes briefly and let the air conditioner breeze wash over me. I had a massage scheduled in an hour, so this situation needed to resolve itself soon or I'd be late for my date with Roberta's hands.

Movement, upper right apartment. Hers. A door flew open, Lee's head moving quickly down the open hall, a blonde head close behind, tugging on his shirt, arms gesturing wildly. I could imagine the words flying out of her mouth. *Lee, don't go. Lee, it isn't what you think!* I wondered if the word 'love' left her mouth, if their relationship had progressed to that point.

He disappeared into the stairwell. I leaned forward, wished I had a drink, something to crack open and enjoy while my hard work came to fruition. This had to work; this had to happen. She couldn't have him; he was mine.

His head bobbed between the cars, his face coming into view as he walked up to his jeep. Face set, features hard, a look I hadn't seen on his face before but knew well. Resolute. Decisive. I clenched my hands in excitement, watching as her face came into view, blotchy and wide-eyed, her mouth moving rapidly, giant breasts heaving as she yelled something and grabbed at his shoulders. I wanted to roll my window down, just a peek, enough to hear this exchange, enough to savor this moment just a little bit longer.

That's right. Turn and walk your pretty self away from this man. He will no longer touch your face. He will no longer make love to your body. He is mine. I will take your place.

I watched him get in, the door slamming hard enough to make her jump. And then, with the screech of tires — the best sound in the world, better than my fantasies — a sound of finality that left her standing in the empty parking spot, black mascara tears staining her cheeks, her scream loud enough to pass through my tinted windows.

Victory is mine. I grinned, giving myself a virtual high five, and put my Mercedes into drive. Pulling into the street, I headed south. Maybe after my massage I'd swing by Brant's office. Drop off a sandwich for him. Plan a dinner to celebrate my victory with the other man in my life.

Chapter 35

By the time I got to the office, Brant wasn't there, a fact that didn't really surprise me. I stuck his sandwich into the office fridge and scribbled a note for him. Then I headed back, away from Palo Alto, up the winding highway that took me home. I ran errands along the way, taking my time, taking a drive through Lee's part of the world, in a slim hope that fate might put us together. *Nothing*. I got back on the interstate and drove into the setting sun.

I pulled into my driveway, my mouth curving into a grin at the sight of Lee's truck, parked on the right side of the drive, his tall build leaning against the door, his head coming up, legs stepping away from the truck as I came to a stop. *That didn't take long.* I got out. Rested my hand on the top of the car and met his look, his hands tucked into his front pockets, his shoulders hunched but his eyes steady, playful, the cool air whipping through us both.

"You lost?" I called out.

"Figured I had to leave the slums every once in a while." He waved a piece of paper, one I had scribbled down my address on a good two months ago. He glanced toward the house.

"You look dirty." I raised my eyebrows. He did. Bits of sand in his hair, like he'd driven the jeep, top down, through the desert. "Sure you aren't just using me for a hot shower?"

He stepped closer, his hands leaving his pockets, resting lightly on my roof. "Sounds like an attempt to get me naked."

I met his cocky smile. "I don't need hot water for that." I shut the car door, walked around, his steps following me up the steps. "Where's the girlfriend?" The words came out right. Casual. Innocent.

"She's gone." He shrugged, but my sideways glance saw the hurt. The way his eyes lowered, the scratch in his throat, the attempt to hide the catch with a short cough.

I unlocked the door. Swung it open and waited for him to pass by. Took my time shutting the door behind me, knowing that — as soon as it shut — the dynamic in this situation would change.

Click. I turned, Lee standing close. So close that when he took a step forward it put me flat against the door, my keys dropping to the floor, my breath catching somewhere in the space between us. He moved forward, the warmth of his body fully against me, one leg sliding in between mine, the hard press of him pleasing, in small part, the ache in my core. He let out a shuddering breath against my neck, his hands dragging down the side of my body and cupping the curve of my ass. Pulling me even tighter to his as he ground even tighter against me.

"I don't want to be your rebound," I whispered.

"I don't want to be your side piece." He bit the words against my neck. "But tonight, I need a fucking rebound. I need to bury myself inside of you and feel whole. And tonight, I am your side piece. So both of us can fuck like adults and both of us can get our brains fucked out and feel like shit about it." He squeezed my ass so hard it hurt, the hitch in my breath bringing his head up, until his mouth was even with mine, the hard breath of him hot in the brief moment before he pressed his lips against mine. Took a deep taste as he ground against my thigh. "You feel that, Lucky?" He grabbed my hand. Put it on his zipper. Held it there until my fingers moved. Outlined him. "That's the level of my need right now. Now, be a good slut."

I fumbled with the button. Got it free and then yanked at his zipper. Pulled it down and dove in. Let out a shudder when my fingers wrapped and pulled free his cock. So hard in my hand. So ready. I wrapped my hand around it. Fucked its length as he ravaged my mouth, the hiss against my lips telling me the tempo he liked. He thrust his hips, the hard beat against my aching cunt not nearly enough. Not compared with the organ in my hand. The one that was pulsing beneath my hand. The one whose tip was wet with arousal, heated with need. I dropped his cock, put both hands on his chest and pushed, his mouth fighting it, one of his hands catching my wrist and putting my hand back on his cock, my name a beg on his lips.

God, I lusted for this man. I needed him. I needed him to be completely mine. I didn't want second best. I didn't want rebound sex. The look in his eyes, domination and lust – I had become addicted to that look. My need for him trumped anything with Brant. I couldn't help that. I couldn't help the different things I wanted from each man. I only knew that right now, I needed more than my hand on his cock. I needed to feel, for at least a short period of time, a full connection with him.

"The bedroom," I gasped. Moved my hand, tried to leave his grip, to move toward the stairs that would take us to my bed.

"No." the resolution in his voice stopped me in my tracks. I looked over. Saw him standing, legs spread, jeans low on bare hips, his cock heavy in his fist. "I need you right now. Lay down."

"Here?" I looked at the floor, at the Persian rug that had set me back a good six figures.

"Christ, Layana. Now. Strip."

I yanked at my clothes, my eyes on his hands. One pressing at the base of his cock, the other moving in slow strokes, the pinch of his face, his eyes closing for a moment before they blazed to life and stared at me, my body almost naked, my hands fumbling with the strap of my bra. He dropped to his knees, pulling me down before him, on my back, the rough kiss of the carpet my welcome party. He spread my legs, held onto my waist and pulled me forward and onto his waiting cock.

God. I knew. So many things wrong with this picture. But God, it felt so good. I stared into his eyes, listened to him whisper my name, and enjoyed every second of the ride. For those minutes, I forgot about Brant, about Tennis Barbie, about anything but him and me and that moment of time.

I was his rebound.

He was my sidepiece.

And both of us wanted more.

At least I did. Maybe anything else was a lie I was telling myself.

Chapter 36

JILLIAN

It's safe to say I never liked Layana. There is something about a woman, when you look into her eyes and see calculation that I don't like. I prefer the open books, the countless women who pass through this office full of smiles and sunshine and optimism. I don't look in their eyes and wonder what they are thinking. I don't listen to them speak and search for hidden meanings. I don't wonder, when they leave, where they are going. But that, from day one, is how it has been with Layana. I had hoped she would pass on. Hoped that another woman would catch Brant's fancy, that he wouldn't go for her long legs and mess of curls. But, alas, he did. She stayed. And now, here we are. Two women battling over this man. I only want to protect him. She loves him. We have differing views on what loving him entails. I don't want to think about what she does to keep him. Whatever it is, it's working. The man won't take his eyes off her.

    I'm sure there are things I could do. To poison their relationship. Expose her lies, put a quiver of death into the perfect existence that he thinks they live. The problem is that she knows the secret. The one that I hug, with the tight grip of a mother bear, to my chest. The one that I have spent years protecting, blood sweat and tears seeping through the iron bars I have built to keep it in. Destroying their relationship? His trust in her? The secret would burn to the ground along with their love. Be exposed in the open air for whoever wanted to grab its papery truth and run wild. In that secret lies nothing but destruction. And so I sit here. Continue paying the men who keep tabs on Brant at all times. Smile when she enters. Help to hide her lies. Pretend to love her with the same vigor that I love him. And hope that one day she fades out of his life.

    I can take care of him. She can only—will only—break him in two.

    Excerpt, The Journal of Jillian Sharp.

Chapter 37

"Stay." I watched his hands slow, the rub of the towel through his hair coming to a stop. He lowered his hands, wiping his face before dropping the towel on the floor and stepping over it, a second towel wrapped around his lower half as he strolled over to his jeans.

"I can't. Stay too long in this place, I'll start thinking I belong here."

"It's one night." One night I desperately needed. How different would a night with Lee be? Would he stay the whole night or leave me in the dead of night as Brant so often did? Would he wrap me in his arms or would he sprawl out on the other side of the bed?

He dropped the towel, my eyes plummeting. Watching the careless movement as he pulled on his pants, uncaring of my eyes, his mouth curving into a confident grin as he tugged them over his hips.

"I have clothes here. If you want fresh ones."

He scowled. "Brant's?"

I had so many answers for that but went with the simplest. "Yes."

He moved over to the bed, pulled at the sheet until it was clean of the bed and my nakedness was fully exposed. "I fuck his woman, I don't want his life." He reached a rough hand out, rubbing a palm over my right breast, the nipple hardening under his touch, the dark look in his eyes turning into a gleam of satisfaction. I sighed, reaching my own hand out and laying it on his cock, the cut of his open jeans leaving it out, stuck out, at perfect eye level from my spot on the bed. It was hot, his skin heated by the spray of the shower and his hand moved from its place on my breast to my hair, gathering the long strands of my hair and pulling me upright, pushing me in the direction of his cock.

"Tell me," he breathed, my mouth reaching his skin, my tongue soft as I licked up its shaft, the organ responding beneath my tongue. "Tell me which you prefer."

I looked up at him. Opened my mouth and took him in. Watched his eyes close, his head drop back as he groaned, his grip on my hair pulling himself deeper into my mouth. Then he yanked painfully, pulling away as he pulled me off his cock and tilted my head up. Dropped his chin and stared into my eyes. The needy look of a man who didn't really want me. "Tell me," he ground out.

"You are better," I whispered, our eyes locked as one, truth in my statement. Raw need in us both. He needed reassurance. I wanted him. I wanted him to stop thinking about Brant and about Molly and focus on me. Want me. The rest would fall into place. It had to.

Push. He shoved back into my mouth. Too hard, I opened wider, tried to take him, my eyes watering at the rough intrusion. He thrust, his hand and hips working together, the scrape of his zipper against my chin, his words falling down on me like forgotten tears.

"Look in my eyes, Lucky. Look in my eyes while you suck my cock." He slowed his motion. Watched with eyes that burned as he drug his wet shaft out, rubbing the tip of it against my mouth before he begged with his stare for more. "You like this don't you? Being my whore while he pays your bills? Letting me use every inch of your body and sending you back to him ruined?" He growled, increased his motion, my airway cut off, my hands pushing at his thighs as my eyes held his clench. His chest heaved, his legs buckled beneath my hands, trembling as he leaned forward, fully in my mouth, gripping my headboard with his right hand, the other on the back of my head, and came down my throat.

My throat was sore. The taste of him still on my tongue, and I watched him move. Tug on his shirt. Button his pants. Run a hand through his hair as he patted his pockets for keys. I wondered, randomly, where he kept his keys. If they stayed in his truck. How they didn't get lost to the wind. He didn't find them in his pockets and that didn't seem to worry him. He paused, halfway through the doorway, and turned back to me. As if he suddenly realized that a goodbye might be needed.

"I'll see you later."

Not what I was expecting. Not what I wanted. They were over. My months of planning complete. Now was the time for *our* relationship. Not for him to bang me and take off, with some flippant reference to seeing me again. I wanted dates. Consideration. Adoration. At the very least a 'Thank you very much' for the two orgasms. I hadn't given Brant two orgasms in one night in the last ... probably ever.

But ... nothing. I didn't respond and he turned, slapped his hand on the custom doorframe, and walked out. Less than a minute later, I heard the tone of my alarm. The alert that let me know that he had left the building.

I lay back on the bed and tried to figure out what I did wrong.

Maybe it was too soon. Maybe he needed time to heal. Maybe he would come back.

I slept alone on sheets that smelled of grass and sex and deceit.

Chapter 38

"What's your opinion on kids?" Brant's voice was quiet, almost inaudible over the wind, his convertible's top down. I glanced over at his profile, his eyes ahead, both hands on the wheel.

"What do you mean?" I picked at a piece of lint on my skirt. Rested my head on the headrest and looked out the open window. A minivan passed, a kid's face pressed against peeling tint, his eyes wide as he stared at Brant's car. I smiled at him, a wave of sadness sweeping over me.

"Kids. When we started dating, you used to talk about having a family. You haven't mentioned it in a long time."

I said nothing. Watching the skyline pass, the setting sun casted a romantic glow over a city with way too many people crammed into its streets. I tried to find the words to say the things that I couldn't say. An impossible task. I finally swallowed, aware that Brant had infinite patience. "I don't really think about a family anymore."

"Why not? You're born to be a mother."

I turned away from the view, surprised at the statement. "Why do you say that?"

"You come to life with the kids at HYA. They love you." He glanced away from the road for a moment, found my eyes long enough to communicate his sincerity.

I looked back at the view. "They're desperate. My own children might feel differently."

"Shut the hell up." The irritation in his voice was so out of character, the expletive causing me to turn back, watch his mouth. "I've never seen someone like you. A woman who is perfectly made for every situation. For standing at my side at the company. For rolling around naked in my bed and letting me please you. For raising children who are loved and adored. For challenging me. For growing old with." He jerked the wheel, the tires growling against asphalt as we whipped off the highway and onto a side lane, the car losing control for a brief moment before it skidded to a halt. He shoved the car into park and leaned forward, grabbing my neck and pulling me onto his mouth, his kiss hard and demanding, my hands pushing against and then pulling at his shirt. We kissed on the side of the highway as if we hadn't touched in days, our hands groping and pulling, the honk and cheers of passing cars combining with wind and lights and sunset, a backdrop to a moment I didn't deserve. I crawled across the center console, my skirt bunching up as I settled into the tight space of his lap, our kiss deepening at the new position, his hands pushing my skirt around my waist, palms and fingers kneading my ass, his mouth greedy as it dominated mine. "I love you so much," he said, leaning his head back to look into my eyes, my hands fisting in his hair, repeating the sentiment back as I lowered my mouth. He stopped the kiss, his eyes arresting as he whispered the question I wanted to avoid. "Is it us, Lana? Is that why you no longer want kids?"

I tried to kiss him, his hands holding me back as his eyes searched mine. I looked into his face and said the only words my heart would permit, the lie slipping harmlessly from my mouth. "No, Brant. No. I promise."

He let out a rough breath, his hand stealing into my hair and tugging me down, his relief felt in the desperate return to my mouth. And, in that moment, with the wind and the cars and the hum of the city around us, I let myself believe the lie.

It wasn't him. It wasn't us. *We* were perfect.

Chapter 39

"Molly came back." His face was dark when he said the words. I looked up from my spot on the couch, a flash of alarm shooting through me.

"When?"

"She showed up at the In Between the other night. A few minutes after I got there. Wanted me back." Lee rubbed a fresh callus on his palm and glanced at me, eyes studying.

Wanted him back. Not a surprise. I tried to keep my voice level. "What did you do?"

"You mean, did I fuck her?" He stood from his spot by the window. Moved closer, towered above me. His eyes contrasted the dark look on his face. More cocky than angry, turning more sexual by the second. He knew I was affected. He stared into my eyes and saw the fear that I so poorly masked. Saw it. Fed on it. Loved the look of jealousy when he saw it. He reached a rough hand out and cupped my head. Pulled it to his pelvis.

"Suck my cock."

"What? Right now? No." I pushed on his stomach with my hand and he caught my wrist. Shoved it down, until my fingers were at his jeans.

"Suck it and see if you earned the right for me to tell her no." We battled with our eyes. I wanted to suck his dick. God, my mouth watered for the taste of his hard cock scraping over my tongue. But I'd be damned if I was forced to do anything.

I pushed against his jeans and he pulled my head harder. Kept me in place. "Suck it and remind me of why I said no."

"You said no?" I looked away from worn denim and back into his eyes. Eyes as tortured as my own.

"Yes." He gritted out, letting out a hiss of breath when my fingers undid the button of his jeans, swiped a needy finger along the edge of his skin. Pulled the zipper down with an insecure motion. "God, I don't know why I did, her beautiful face just begging for me to bend her over and fuck—" the rest of the sentence was lost in the groan that came when I buried his cock in my throat. He fisted my hair, stared at my face, and rocked against my mouth, his words of Molly replaced by my name.

"You fuck him," he said, as his cock fully hardened, as I gripped his thigh and his shaft and prayed the tears in my eyes were from sucking and nothing else. "You fuck him all the time and then expect me to be a saint." I ignored the comment, focused my attention on redirecting his, the soft moan from his lips letting me know I was on the right track. "Why?" he asked. "Why should I?"

I never answered his question, only his need. And ... when his orgasm was over and he pulled me above him on the couch, his arms enveloping me into his chest, my wet mouth against him, the answer didn't seem to matter any more.

Chapter 40

ONE YEAR, THREE MONTHS AGO

My house was unaccustomed to a man's presence. The weight of one on its couch pillows. The sprawl of dirty shoes kicked off in its foyer. Lee's scent invaded its hallways, competed with the scent of polish and flowers, masculinity meeting delicacy and crushing it into dirt. The male impact was new to my home; Brant had visited twice, early in our relationship, then never returned. I still had a few of his things hanging in a guest room closet, all items I had worn home in my early days, before I had a closet at his mansion.

I'd seen Lee almost every day of the last week, sucking up my time with him while I could take it. Brant had been MIA. Jillian said she'd only seen him a few times, darting into the office at sporadic times, not answering calls or texts. She said it was normal—that he got like this. Mostly at times of high stress. And, with iTunes negotiations at a breaking point, a few billion dollars up in the air, now was a time of stress. A time when he should be around, but he was not. Life went on. She handled it.

I didn't mind. It gave me time with Lee. Time I was embracing with both hands. Holding onto, unsure how many more instances I would have left. I could feel the end of our future. It sat on a ledge of probability. He would disappear. I knew it, could feel it in every moment of perfection. And then, this entire cycle would start over. With a new man, a new someone that would be my side piece to Brant.

He stood in front of the fridge, a hand on the top, his eyes skimming, the float of cool air frosting through the space. "You have nothing," he announced.

"It's full. That hardly constitutes as nothing."

"No beer. No junk food. No ice cream. I could eat every bite in this fridge and lose weight." He shut the door, sauntered into the living room. "Let's go grab dinner."

"Now?" I glanced at my watch. "It's almost nine."

"Which is why I'm hungry. That pathetic excuse for dinner we ate four hours ago didn't count."

I rolled my eyes. The 'pathetic excuse for dinner' was foi gras that I spent three hours preparing. It was Brant's favorite dish. I should have known, in this complicated scenario of conflicts, that Lee would hate it. "Fine." I stood, tossing the remote down on the sofa. "I'll go change."

"Uh uh. You're fine." He grabbed my elbow, steered me towards the door.

I glanced down at my jeans. "Where are we going?"

"Let's just drive. There's got to be somewhere around here that's got the game."

I stepped out, grabbing my keys off the counter and pressing the button for the garage, my pull on the front door pausing when I saw Lee, standing in the driveway. His head was turned toward the garage, the full range of cars slowly revealed as the doors swept up.

I yanked the door shut, stepping down the front steps in time to hear his low whistle. "Damn, Lucky. I might start fucking this guy."

I moved past him, irritation sweeping through me. "I do have my own money. Not everything is from Brant." A ridiculous defense to say to Lee, made more so by the fact that three of the four cars were gifts from Brant. I stepped toward my Mercedes, my everyday car, his hand reaching out and stopping my movement. "Let's take the black one."

I came to a sudden stop, whipping my head to him. "The black one?" I stalled.

The black one in question was a 2004 Land Rover Defender. It was the only car in the garage I've paid for, traded my last vehicle in on it. And, as awkward as this situation now was, I purchased it as a gift for Brant. Wanted to, in some small way, repay him for the gifts he had a tendency to lavish.

Unfortunately for me, Brant hadn't been a fan of the vehicle. In the brutally honest fashion that I loved, he had told me as soon as I had handed over the keys.

"SUVs aren't really my thing." He held the key awkwardly, glancing from it, to the black vehicle, and then to me, a sheepish look coming over his face. "I don't like the insecurity of them. And the IIHS safety rating placed them in the worst classification for risk of rollover. The—"

"It's okay." I smiled at him. Reached out and took the key back. "I should have asked."

"I just don't need a vehicle I won't drive." He leaned over, looped a hand around my waist and kissed the top of my head. "You mind?"

Mind? I had stared blankly at the truck, a good ten grand of depreciation occurring in the two days since I had signed the bill of sale. I looked up at him. Let him bend down and kiss me. "No babe. I'm glad you told me."

A BSX employee had driven the vehicle to my house, where it had spent most of its life in the garage. Now, Lee was in my driveway about to come over the damn thing. I took a few slow steps in the direction of the keypad. Lifted the Defender's keys from the box and handed them to Lee.

"Here. You drive."

He snatched the keys without acknowledgement, jumping into the vehicle, his hands running over the leather-wrapped steering wheel and adjusting knobs and settings, the roar of the engine loud in the garage. I watched him warily. Waited for him to pull out of the enclosed space before walking around to the passenger side. Stepped up and into the five thousand pound vehicle of pure masculinity. The vehicle that Lee seemed made for, his frame loose and in control, his hand gripping the shifter with a comfortable ease.

This was exactly what I imagined when I bought the truck. And maybe that's why I bought it. Maybe I was trying to take my genius and dump him into a tub of masculinity and danger. Roughen up his smooth edges. I fastened my seatbelt and swallowed my side of guilt.

With the squeal of tires, Lee pulled out through my gates.

Ten minutes later, the blare of the radio competing with the whip of wind, I hit Lee's arm and pointed. "There." In the shopping center, a sports bar. Lee followed my hand, whipping the truck into a spot and hopping out, his hand resting on the side of the Defender a little longer than necessary, a bit of longing in his eyes.

I joined him, our hips bumping as we walked toward the restaurant, his arm looping around my shoulder, the gesture casual yet familiar. A few weeks of fucking and we were at ease in each other's presences. I blushed, leaned over and pressed a kiss against his cheek. Felt the pull of his arm as he squeezed me into the kiss.

This didn't feel like a rebound. It felt like it should. Complete. This would work. He would fall in love with me and only me. I came to a sudden stop when my eyes met Jillian's.

***

Jillian's eyes brushed over both of us, noticing everything about Lee in one long glance. A change, invisible to anyone else, but a billboard of emotions to me, swept across her face. I was unable to look away, unable to move. I stared at her until the moment that her critical gaze found its way to my eyes. There, we held each other, two women on opposite sides of a battlefield, my weapons sex and passion, hers the ties of family and history. We held an entire conversation through that stare. A heated battle of emotions, arguments discussed with tightened lips and silent looks. Then, the battle ended, the older woman closing her eyes in one, long, pained moment. I felt her disappointment. Her anger. Her frustration. I knew it because I felt it in my own heart.

I pulled away from Lee, tucking a strand of hair behind my ear, my hands dipping into my pockets, his eyes reading the motion. "What?" He glanced over, his eyes seeing and skimming over Jillian, the woman not registering in his search for problems.

"A friend of mine. Go on in. I'll be there in a minute."

He shrugged. "Whatever." Tossed me my keys and turned. I would have bet, from the cringe on Jillian's face, that he winked at her in passing.

I waited, stepping forward, seeing—out of my peripheral vision—him enter the bar, heard the rise in music and voices until the door swung behind him and we stood in silence, two opposing forces separated by four feet of concrete.

"What are you doing Layana?" her voice was tired. Beaten. As if we had had this argument a million times and she couldn't bear to go through it again.

"I can't..." I stopped. Tried to find my words. "You know what Brant's like." I dipped a head toward Lee. "He's different. I tried ... I can't stay away."

"You love Brant." She sighed, her exhale a trip of congestion and old lady. "I know you do."

I nodded. "I do."

She glanced over her shoulder. "And him? Does he have any of your heart?"

I swallowed. Searched the recesses of my heart that I didn't want to exist. "Part of me loves him too. I can't really separate that."

Her mouth tightened. "You're playing a dangerous game."

"It's my game to play. I'm the one in the relationship." I regretted the moment the flippant words left my mouth.

Her eyes fired. "You selfish stupid girl." She pointed a strong finger toward the bar. "He'll leave you, Layana. One day, you'll wake up, and that boy in there will be *gone*. Brant loves you. He'll be with you forever."

I nodded. "I know." I turned, tucked my purse under my arm because I needed something to do with my hands, and walked toward the neon. Her voice, quiet but firm, stopped me.

"Brant told me he proposed again."

"Yes." I turned. Met her eyes. "Should I marry him?"

She let out a huff of laughter, a cold and brittle sound that spoke of incredulity and hopelessness. "Lana, you know that I don't particularly care for you."

"I'm well aware."

"But I don't know that I'd be in support of any woman dating Brant. You could have left him. Back in Belize, when you found out about him. But you didn't. You stayed with him. Five minutes ago I would have said yes, marry him. Now? Seeing you with *him*?" She jerked her head toward the bar. "You are threatening everything you have because you want everything you don't. You don't get everything when it comes to Brant. You get what he shares with you. And you have to be happy with that."

I found my voice somewhere around the pit of my shame. "I don't know that I can be happy with just that."

She shook her head, her eyes filled with disappointment. "Love isn't about being happy. Be single and be happy. Love is about putting him, his sanity, his happiness, first. If you aren't willing to do that then you aren't really in love."

And, with that justified blow, she turned, her heels clipping through the parking lot, her head down, shoulders hunched. There was a part of me that loved that woman. That loved her fight for Brant. There was another part of me that hated her guts.

I turned and headed for the bar, my path to hell lined with neon signs and temptation, all in the form of Lee.

Chapter 41

ONE YEAR, TWO MONTH AGO

"Layana." Jillian looked up from her desk, raised eyebrows pointed in the direction of her admin, a male who positively quaked next to me. "What a ... surprise."

I stepped forward, perched on the edge of the closest chair; any further time spent standing would have felt too similar to my time in the headmistress's office. "I'd like to speak to you about something."

She stood, spreading her hands. "Absolutely. I'm always happy to see you. Chad, please leave us, and hold any interruptions."

I heard the flee of steps, her hard eyes returning to mine. "What is it?"

"Thank you for not making a scene last night."

She nodded stiffly. "I didn't really have an option."

"I do a lot for Brant. For you. For BSX."

She pursed her lips. "You keep a secret. Don't blow it into a monumental feat, dear."

"I need something in return. From you."

"And that is?" She moved to an antique desk, set along the right wall of her office, and began the process of pouring a cup of coffee. She didn't offer me any, and I smiled at the petty snub.

"I need to know how many men..." I glanced at the door. "How many men Brant has..." I try to find the right word to use in this public setting. "...been in contact with. If Lee is the only one. What the possibilities are for more."

Her forehead creased and she motioned for me to close the door. "Do you plan on collecting more boyfriends, Layana? Juggling a handful of men at once?" She stirred a spoonful of sugar into the black liquid. "You're not intelligent enough for that. Trust me on that. No one is."

"Just answer the question, please." I couldn't shed the manners; they lay on my skin like grease that only smeared when attempts were made to wash it off.

She set down her spoon. "Lee is it. There were some other boys in the past, but they have all left. That's why I tried to warn you before. This part of Brant's life ... you need to forget it. Focus on building, on strengthening your relationship with him, and forget about anything or anyone else."

"How long did the others last? The other boys?" I swallowed, suddenly scared of the answer.

She shrugged. "It's hard to say. They don't exactly speak to me. I would guess two to three years on average, some as long as five. And Layana?"

I met her eyes.

"Lee is the weakest of them. A couple of them have been ... ugly. Violent. You can't save them all. You snagged Lee, congratulations. Don't get cocky and think that the next boy will be the same. The next boy is just as likely to bend you over and rape your ass."

I felt sick, the crude words rolling off her tongue as jarring as the image that accompanied them. I imagined all of the possibilities, all of the unthinkable things I had never considered, my life too clean to know true depravity.

"It'd probably be best, at this time, for you to either walk away or put your big girl panties on. You need to make a decision. You either love Brant despite this, or you don't. How *much* do you love him?"

The room refocused on her words, her challenge. I closed my eyes and pictured Brant's face. The man behind the brilliance. The man who I loved in a way I didn't think was possible. The man who I would fight for, would lie and cheat and steal for. The man, who, in some way, shape, or form was savable. I knew he was. He had to be. I opened my eyes and met Jillian's. *How much do you love him?* "Enough. More than enough."

She sighed. Set down her coffee cup. "I certainly hope so."

Chapter 42

Lee was drunk. When he stepped he stumbled. When he leaned on the bar his arm slid. I glared at the bartender, the same asshole from a year and a half ago, and asked for a bottled water. I got a dirty glass and a nod toward the bathroom. Fuck it. I slid the glass back.

I sat on the closest stool. Moved close enough to break his fall if he fell over. "What happened?" I pulled at his chin, his face moving enough for me to see what looked like a busted lip and swollen jaw.

"Asshole homeowner. Said I left last week with only half the grass cut."

"Did you?" The sharp look he gave me answered the question. I raised my hands. "Sorry." I glanced at the bartender. "Could I get some ice?" That, the man provided, a few handfuls dumped in the bottom of a garbage bag. I twisted up the package and pressed it gently against his mouth. "How did that lead to this?"

"The dickhead threatened to tell the rest of the neighborhood." He shrugged. "So I punched him."

I blinked, the intelligence level behind this story staggering in its immaturity. "Why didn't you just walk away?"

He pushed away the ice, worked his jaw from side to side while glaring at me through watery eyes. "I need work. Need cash." He tried to reach for a beer that was no longer there. "From someone who's never worked a day in her life, I wouldn't expect you to understand."

Never worked a day in her life. It's true. I moved from Stanford to a part-time job to the life of a pampered retiree. My full-time job being Brant and now Lee. Lee's finish to the sentence came with a side of disgust, as if my lack of a day job made me less of a person. It was something Brant had never mentioned, and I suddenly wondered if it was something he thought. Emotions and feelings often got hidden. Pushed down until they found another outlet to creep back up into.

I moved the ice to his lip, his eyes flaring as the cold compress hit the open cut.

"Shut up," I whispered. "Take it like a man."

He leaned into my hand, the smell of alcohol and grass and dirt and man invading my senses.

"Mind giving up that seat princess?"

Lee's eyes flicked back open as I broke contact, turned to see a man behind me, his tattooed arm wrapped around a woman I'd politely describe as hard. The stranger's other hand gripped the edge of my stool, as if he was contemplating giving it one firm yank that would flip me onto the germ-infested floor. My eyes took in the bar, bodies filling the small space, the landscape unbroken by the rough man before me. I was the only break in this scene, in my linen pants and Jimmy Choos. The bag on my arm that cost more than half the vehicles in the parking lot. It was stupid for me to come here, on a Friday night at midnight. Stupid of me to walk into an atmosphere of alcohol and rough men and expect to not be noticed, pushed around. Put in my place.

I slid off the stool, my heels finding the floor, my hand catching the bar. "Sure." I smiled, the man's face unchanging, his delight at gaining a seat hidden by scruff and dirt and tough.

"Sit back down." A growl of a statement from Lee, who lifted his head high enough to catch my gaze. Stared at me with an order in his eyes.

"I should be leaving anyway," I said, my voice low enough not to carry. God, I didn't need this. Drunk Lee, who's already bloody from one stupid fight, defending my honor in a place I should have been intelligent enough to avoid.

Lee lurched to his feet, swaying slightly as he turned to face the man behind me. A man who, unfortunately, hadn't budged, still only a step away, girlfriend still suction-cupped to his side. "What the fuck's your problem?"

I pulled on his arm. "Lee." A word that earned me a moment, a glance in which everything froze and he looked at me and I saw everything he couldn't say in that one moment.

He couldn't buy me cars. Couldn't drown me in diamonds and buildings and trips to Dubai. Couldn't even pay for the beers filling his stomach. But this, this was one thing he could do. He could stand, fight, bleed for me. This, something that Brant would never do. A situation our alternative life would have never put ourselves in. This was Lee's world. Here he was king. Here he would slay the tattooed dragon and be my hero. His eyes burned the air between us and I let out a shaky breath. Released his arm and sank back onto the highly contested stool.

"You guys ain't drinking. Make room for someone who is." In two sentences I saw yellowed teeth, a sneer I would cross the street to avoid, and a tightening of Lee's entire body. I saw his punch telegraphed a million ways from Sunday. Had a moment of admiration at the flex of his back muscles when he lunged forward, a right hook missing my insulter by a good two feet, the man leaning back and easily avoiding the punch.

I closed my eyes. Couldn't see any more. Pushed off the stool as the smack of fist against flesh sounded in the loud space. A space that suddenly fell silent, the push of the crowd inward as a dozen bodies quieted and strained for a better view. I opened my eyes in time to see Lee stagger forward and land a punch, the man's head snapping back in an unnatural fashion. I surged forward, plowing between the two, my eyes catching ahold of the other woman in this equation. She snapped a wad of gum and looked away, bee lining for my open stool, her concern for these men nonexistent as long as her seat was secure.

"Stop, Stop!" I screamed the words into Lee's face, his pause long enough for me to shove him back into the crowd, the sea of bodies swallowing the two of us whole, the bar not big enough to accommodate a crowd shift without relocating the population, the swell cutting us off from the offending party. I linked my arm through his and pulled, dragging him to the door and out to the street.

I expected curses, exclamations of male power, an attempt to return inside, but he only stumbled. Once forward, once backward, then sat, his knees buckling in such a fashion that his descent to the ground was almost graceful, a plié leading to his seat, on the dirty curb, his arms resting, folded, on his knees, his head falling to his forearms.

I sat next to him, as carefully as I could. Aware, as my butt hit the concrete, that I was condemning my linen pants to an early death sentence.

Silence. I was at ease in the silence. It fit in this moment in time, reminded me of other times, other places. A reprieve from the insanity of tonight. I hung my head and wondered what I was doing. I should be at home. In my quiet home, neck-deep in a bubble bath, a book in hand. Or curled in the hammock on my back deck. Listening to the ocean until I fell asleep.

"You'll never do it." His words were a slur of depression, thickened by alcohol and desperation.

"Do what?" I kept my head down, eyes closed. I didn't want to see the face that accompanied that statement. Didn't really want to know the answer to the question I had just asked.

"Leave him." A long silence, broken somewhere in the darkness by the crunch of glass and a curse. "You won't, will you?" I felt his eyes on me, forced myself to lift my head and give him the respect of eye contact.

A destroyed man sat before me, his arms around his knees, a shiver against my soul. I had seen this man in so many different lights, but this was the weakest. This is the one that touched me deepest and hurt me the most. The one that I, in some ways, loved the most.

I stared at him and said the only thing I could. "No, I won't. I won't ever leave him."

He broke the contact, rested his head back on his hands, and silence fell back over the street.

Then, with a forward heave and strangled cry, he tipped forward and vomited onto dirty asphalt.

***

A cab took us to my house. I hated leaving my car, but didn't want a drunk Lee in the vehicle while I was driving. I needed both hands, in case of a hiccup during the twenty-minute drive. There was no hiccup. He laid down across the seat, his head in my lap, a loose hand resting on my thigh, as if to reassure him of my presence.

He snored a few times during the drive, hard bumps silencing his sleep, his head rolling against my lap, prompting new fears of a second vomit incident. But the cab pulled through my gates without event. It dropped us at the front, an extra twenty bucks convincing the driver to help me carry him to my bed. And there, his clothes stripped off, my duvet pulled up over his bare chest, he slept. I laid on my side in bed next to him and stared at his beautiful face. Stared and thought and tried to sort out the mess of feelings in my head.

***

When I woke up in the morning, he was gone, along with the cash from my wallet.

Truly gone. His cell phone dead. Jeep found, supposedly abandoned, by my private eye. No sign of the man who held a large piece of my heart. I didn't see again for seven months.

I tried to forget him.

Tried to accept his disappearance as a blessing.

Things in my world with Brant went on. Life was smooth, no stress. The iTunes deal closed, Brant doubled his wealth, and life carried on. But every time I was away from Brant, I thought of Lee. Wondered. Missed. Turned down another proposal from Brant, this one over candles and lobster on the upper deck of his yacht. I almost accepted. With Lee gone, I had to fight from saying yes. But I didn't.

I had to know if Lee was out still there.

Had to dig back into the darkness, verify his existence, find out more.

I just wasn't cut any other way.

Chapter 43

BRANT

I keep the ring in my office, in the main drawer of my desk. Its box is worn, my hands turning the velvet over too many times to count. More than it was built for.

I bought the ring thirteen months ago. On a whim, my head clearing enough to realize that I was downtown, for a reason I didn't know, a swarm of people around, the daily grudgefuck that was San Francisco. I hate this city, its shove of too many people in too tight a space, the fight for air claustrophobic in its necessity. I stood on that crowded street, dirty cracks underfoot, and saw the jeweler, across the street, a silver sign of black and white calm against the madness that was the crowded street. I worked my way through the crowd and stepped inside. Earrings maybe. Something to glint among the dark curls of her hair. I stepped into the calm and quiet of expensive and breathed easier. Smiled at the man who greeted me. Stepped, not to the display of necklaces and earrings, but to the left, my legs pulling me toward the glittering expanse of engagement rings.

I didn't know what I was thinking. I couldn't propose without coming clean. Without telling her about the black in my soul. I am damaged goods. I know that. She deserves to know that. To know what she is stepping into. The pain that I will drag her through, should the medication ever stop working. But all that left my mind when I stepped up to the glass. When my eyes scrolled over mediocre rings and stabbed the surface above one cluster of settings. "Let me see those."

I walked out without a ring. There hadn't been anything worthy of her. But they had worked with me. Tracked down a stone that fit her. A natural blue diamond. It took them three weeks to find one large enough. 2.41 carats, in the shape of a shield. A unique shape, a unique stone, perfect for her. They put it in a simple setting, then delivered it by Brinks trunk. It sat in my desk for another month before I felt secure, felt right. The biggest decision of my life, more important than any deal, any development. I carefully weighed the decision, analyzed pros and cons, examined every facet of my relationship with Layana. Looked at it as a business decision, even though marriage should be anything but. But I already knew what my heart felt. No point in holding it underwater to drown in an unwinnable situation. I needed to go through an analytical process to ensure success.

Before proposing, I completed the analysis for me (positive result), and then for her. Tried to determine if this was a smart decision for her. Tried to anticipate the fallout that would occur if or when she discovered my secrets. Maybe she would be fine. Maybe she'd understand.

Or maybe she'd run for the hills.

I had stewed over it, worked through scenarios, turned that ring over a thousand times ... then I had gone for it. Made a decision, let my accountants and family know, and said goodbye to all logical reason.

Love. It makes us do crazy things.

I rolled the ring against the pad of my thumb, watching the unclaimed diamond flash in the light from my desk lamp. Then I set it back in its box, closing the lid, and returned it to its semi-permanent home. I turned off the lamp and sat there for a long moment, my office and my heart empty and silent.

Chapter 44

SEVEN MONTHS AGO

The next time I saw Lee, he came to me. His frame leaning against the back wall of my house, the early morning light casting golden shadows on his body. Bare, just shorts on, salt water drying on his body.

I came to a stop, my sports bra sticking, sweat running hot down my face. I wiped my face and met his eyes, my breath hard from my final sprint. "Hey."

"Hey."

"You're back."

He stepped out of the shadows, the sun illuminating his skin, his eyes squinting when he came to a stop in front of me, his hand reaching out and tugging on my ponytail. "Yep."

"I missed you." I couldn't hold the sentence back. It was true, not matter how much I hated it.

His grin broke, as he looked down, tried to hide the reaction. His dimple winked at me, the combination one that made my legs weak.

"Don't leave me again." The weakness in my voice showed and he looked back up. Studied my eyes with a somberness that was more Brant than Lee.

"Okay." He nodded.

***

I came down from my orgasm, his cock deep inside, his body draped over mine, two shapes, both bent forward against the bedroom window, his mouth at my neck, the heave of his chest against my back as he thrust, groaned, moaned my name as he fully marked me as his own. Shuddered inside me before pulling out, whispering my name with a kiss against the back of my neck.

My legs gave out, his hand catching me before I fully dropped, dragging me backward until we were both flat on my bed.

"God, I love fucking you." His breath was heavy and the bed shifted when he rolled, pulled me closer.

"Same here." I closed my eyes. Appreciated the drift of air across my skin. Recovered.

"I need a shower."

I grinned. "Me too. Give me a minute."

"I don't have a thing to do today. Take as long as you need."

I kept my eyes closed. Felt him lift my hand. Trace his fingers over the lines on my palm. Pressed his lips against the spot, my fingers closing around his mouth.

"I love you like this." His mouth against pillows, muffled slightly. I kept my eyes closed, my mouth curving into a smile.

"Like what?"

"Naked. Satisfied. Nothing on, nothing to make me feel inferior."

That opened my eyes. I turned my head, tilted it up to him. "Inferior? Why would you feel that way?"

"We live in different worlds, Lana. Don't insult me by ignoring that fact."

I kept quiet. Felt the soft trail of his hand over my back that apologized for the tone in his voice. "But you're here now."

"Yeah. I couldn't even tell you where I've been. Everything..." he grew quiet. "Everything fades unless I'm with you."

It should have been a compliment. Instead, it felt more like a prison sentence. A statement of fact. I didn't respond.

"I wish my mom could have met you."

I forgot, for a moment, to breathe. Waited to see what would follow. Which path this conversation would take.

"She was so beautiful. Hair like yours—curly. Never in control. She used to chase me around the house and it would bounce, like a third person in the room." His voice dropped, as if he had fallen asleep, and I strained for more. When he next spoke, I could barely hear him.

"I can't really remember my father. I was eight when they were killed. A drunk driver, some country-club asshole on a Sunday afternoon ran headfirst into their car. He lived, they didn't." The hand on my back had grown hard.

Silence.

"I'm so sorry, Lee." I didn't know what else to say.

He ignored the sentiment. Continued speaking like the words were bottled up and needed an escape, his voice tight and quick, each syllable dipped in anxiety. "I didn't have any other family. Got put in the foster care system. I had eight different homes by the time I turned eighteen. Three of the homes were okay, five..." I heard the sound his throat made when he swallowed. The hand at my back was gone and I rolled over. I rested my head on his shoulder and wrapped my arm around his chest. Wound a leg through his, until every part of my body was linked with his. Gave him comfort in the only way I knew. "Five ... were bad. I disappeared when I turned eighteen. Got a few thousand bucks from the state and took off." His hand returned. Drew a line down my spine. "You and I ... we've lived different lives. I've never been taken care of. Have never had enough to take *care* of another person, much less spoil a woman like you. My entire life has been about survival. Fighting to get where I am. To get to the point where I will be good enough for someone else."

I said nothing. Just laid there, wrapped in his arms. Felt the moment when he stopped waiting for a response and fell asleep, his hands going limp and heavy against my skin.

It was a wonderful story. Poetic in its portrayal of his life. Endearing. The creation of this tortured, confused man before me. Perfectly explained his desperation for love, mixed with a side of I'llNeverBeGoodEnough.

Too bad it was all a lie. I laid in his arms and wondered how many women he had told it to.

Chapter 45

BRANT

In some ways we are so close to everything, to a life in which one starts and the other finishes, a joining so complete that we are one. In other ways...

We are a world apart.

Lies. Lies are keeping us apart. I started this relationship with one lie, a part of my past that I have locked away and hoped she would never find out about. She started this relationship clean and innocent, and has piled on the lies since then.

I want to rid us of all of the lies, wipe our slate clean with one confession session. But I am terrified to tell her my secret. And I am terrified to hear her tell me hers. I know it, but I don't want it spoken, don't want it any truer than what I already know.

I just want to know why. Why does she cheat on me? What do I not provide for her? What part of me is not good enough? Why, when her love for me burns bright enough to singe ... does she sneak off with a stranger? My biggest fear is that she loves him. My biggest fear is that he has wormed his way into her heart.

I love her too much to share her. I hate him with a vengeance that turns my blood white.

I've had her followed. Met with a private investigator and had him spend a month tailing her. But she was too smart, his report revealing that she has spent time with only one man: me. Now, I have Jillian watching her. Tasked with finding out anything and everything about the man who holds the love of my life in his hands.

I am an intelligent man. I have been called calculating. But I am not cold; I am not unfeeling. My love burns as bright as hers, as does my possession. But my anger, my emotion, doesn't simmer on the surface. It hides, in wait, for the moment when it needs to erupt.

Chapter 46

FIVE MONTHS AGO

"You won't marry me."

"Is that a question or a statement?"

"It's the beginning of a question."

"So ... finish it."

"I would, if you'd stop talking long enough to let me."

I looked up from the pile of fruit before me, my hands on an orange that would have to be good enough, nothing else in the pile soft. I grinned at Brant. "So talk."

He tossed a mango my way, weaving through the roadside stands until he was closer to me. "You won't marry me ... but why aren't we living together?"

Yes, why Layana? I searched my brain for an acceptable answer, other than Lee. Pretty sure Lee wouldn't agree to fucking my brains out on Brant's bed. Then again ... I had my downtown condo, the one that Molly and Marcus didn't break in properly. It deserved a good round of fuckery. "Maybe," I finally said, moving to the side, in front of the limes, Brant's hand pulling at the back of my sweater, moving cashmere in a way that shouldn't be moved.

"Maybe?" He wrapped an arm around me. Nipped at the back of my neck before staring down at me with a somber expression. "Maybe is your answer to my proposals."

"It's a good answer." I smiled up at him. Raised onto my tiptoes and kissed his lips.

"It's a horrible answer," he grumbled, pulling me back when I tried to turn away. "Do you love me?"

I stopped. Set my basket down and wrapped my hands around his waist. Looked up into his face, the face that I loved more than life itself. "Of course I love you. Don't ever doubt that."

He leaned forward. Brushed my lips so softly I closed my eyes. Needed more. "Then move in with me," he whispered. "Be my illegitimate girlfriend."

"That wouldn't be proper," I said against his mouth.

"Then marry me," he said, giving me a strong kiss and pulling off. Glancing around us with an exaggerated expression. "Do you want me to do it? Kneel down right here?" He patted his pockets, pretended to fish for a ring I knew damn well was in his office safe.

"No!" I cried. "For God's sake, no. I will move in with you," I vow, wrapping my arms around his neck and stealing one last kiss.

"You promise?"

"I promise." Then I shrieked, his hands swooping me up, our basket tipping over, fruit rolling to all ends of the aisle. "Brant, what are you doing?"

"House-hunting." He hugged me to his chest, deftly moving through the crowd, my head craning for our basket.

"What about the fruit?"

"I'll buy you a house with an orchard," he promised, setting me gently down on the ground next to his car, his hand opening the door and holding it open for me.

"Now?" I asked dumbly, stepping up into the cab, watching his face as he shut the door and moved around to the driver's side.

"Now."

"I thought I'd just move into your house." House was really the wrong word for it. Mansion. Fifty thousand square feet of space he barely used. A basement lab he had spent ten million dollars outfitting. He couldn't move. Wasn't possible.

"It's *my* house. I want *our* house. A place to build our future. A place you pick out." He shifted into gear and tossed his phone into my lap. "Call Jill. Find out which realtor I should use, then get them on the phone."

Our house. I dialed Jillian and wondered how well this would go over with Lee. Maybe I was making a mistake.

***

I bought my first house a week after my twenty-fifth birthday. Had a budget of three million dollars. Went crazy and spent four. Looked at twelve different homes before coming to the difficult decision of choosing one. With Brant, I expected even more of a production. It turned out to be ridiculously simple.

In my prior, paltry price range, I'd had to make decisions. Did I want the outdoor kitchen or the sun porch? The indoor theatre or a library? An oceanfront office or spare bedroom?

In Brant's price range, every house had everything. And there were only three to choose from. The realtor offered a limo, but we drove Brant's Aston Martin, winding toward the coast, the homes fifteen miles apart. Everything we could ever want for thirty million dollars.

It was an easy decision. The first one was a palace of ostentatious details, hand-painted ceilings, and heavy velvet drapes. It screamed old wrinkly money, and came complete with maids' quarters and an entire floor dedicated to formal rooms we would never use. It did have a ballroom, a huge expanse I envisioned using in a variety of ways, the foremost being a skating rink for our future children. But the consensus, a look shot between Brant and I upon our exit, was that it was a no.

Windere was the second property, an estate high on the cliff, owned at one point in time by the Kennedys. It had four gated acres, nine bedrooms, tennis courts and an elevator that carried us the 42 stories down to the beach. It also came with a two-bedroom beach house, at the base of the elevator, a twelve hundred square foot gem with an attached spa and second pool. It had privacy, needed a staff of at least eight, and was a good half hour from Palo Alto, but it was comfortable. Modern. Us. It also had a six-thousand square foot basement. We were sold.

"This is it." Brant clapped the realtor, a small woman with a large overbite, on the back. "Good work."

"I have one more property to show you ... in Santa Cruz ... it's a beautiful house..." Her voice faltered, and she looked to me for help.

"This one's perfect," I echoed Brant's opinion. Looped my arm through his and beamed up at him.

"Draw up the contract." He slid an arm around my shoulder, leaned down and kissed my mouth. "I love you," he murmured, the realtor stepping away to give us privacy.

"I love you too."

"First steps, right?"

I grinned. "First steps. Baby steps."

He growled against my mouth. "Don't say baby. I'm already wanting to see you pregnant, kids running through this house."

The light in my heart faded slightly, and I pushed myself up, stealing a kiss before the emotion hit my eyes. "Let's get one last look at our future home."

Chapter 47

"What's going on?"

I looked up from my place on the floor, mid-wrap of a picture frame. Lee stood in the doorway, hands out in confusion. He looked around the empty living room, half the furniture removed last week and sent out for consignment. I leaned back. "Frank?"

A moment later, a shaved head stuck its way into the room. "Yes ma'am?"

"Can you round up the guys? Take them to lunch? I need some privacy."

"Sure." He nodded a hello to Lee and exited the room.

I hopped up, setting down the frame, and brushed myself off. "Hey babe."

"What's going on?" he repeated.

"I'm moving. I tried to call you. Been trying to call you. You should get voicemail."

He looked around like he didn't understand the concept, taking a few steps into the kitchen before returning. "Almost everything's gone. When are you leaving?"

"Friday."

"So, where's your new place?"

"Not far." I stepped forward, wrapping my hands around his body, my body flush with his, his reaction immediate.

He looked down, leaned over and pressed a kiss on my mouth. "Show it to me."

"Now?"

He shrugged. "Sure. You look like you could use a break."

I looked around, at my house full of half-packed. A house that Frank and his team could handle. "Okay. Let me grab my keys."

We took the Defender, Lee's hands familiar on the wheel. I was tempted to give him the vehicle, his love of it apparent every time he sat behind the wheel. Maybe later. Now it would only cause a fight. Questions from Brant. Too much confusion, too much rocking of the boat.

A silent drive, the only words coming when I'd point out turns, give directions. I snuck glances at Lee as we drove down manicured streets, a world away from his part of town. His eyes moved constantly, his expression brooding. I knew this Lee. This was the insecure Lee. The one who grew hostile and irritable at my general life of luxury. The one who hated Brant with a fervor that scared me. Maybe today was the wrong day to show him the house.

"I'm starving." I reached over, looped my hand through his. "Want to grab lunch first?"

"I'm not hungry." He pulled his hand free. Down shifted. "Doesn't your new place have food?"

I looked out the window. Swallowed my response. This was going to be a disaster.

***

I saw the hesitation in Lee's turn as I pointed toward the new house, the slow stop of the Defender at the gates, the guard stepping from the small hut, seeing the two of us and waving, the gates starting their slow movement, unveiling the beauty that was Windere.

His shift movement was delayed, the crawl down the driveway slow, the crunch of dead leaves audible in the absence of wind. When the truck came to a stop, before the six-car garage, he jerked it into park, turned off the key, and sat there, the engine dead, his hands on the wheel.

"You're moving in with him." A dead sentence.

"Yeah. You can come in. I want you to be comfortable here."

He chuckled. Dropped his hands from the steering wheel and looked at me. "I'm not coming in, Lucky. I didn't know ... didn't realize. You should have told me."

"It's just a place to live. It doesn't change anything with us."

"It does. Your house ... I was okay there. This place..." He tilted his head and looked up, at four floors of excess. "This place has its own guard shack for Christ's sake. You think they're going to let your side fuck in?"

"It's fine, Lee. You can come and go anytime."

"Anytime he's not here. Fuck that." He let out a heavy sigh and turned in his seat. Stared into my eyes. "I'm never gonna be able to give you this. Shit, I'm never gonna be able to give you anything."

"I don't need you to." I shook my head. "I only need you to love me." The words stuck on the way out, my mouth regretting them as they fell from my lips. He wouldn't understand, he'd think it more than it was, the statement putting too much weight on our affair.

"Love you?" He looked down, laughed softly under his breath before peeking back up at me. "Lucky, I've loved you for as long as I've known you. I just never thought I could have you."

I lost a heartbeat, crawled over the center console, sitting in his lap and wrapped my arms around his neck. Kissed his mouth in full view of the guard shack and a threesome of movers who I'd never see past next week. His hands slid down my body. Squeezed my ass while his mouth claimed my own. It had been the wrong statement for me to make, his admission one that broke my heart and made my year, all at the same time. I pulled off, breathing hard, my eyes meeting his, and told a twisted version of the truth. "I love you too."

"All the good that does us."

"Come inside," I begged. "You can christen it, fuck me in every room of the house. Make it yours."

His body tightened underneath me. "Hasn't he already done that?"

I smiled against his mouth. Took a final taste of his mouth. "Not in any way," I whispered.

"I take back any time I ever called him smart." He wrapped his arms around me, shouldering the door open and carrying me out of the truck. Set me gently on my feet, his hand shutting the door while looking warily up at the house. "Rich prick," he muttered, leaning back against my pull of his hand, his strides slowly taking him up the entrance steps, a mover passing us on the way, professional smile flashed at us both in turn. "Ms. Fairmont. Mr. Sharp." The woman chirped, steps continuing, no pause in her stride.

I felt the start in Lee's step, pulled him fully into the house. "She thought I was Brant," he hissed, glancing over his shoulder at the woman.

"You're with me. He hasn't been here. The movers will probably assume it," I nodded at the room before us, a three-story entrance hall, with as many as four men actively unpacking before us.

"Meaning I can fuck you right here and none of them will be the wiser?" He moved closer, pushing me against the closest column, the press of his body making it very clear where his thoughts lied.

I giggled, pulled away from him. "Behave," I mouthed, stepping away to tap the arm of the closest individual.

"Yes, Ms. Fairmont." The man turned, giving me a wide smile while nodding respectfully at Lee.

"We'd like some privacy. Can you find Ann and have her clear the house of staff?"

"Certainly." The man scurried away, Lee watching him in amazement.

"Does everyone do everything you tell them to do?"

I stepped back against the column and pulled him back before me. "Kiss me."

His eyes hooded, he obeyed, returning the crush of his body to mine, his kiss hard and possessive, his hands blatantly groping me over the thin cotton of my sundress. "I guess that's a yes," he muttered.

"Yes," I agreed. "Now, fuck me eight ways to Sunday."

"Yes, Ms. Fairmont," he drawled, yanking down my panties with one firm hand. "With pleasure."

Chapter 48

I know you don't understand. I know you hate me. But you will soon find out Brant's secret. I can't keep it hidden. It won't stay quiet, is screaming silently until the plug is pulled and its howl will fill the air. And once you find out, you will understand. You would have done the same thing.

***

I'd spent almost two years on Lee. Breaking into his life. Removing all obstacles. Making him fall in love with me, forcing that love to squeeze from his pores and envelop his heart.

I had succeeded. I had him fully in my hands. The only issue was, I didn't know what to do with him at that point.

You could only control, manipulate, a man so much before your leash of control broke. Especially a man like Lee. A man who grabbed at everything he could and wanted more. I could feel the twinge of my leash. The crackle of weakening threads as he pulled hard against my ties. Hard in the direction of Brant. His hatred for him grew the more Lee felt for me.

Jillian was right. I was playing a dangerous game. And risking everything for my own selfish goal.

Chapter 49

TWO MONTHS AGO

The oceanfront guesthouse became our fuck den, far enough from the main house to be our own oasis. Sometimes Lee visited twice a week, sometimes twice a month, his appearance as sporadic as the sun. Lee's stress at getting through the guards subsided the fifth or sixth time he pulled through our gates without a moment's hesitation on their part, a friendly nod the only indicator of his presence.

"Your guards suck."

"What do you mean?" I craned my neck back, my head in his lap, meeting his perturbed gaze.

"I could be killing you in here."

I laughed. "Then I'd have been dead months ago." I flipped the channel. Found ESPN and stopped. I'd watched more sports in the last year than I had my entire life. Brant read and invented in his free time, while Lee watched mindless games that had no impact on anyone's life.

"I'm serious. What's the point of having guards if they just smile and wave at anyone who pulls in?"

"I told you, they know who you are."

"Which is what? Your fuck buddy?" The bitter tone in his voice gave me pause. I muted the TV and turned, rolling onto my side and looking up into his face.

"I'm not intimate friends with them, Lee. I told them to always let you in. Isn't that good enough?"

"Why aren't they loyal to Brant? He's the one who pays their salary. Pays everyone's bills in this place. And where the fuck *is* he?" This was angry Lee. Moody, gets pissed off at anything and everything Lee. My least favorite version of him, a side effect of a passionate man. Brant never got mad. "I've been over here ten times, and he's never been home. Does he even live here?"

"You know he does." I dropped my head back, stared at the ceiling and wondered how I got myself in these situations. How many more impossible questions Lee would have for me today. "Remember? That was a fight in itself." I've fought with this man ten times more than I've ever fought with Brant.

"Rich fuck." He shoved me off his lap as he stood, my body falling from the couch, a hand catching me as I flipped up my head and glared at Lee. He paced to the window, hands on his hips, the pose accentuating every cut of his bare upper half. "I swear Lana, you better hope I don't ever run into him ... you send me down here like some fucking pool boy while he fucks you up there in that mansion—"

"You hate the main house. That's why we come down here."

"Has he fucked you down here?" He turned abruptly, the light dimming in the house as the sun moved lower. Stared at me with eyes full of hatred and hurt.

"Please stop saying fuck," I whispered.

"Has he *fucked* your sweet little *cunt* in this house?" He stepped closer, emphasizing every word, his voice a snarl as it finished, his hands dragging me to my feet and lifting hard on my waist, his grip so hard it hurt, the lift carrying me to the granite island counter, where he deposited me, his hands pushing open my legs, his body taking its place between them.

"No." His hand captured my face when my answer came out, gripping me hard, his mouth following suit, crashing down on my lips with a neediness that ached.

"Promise me." His other hand came hard on my ass, dragging me forward, to the edge of the counter 'til he held me fully against him, the soft material of his shorts doing nothing to disguise his arousal. I hated the way he could do this. His need instantly turned me into a raw cavern of want.

"He hasn't," I gasped. "Please, I need..." I clawed at him, wrapped my legs around him, pulling at his neck to bring his mouth back to mine.

"Tell me."

My hands fumbled at the top of his shorts. Reached inside and gripped him, his hold tightening on me the moment I had him fully in my hand. "This."

"You know what I think you need?" He pushed into my hand. "Is to be bad."

"Yeah?"

"Yeah."

I swallowed a mouthful of lust. "Then make me bad."

"I'll make you worse."

Then he fucked me. Right there on the counter. And I screamed my orgasm against the waves and the gulls and the wind. And forty-two stories above us, the colossal mansion on the cliff was silent and empty.

Chapter 50

Living together changes a relationship. Brant and I didn't have the normal relationship issues. There were no dirty dishes to argue over. No laundry left on unswept floors. No, the traditional sources of strife were handled by our over-attentive staff of seven. But even without fights, our relationship changed, improved as a result of our addresses merging.

If I had any doubt of my love, it disappeared with every morning I woke up next to this man. His focus best in the morning, when he woke me with gentle swipes of his fingers through my hair, soft kisses placed on the surface of my skin. I'd roll into his arms, and there we'd spend an extra hour in bed, blinking the sleep from our eyes as the warmth of coffee flooded our veins. Sometimes he read, my body curling into his as I fell back asleep on his shoulder. Sometimes we fucked, his hard-on impossible to ignore between us, playful kisses turned into much more by his hands. Mostly we talked. About his day or mine. About HYA events or BSX projects. About our future and whether we would have two kids or four. Private or public schooling. Stanford or Peace Corps.

In the evenings, on the nights he came home, we cooked. Christine, the chef, acted as instructor, our skill growing with each dinner. My skill was implementation, Brant's prep. We put on music; Christine kicked us off with general instruction, and then let us fail horribly.

Sometimes he'd get home too late. I'd save him a plate of her creation and sit with him on the upper porch. Listen to the crash of the ocean and talk while I sipped wine and he ate like a teenager. His appetite was huge. I never knew that before we lived together. Never knew that he snacked constantly then ate large, as if he was burning a thousand calories a day, his taste in cuisine as varied as my own.

He also worked impossible hours. Couldn't recall half of his days when we sat down to talk. Lost track of time when steaks were on the grill. Loved, above all else, the sound of my orgasm. Wanted, above all else, to spend the rest of his life with me.

The closer we grew, the more I wanted to really talk. About the secrets that lay between us. There was a way for us to have a real future. I knew it. Fuck Jillian and the things she had told me. I believed our love could carry us through it. I believed I could be the glue that held him together when his world fell apart.

I wanted to kick at the support beams of all that he knew. Expose the truth behind all of this. Tell him everything. And see if he survived. See if he stayed.

I risked losing him.

I risked destroying his life.

I risked saving our love. Our future.

Chapter 51

BRANT

I am not a simple man. I know that. We all discovered that the summer of my eleventh year. The summer it snowed in San Francisco. The summer the three girls disappeared. The summer my parents bought a computer, and I stopped playing outside. That summer, everything as I knew it changed.

The simple Apple II processor, set up in my father's office, unlocked an entire world for me. The introduction to advanced technology took my childhood obsession with calculators and small appliances to an entirely new level. A switch turned on in my mind, and I opened the door wider, letting a pent up sea of 'what if' thought processes loose. I dismantled the expensive new purchase, its guts stretching out across my father's desk, and learned its language in days. My parents were furious, then confused, then saw the genius, and moved me and the computer down to the basement. Gave me a workspace, tools, and freedom.

I learned at a furious pace. Visited the library, checked out every book on technology I could get my hands on. My interest became an obsession, my passion a madness. The more I learned, the more I unlocked different pieces of my mind and learned of their potential, the further I pushed my intellectual limits. Chaos began to reign in my mind, a complicated race of intellectual competition, as one thought process competed with another, all in an attempt to fight to the front of my subconscious first.

I worked harder. Didn't eat. Barely slept. Ignored my parents, became irritable. Spent every spare moment in the basement. It was as if technology spoke the only language that my newfound madness understood. And inside those basement walls the chaos—for one brief moment—stopped. Focus came. Everything else disappeared. I worked in my new home, and my parents called specialists. Discussed me in hushed tones as if I was sick.

Then, October 12th occurred. Our little family's version of Armageddon – a disaster of epic proportions. I was taken to doctors, a slew of them. Dr. F was the face that stuck. A constant presence in the carousel of different tests and meds. He was a psychologist, asked questions, examined experiences. Tried to sort through the kaleidoscope of my mind and understand its structure and balance. I told him a hundred stories, walked him through every piece of my past. Everything except what happened on October 12th. On that subject, on that date, I remained mute. It wasn't a conscious decision, I wasn't being stubborn or secretive. I didn't tell him because I didn't know what happened. It was as simple as that. I couldn't remember. Or my subconscious wouldn't let me remember.

Eventually, life took on a new reality: Jillian and I against the world. I built computers, she brokered deals, and we redefined success. Any deceit we orchestrated … it didn't seem to matter. Money was rolling in, I was well-adjusted, and my parents believed anything we said.

I lied for almost a decade, Jillian covering my sins with a smile and words so smooth that I almost believed them myself. Then, the lies stopped, medication fixing all of my problems.

It'd been 27 years since October 12th.

And I was now in control. I was in love. I would convince her to be my wife.

Never better.

Chapter 52

ONE WEEK BEFORE

The crash of a plate cut deep to my spine, Lee's arms sweeping everything off the table in one angry sweep. He was drunk, his eyes bleary, his announcement made by a steady and consistent lean on the doorbell between the guest house and main home. I had pulled on a robe and taken the elevator, the incessant buzz of the bell ringing through the elevator, the only foreshadowing of the train wreck that greeted me.

"I never wanted this! You wormed your way in my fucking life and now that you have me, you don't want me!" Lee breathed hard, his chest rising and falling, eyes wide, the hurt twisting his features.

"Of course I want you. I love you."

"But you're still with him! What kind of sick twisted girl are you? I swear to God, I can't ... I can't take this. I can't know that you're going back and fucking him. It is killing me. I can't think of him touching you." He stared at me, his eyes pools of hurt, so much emotion swirling through them. His chest shook when he gasped, and he exhaled hard, his fingers shaking as he reached out, pulled me to him and looked into my eyes. "Tell me you love me."

"I love you." I met his stare and wished that he understood, my own eyes filling with tears.

"Tell me again."

"I love you."

He ripped at my pants, pulling the material down with one hand while the other gripped my neck so hard that it hurt. He was frantic, he was needy, and when he pushed inside of me I was not ready, and he was so hard, and I gasped for a different reason but ohmygod I did love this man.

"I can't," he gasped, pulling me to the edge of the table, the edge biting into my ass as his hands held me in place, and his hips started to move. "I can't lose you, Lana. You are my everything." His mouth shuddered against my collarbone as he dropped his head, the soft touch of his lips on that skin different than every other piece in this equation and I arched underneath his hands, pushed against his cock and pulled his head against my neck, his mouth following suit, kissing and biting the skin, making a possessive trail and he pulled and pushed and branded me with his cock, the rhythm increasing and I moaned, my hands holding onto his skin, the muscles under my fingers flexing as he fucked me with his feelings.

Then his mouth opened against my skin and he cried out, a moan of my name, his thrusts slowing as he emptied himself inside of me. Our bodies slowed, his final thrusts hard and deep, and then he stopped. Stayed inside of me while he gasped against my neck. "Tell me."

"I love you."

Then he picked me up and carried me to our bed. Laid me down and rolled me, so my back was against his chest, his arm wrapped around me, pulling me tightly in. He was so much larger, the tuck of my body putting his mouth against the top of my head.

"I don't know what to do." His voice was blurry and soft in the dark room, words almost lost in the hum of the fan. "I love you too much to leave you. But I can't do this. It is killing me." Then he said the words I dreaded, the ones I never wanted to hear but that had stalked me in my dreams. "You have to choose. You have to."

Ten minutes later, his breath evened out. I laid there, his arms relaxing around me, and began to cry. Sometimes getting everything you ever wanted sucked.

It had been long enough. Any love there was would have to be strong enough. It was time. I needed to rip the roof off all of our lies.

PART 3

It was time to pull the roof off of all of our lies.

Chapter 53

TWO YEARS, FOUR MONTHS AGO

The moment Brant turned, in that Belize hotel bar, at 1:43 AM, I knew something was wrong. I just couldn't place what. Couldn't figure out why the hairs on my arm stood up. Couldn't figure out why the noise of the bar suddenly seemed to fade. I stood there, stared at him, and tried to place the problem.

"Hey." He grinned. A wide grin that showed his dimple and white teeth and carefree games of football on Saturday nights. When he smiled his eyes carried the gesture, crinkling at the edges, the total effect one of a man who knew his charm and carried it easily. "You look lost sweetheart." His hand reached forward, cupped the edge of my elbow and tugged me closer, my hand reaching out and touching his shirt. Pushing on it without any force. Just trying to stop my forward motion while allowing my mind to sort out what about this situation felt wrong. My eyes flicked right, to a polo-wearing blonde perched on the closest stool, whose outfit screamed resort employee, her hand gripped around the neck of a beer that I'm pretty sure she wasn't old enough to drink. His other hand, the one not dragging me into his space, was resting on her bare thigh. I stared at that hand and wondered why he didn't move it.

"Honey." A call of a name designed to get attention. My eyes snapped up to his face, that wide smile still there, his eyes on me. He had been talking to me. Called me honey. *Honey.* That was a word I'd never heard roll off his lips. I looked back at his hand. Watched it as his fingers moved. Caressed the skin of her thigh. As I *fucking* watched.

I ripped my eyes from the sight, plastering them back to him, my eyes raping every surface of his face, looking for clues. Was he high? Pupils normal. Drunk? Didn't really look it. He looked normal. If normal had a face that looked nothing like Brant. If normal looked flirtatious and easy-going.

Like a man who had friends and watched sports. Like a man whose hand was moving further up blonde tennis chick's leg.

I pushed hard against his chest and snapped my fingers at the girl. "You. Get out of here before I have you fired." She blinked. Looked at Brant. Then back at me. I didn't wait for a response, I turned to Brant and prepared to give a full ration of every pissed off emotion in my body.

His face tripped my tyrannical plans. It was irritated, his hand reaching out and grabbing the shoulder of the blonde, pushing her back down on the stool when she went to stand. "Stay Summer," he said under his breath, the name combined with the action raising my level of pissed to a point I have not reached in ... forever. *Summer?* He rose to his feet, towering above my hotel slippers' height. "Miss, you should probably be the one to leave."

Miss? I gawked at him. If Honey had thrown me off, Miss kicked me into next week. I avoided looking to my right, hating the feel of the blonde's eyes as my boyfriend made a complete ass of me.

"Miss?" I sputtered. "What the fuck's wrong with you?"

He shook his head, looked at the people next to him, strangers he had never met, as if I was the crazy one in this situation. He stepped closer to me, lowering his voice as he tilted his head down and stared directly into my furious glare. "Did I miss something? Did I do something to you without realizing it?" His eyes dropped, and I flushed for a quick moment when I realized he was staring as the sheer fabric of my top, the robe gaping open enough for him to see cleavage. I stepped back, wrapping the robe tighter, my mouth working, my hand thrusting his cell out, incoherent thought manifesting itself into speech, anger in the form of words, spilling out.

"I don't know what kind of sick game you're playing Brant, but we are through. Take your cell and get your own fucking room."

"Brant?" His eyebrows met in a way that I'd never seen but was incredibly hot. The image almost distracted me from the next line of bullshit out of his mouth. "My name isn't Brant."

My name isn't Brant. The most idiotic sentence that, I could guarantee, had ever come out of that man's brilliant mouth. I laughed. "Your name isn't Brant?"

"No." Such absolute certainty that, for a minute, I thought I might be the crazy one in the room. "You have me mistaken for someone else." He held out a hand as if I would have any interest in shaking it. Stared into my eyes. "Who are *you*?"

The night had left Crazytown behind. I blinked at him and understood nothing except that everything was broken.

***

"You know my name," I whispered the sentence.

He tilted his head in a gesture of recollection, then shook his head. "No. I'm sorry. Did we already meet?"

I glanced from his innocent face to the blonde, her brows raised in an expression that indicated her impression of my sanity. Then my eyes moved, the crowd around us all carrying similar expressions, their perplexed pity fixed on one common source: me. Not Brant, who appeared to be in the middle of a nervous breakdown. One in which he appeared sane, just lost any concept of who he was. No, everyone thought I was crazy. I crossed my arms and pinched my skin, just north of my ribs, just to make sure I wasn't dreaming. I wasn't.

I looked at Brant's cell, still stuck out, ignored by everyone but me. Without a word, I slipped it into my pocket, turned, and fled the bar.

Hot tears slipped down my face, tears bred from confusion, mixed with a side of loss. I veered, seeing a stairwell door and pushing on it, my butt hitting the first step it found, my composure held together until the door shut and I was fully alone. Was this the end of us? Not Jillian, not an affair or disagreement over wedding invitations? This insane middle of the night confrontation with a man who didn't know my name?

I stopped the rocking motion my body had begun. Was that who I just met? A man who didn't know my name? I analyzed. His face. Reactions. Words. My senses. I believed the words that came out of his mouth. Believed that he believed them. It was what had made the entire scene maddening. But if he believed the words he had spoken, if he believed that he didn't know me, believed that he wasn't Brant....

Was this the secret? If so, it meant it was real. That this was not a blip of abnormality but a ... lifestyle. A forever. I pulled out my phone, dialed Jillian's number, and damned the consequences.

She answered on the last ring before I lost my nerve to voicemail.

"Hello?" Her voice had aged, or maybe it was just the fact that it was two in the morning.

I cleared my throat. "It's Layana Fairmont."

"I have caller ID. I'm well aware of who you are."

"I just ... Brant ... he was downstairs in the bar. And he didn't recognize me." I closed my eyes and hoped that those sentences made sense. This was the test. Where she either knew exactly what I was saying, or jumped to the conclusion that I had driven my boyfriend insane. Which, from where I was sitting, was still a fairly good possibility.

Her sigh told me everything I needed to know. Not surprised. Not irritated. Resigned. Expectant.

"Who was he?"

"What do you mean? He said he wasn't Brant."

Another sigh. "I had hoped this wouldn't happen."

"Excuse me?"

She was silent for a long moment. When she finally spoke, it was the voice of an old woman. "There was a reason I didn't want you to go away together. You think I hate you. You think I'm trying to fight your relationship. But you were wrong. I was just trying to keep this moment at bay. Trying to salvage any chance of Brant having some normality."

"I don't understand." The understatement of the century.

"Brant has dissociative identity disorder, DID. He's had about five different personalities over the last three decades. I wish you'd gotten the name of the side you met tonight. I thought he had improved..." She stopped for a moment, the line going so quiet I worried I had lost her. I glanced at the screen. Cursed the low battery icon that displayed. "I don't know as much as I'd like. He's very good at hiding; his personalities are even better. They are still, to this day, hiding from Brant."

"Hiding from Brant?" I stood. Squeezed my hands into fists and tried to slow the racing of my mind. "He doesn't know?"

"No." Her voice had sharpened to a fine point in that one word. "And he can't find out. His doctors have been very clear on that. His conscience walks an emotional tightrope. Finding out ... it would be counterpart to pushing him off the edge of that rope and having him crash. Everything would collapse. His gifts, his personalities ... the doctors don't even know if Brant would be the one to stay in control, in the forefront. We risk, at that moment, losing the Brant that we know—the Brant that you love—possibly forever."

I sat, on wobbly legs, unable to hold up anything other than my sanity. Pressed my fingers into the lines of my forehead. Closed my eyes and wished for a dream.

The secret. I'd dreaded it. Avoided it while digging for clues.

It had arrived. I had met it. And I wanted nothing but to turn back the clock and recapture the pieces of my heart. They lay, like broken glass, back in that bar, being crushed underfoot by Brant and that woman's feet.

"It won't last long," she added. "Normally he's only in a personality for a few hours. He'll switch back soon, depending on how long he's been out."

"I've got to go," I mumbled into the phone.

I don't know what I expected. Jillian to grow a shard of compassion and treat me as something other than a money-grubbing piranha. But she said only three words.

"Keep the secret."

***

"Layana?" His voice was confused. I lifted my head from my arms and looked up at him.

My boyfriend stood before me, hands in his pockets, concern in his eyes. *Layana*. He had said my name, framed by the gray dust of the empty stairwell.

I stared at him, accessing. The wide smile was gone, as was the girl. *Summer*. I tested his name on my tongue. "Brant?"

"What are you doing in here?" He crouched down until he was at eye level, his hands running over my arms in a method that typically created warmth. "Are you okay?"

I nodded. Okay was about as far from my current state as possibilities allowed. I smiled, searching his face, finding everything there that I knew. Responsibility. Gravity. An unwavering aura of calm. I reached out, wrapping my arms around his neck, breathing in his scent, the hang of smoke still on his clothes. I tightened my grip as his hands slid around my body. Pressed my lips against his neck as I wondered if he had kissed her.

He lifted me off the stairs and carried me, like a child, to our room. I curled against his chest and, when he laid me on the bed, I pretended to be asleep. Didn't want questions, had too many questions inside my own head that might burst to the surface. I laid on the soft pillowtop. Let him drag the blankets over me. Felt the sink of the bed when, a half hour later, his skin smelling of soap, he crawled in. Wrapped his arm around me and pulled my body against his. Heard the whisper of his voice as he spoke in the quiet room.

"I love you."

I love you too. I kept my body still, my breath even. Waited for him to fall asleep and tried not to think about the ring in his suitcase.

Chapter 54

The next morning, I stayed in bed. Groaned when Brant's lips brushed the back of my neck.

"Come on baby." His voice sweet against my skin. "Big plans for today."

I curled my knees to my chest, thought of the ring box. *Big Plans. Terrifying.* I pulled the blanket tighter. Let out another groan that sounded more alarming.

"What's wrong?" His hand, soft on my hair. Probably the same hand that had slid up that woman's leg. Caressed her thigh like he wanted to fuck her.

"I don't feel well."

"Really?" Concern mixed with disappointment.

"Please call the front desk. See if they have a nurse on staff." I didn't lift my head, let the pillow muffle the words, certain their meaning would carry.

"A nurse? You're that bad?" His hand moved higher. Gently touched my forehead, like it would be warm, like a fever was a symptom of heartbreak.

"Hurry," I whispered the word and heard the rustle of sheets, the bed lighten as he moved to the desk. Spoke with hushed words that I strained to hear.

"Someone will be here in a few minutes. What can I get you? Water? Aspirin?" There was panic in the lining of his words now.

I did nothing but groan in response.

Five-star service got me two nurses and our butler. I made a pained face and asked Brant to give me privacy with the nurses. Five hundred bucks in cash, split between the two of them, got me serious faces and an announcement, upon Brant's return to the room, that I needed to return home immediately. The butler stepped forward, offered his services to secure a chartered jet. Brant accepted, more tips changing hands, the duo of nurses getting double-compensated, then everyone jumped into action, the nurses starting the business of packing our items while Brant knelt at the side of my bed, his face at eye-level, his hand gripping mine. I winced for good measure, tightening the curl of my body. "I'm so sorry, love. I wish there was something I could do." I closed my eyes, hoping he would stop. Step away. "I love you so much. If anything happens to you..." There was a break in his voice, a desperation. I peeked out of my lids, saw him patting his pockets, looking around wildly. *No.* I pulled on his hand, pulled his attention to me.

"I just want to sleep right now," I mumbled. "The nurses gave me something for the pain..." I closed my eyes and let my hand slacken in his grip. I felt the shift of his hand as he stood. The press of his lips against my head. Then, both touches left and I heard him begin to bark orders to the room.

The return trip was made by private jet, a charter that probably set Brant back thirty grand. No lines for security. No baggage claim. The car pulled into the private airport and we were airborne fifteen minutes later. The flight attendant settled me in on the couch, Brant at the other end, his hands pulled off my shoes and set my feet in his lap, his hands gentle as they rubbed my soles.

I avoided him. Avoided looking his way, hearing his voice. Recoiled at the touch of his hands, terrified of doing anything to encourage him to pull out that ring box and ask the question I had spent six months wanting. I closed my eyes and avoided him and counted down the hours until landing.

...Dissociative personality disorder. Given the time and different stages of his life, he's had as many as five different personalities ... The man I had met downstairs. His hand on her thigh. Smudged lip-gloss. How many women had he fucked during the last year?

He's very good at hiding, his personalities are even better. Missed dates. The things I'd blamed on forgetfulness. So many times he'd left during the night...

We risk ... losing the Brant that you love ... forever.

I wanted to be home. I wanted my house and my solitude and to figure this mess out, and to examine whether there was any chance of pulling my heart back in one piece.

What would you have done? When, three months later, Lee stepped up in that gas station store and flashed his smile? I had loved one side of Brant. Was it really that strange that I fell in love with another side of him?

Chapter 55

PRESENT DAY

It is time. I have to do it. Have to sit down with Brant and talk this through. He is an intelligent individual. He loves me. Lee loves me. I should talk to Jillian about this, but I don't want to. I am too worried about what she would say. The orders she will shove down my throat. Orders I have no intention of following. I know what the right thing to do is: to allow Brant to live his separate lives without interference. I understand that. But it is too late for that. I fucked up this entire situation two years ago. When I saw Lee and stepped closer. Fucked him in a parking lot and fell in love with his smile. Chased him down and wrestled his heart into submission.

My options are limited. Lose Lee or tell Brant. Put Brant's psychological well being in danger because I am too selfish to lose Lee. Again, I know what I should do. What path Jillian would scream at me, her hatred compounding with every unjustified shake of my head.

Am I that horrible? I think the answer is yes; I know it is wrong, but my love is too strong to feel anything but right. I can't lose Lee. And I did all of this out of love for Brant.

Yes, this is selfish.

Yes, I am putting Brant in danger.

Yes, I am possibly saving my relationships in the process.

Yes, I am taking the biggest gamble of my life.

I love them both too much to do anything else.

I cradle two glasses of wine in my left hand and step through the open glass sliders, the wave of ocean wind crisp in the dark evening. Take my place on the outdoor couch next to Brant and tuck a bare foot underneath me. Handing him his glass, I try to figure out where to begin.

Chapter 56

His wine is half gone by the time I finally speak. "I've been keeping something from you." I set my glass on the table before us and turn toward him. I don't need to draw attention to the conversation, his focus is complete, as it always is. He follows suit, setting down his wine, his eyes settling on me, the clench of his jaw the only sign of tension. I stare at that tightening muscle and wonder at the it, the tic rarely seen in Brant. I swallow, trying to find the next sentence, my hands moving nervously as I attempt to pull together intelligent thought.

"Is this about the other man?" His voice is deadly calm. A calm I have never heard from him but would have expected in an angry version of Brant. Calculated. Controlled. Angry.

I blink. "What?"

"The other man you've been seeing." He says the words casually, but I see the tightness in his face, the stiff line of his mouth.

"What are you talking about?" *Of course he knows.* The man is brilliant. Can spot minute changes in a hundred pages of code. I haven't exactly hidden my behavior. I figured an absent man can't catch someone who—in his mind—doesn't exist.

"We're both intelligent adults, Layana. Don't play stupid." His voice is harder than I've ever heard it, yet quiet. He isn't a yeller. I swallow.

"Okay. Yes, in part this is about him. Just ... bear with me for a minute. I'm getting there."

"I've been waiting for you to tell me. Waiting for you to explain what on Earth I am not providing for you." I can hear the threads of hurt in his voice. Small. Easily missed, yet in the structure of Brant's voice I hear them as loudly as if he is screaming.

"It's not what you think. I—"

"How long has it been? Five months? Longer? I suspected before, but didn't know for sure until we lived together." He leans forward, resting his elbows on his knees, his eyes intent on mine. Analyzing. Searching for truth among so many old lies.

"Two years."

That hurts. I see the flinch in his features. The swallow in his throat, the moisture that comes to the edges of his eyes. He drops his head to his hands. "Is this why you won't marry me?"

"Not in the way you think." I hadn't intended on my relationship with Lee to be the catalyst that started this conversation, but I move on. Let it open the door wider.

"Do you love him?"

I lean closer, hold Brant's hands and force his eyes to mine. "I love *you*. Everything about this has been about you."

He pulls his hands away. "Stop talking in fucking riddles, Lana, and tell me why."

"I need you to look at me. I need you to listen."

He does. He stops talking, he looks me in the eyes, and he focuses. Loses his ego, loses his hurt, and focuses on my words. Does what Brant was built to do. Analyze and interpret.

I give up the quest for the perfect words and dive in.

"His name is Lee. I met him in Mission Bay. He does odd landscaping jobs out there for cash. He was dating another girl for a large part of last year. I've been sleeping with him off and on for two years. I used to do it at my house, now I do it in the guesthouse. Lee is not his real name, it's an identity that he's adopted." I swallow, then go in for the kill. "Brant, his real identity ... it's you. He's a personality your brain created, an identity that you adopt at times. Mostly during times of stress. You have a condition called dissociative identity disorder. It's what used to be called multiple personality disorder. I haven't been cheating on you. The other man ... it's you. It's just a different side of you, one who has his own personality."

His expression doesn't change when I stop talking. He just stares into my eyes and listens to silence. Blinks a few times, long intervals between. "I'm thinking," he finally says. "Trying to decide if you are lying or if you sincerely believe what you just told me."

"I'm not lying."

His eyes hold mine. Studies them. Moves slightly as a process occurrs behind them. "I believe that you mean what you're telling me," he says slowly. "That doesn't mean you aren't insane."

I smile slightly. "I'm not insane."

"One of us is. I'd much rather it be you." My smile drops.

"You're not insane."

"I'm absent-minded, I'm not living separate lives."

"I've been fucking your other personality for two years. You are."

"Do you love him?" The question, when repeated a second time, has entirely different tones.

"Yes." I blink, tears suddenly present, the wealth of my emotion at an all time high. It isn't fair to love a man in two different ways. One way is hard enough.

"More than me?"

"No."

"You are mistaken." A stubborn stick to his jaw.

"Jillian is the one who told me." A gamble, but those words are the ones that truly get his attention. He turns back to me.

"*What?*"

I move to the ground before him and kneel, my hands on his knees. "In Belize. The weekend you were going to first propose. I woke up in the middle of the night and couldn't find you. I went downstairs ... and saw you in the bar. But you weren't yourself. You didn't recognize me. Introduced yourself as someone else—"

I stop, his form rising above me, stepping to the side, his hand roughly pushing me aside. Like Lee, not like Brant. I choke back the rest of my sentence.

"You're wrong. You were confused. Probably drunk."

I struggle to my feet, reaching for his hand and miss, frustration spreading through me. "No! I stood in the bar and you told me *you didn't know me*. You made a fool out of me, made me look crazy. You introduced yourself as *someone else*. Had your hands all over another woman. I left the bar and called Jillian. She told me." I lower my voice, his gaze finally back on my eyes. "She told me that you've suffered from DID since you were eleven. Since you became a savant. She said the doctor said you must never know. That you might have a mental break, lose Brant and adopt one of the other personas. Your parents, Jillian ... they all know. They keep the secret to protect you!" My voice gives out on the last word, the hoarse rasp breaking the sentence in two.

He steps closer, his hands fisting, the calm stride of his voice no match for the frustration in his tone. "So why then, Layana, are *you* telling me this?"

"I can't..." I lose my nerve. Don't want to give voice to my selfish thoughts. "Lee ... he wants me to choose. What you do in your other lives ... I can't ignore that. I can't be your wife and know that when you are away from me, when you are living another life, that you are touching other women. Loving other women. I need you to be fully mine. I need you to love only me. Right now, I have you both. I love you both. But Lee ... he wants me to choose. I can't lose him, Brant. I need to find a way to have you both, without losing either of you."

"So your plan was to tell me. To burden me with this."

"A part of me hoped it would be freeing."

"I want to speak with Jillian. I don't believe you."

"How can you love me, want to marry me, and think that I would lie about this?" I stare at him, wanting more, wanting the man I love to recognize the man I can't live without.

"It's inconceivable, Layana. What would you do if I told you that you had another person living inside of you?"

"But I don't."

"That's how I feel. I'm in my head all day long. Have been for almost forty years. Trust me, there's no one else up there."

With that, he turns away from me and heads inside. Less than a minute later, I hear the roar of his car.

I listen to him leave and wonder who will return.

Chapter 57

BRANT

This is not possible, yet she is not lying. Can't be. Everything about that interaction screamed truth. I need Jillian. I need to look in her face and find out the truth. I feel stress, pushing on my chest in ways I cannot cope with. Now is the time for a pill. I can feel a blackout coming, pushing on the edge of my sanity with greedy feelings, my mind's source of relief simple in its black oblivion. I fight the urge, suddenly suspicious of the only relief I've ever known, the pale pill that calms my world. Refocuses my anxiety. Lets me sleep. Lets me continue my uninterrupted life.

Is everything I've known a lie? How deep does this level of deception go?

On October 12th I blacked out. Woke up with half of Jillian's face beaten in. They said I had gone crazy. She had tried to pacify me and I had turned on her. Punched and kicked and knocked her backward. I woke up in a children's pysch ward with absolutely no memory of the exchange.

That was back when I used to have blackouts. It was explained that they were my brain's way of coping with the pressures that my intellect forced on it. Spots in time where I would act in a manner that made no sense. The longest lasted five hours. Two decades ago Jillian found a doctor who solved my problem. Provided a cocktail of meds that calmed my dark demons. The blackouts stopped, my only moments of dark occurring when the drowsiness side effect knocked me out. I've lived without a relapse for decades.

Blackouts. That is what I was told, what I believed.

I push harder on the gas, my hands trembling against the steering wheel. Jillian. At the root of all of this, is Jillian. She will have the answers.

Jillian is standing before her home when I pull in. Wind buffering the long coat around her, her hands tucked in its pockets, a resolute look on the face of a woman I love like a mother. I turn off the car and we stare at each other through the glass, a long look where I read fear and try to understand it. I am so confused. I am so lost. I need Layana. I open the car door and stand. Watch Jillian step backward until she reaches the steps and turns, moving rapidly up them, her black-coated figure framed by her colossal house of white. Around us, dusk hit and lights suddenly come on, illuminating trees and pillars, accents of drama that are unneeded in this clusterfuck of a situation.

I step away from the car and tuck my hands in my pockets against the chill. My shoes are heavy as they take the stairs, her profile illuminated in the open doorway, her hand bracing open the front door. I meet her eyes as I step in. "Jillian."

"Brant," she says with a resigned sigh. "Come on in to the den."

Den is a word used by a woman who doesn't understand what it means. Dens should be comfortable, not the formal atmosphere that is the bones of this room. I sit on the edge of a divan and watch her face as she settles into an upright chair.

"Layana called me," she says. "She told me what she told you."

I watch her hands smooth the front pleats of her pants.

"I never wanted you to date that woman, Brant."

Not the words I am expecting. "Is she telling the truth, Jillian?"

She looks at her hands, then up at me. "You wouldn't even believe me if I told you, Brant. She has you so twisted around her finger. Multiple personalities?" she scoffs. "It's her delusional attempt to explain an affair." She stands and paces before me, her shoes clicking on the floor like a metronome. "You're the one who suspected her of cheating." She points a trembling finger at me. *Trembling.* From anger or fear? "You know what's going on here, Brant. She's found someone else and doesn't want to lose you over it."

I match her stance, rising to my feet. "So she invented *dissociative personality disorder* to explain it? Do you have any idea how insane that sounds?" Jillian won't meet my eyes. Her gaze skitters over the room. "She doesn't know," I continue. "About my blackouts. Has no other ground to stand on. She looked me in the eyes and told me something she thinks to be true. Told me something she says that *you told her.*" Breath pushes out of my chest in hot waves, the pounding in my head hurting. Rage. That is this emotion. A foreign emotion that I haven't felt in a long time. Don't understand. I feel a peeling of my psyche, a loss of some of what I understand to be control. I blink, focus on Jillian, can feel the snarl in my voice as I step closer.

"Brant ... you don't understand." She falters. "Your medicine stopped all that."

"All *what*? The blackouts? Or my stepping into another persona altogether?"

She holds up her hands, and I stop. Realize how close I am to her. How the wide white of her eyes is fear. Of me? A laughable thought. I will my fists to relax and focus on my breathing.

"I don't know anything about another persona. All I know is that you've been doing perfectly. Your work has never been better, your focus more crisp, your creative insight more in tune."

"Fuck the work. I'm talking about my life, the person I am when I lay my head down to sleep."

"You don't mean that," she straightens. "Your work is everything, Brant. You and I... we're changing the world."

"We're building computers, Jill." I reach out. Grip her shoulder and force her stare to meet my own. "What's going on with me? Is she right?" I beg with my eyes for truth and see a falter of indecision in her own.

Fury boils through me at the tell, ripping apart the veins of my composure and I grip her other shoulder with my left hand. Rattle the small bones of a woman I thought I knew. "Tell me!" I scream into her face. "Is there someone else inside of me? Tell me!"

I watch, in slow motion, the snap of her chin, its jerk as I shake her shoulders. The feeling, an overwhelming hatred of the unknown, shatters every tie of self-control that I had in place. I notice, for the first time in decades, the strip of my world as it breaks into pieces. The dark sweep of oblivion as it takes my anger and dissolves it into a sea of black.

Black.

Nothing.

Maybe it is another personality taking over. Or maybe it is the injection stabbed into my back, Jillian's eyes leaving mine for a brief second to look over my shoulder and nod.

***

I wake up restrained, my wrists and ankles given a limited range of movement, about two inches, best my drugged mind can determine. I jerk and pull, the action worthless, other than earning movement from the man in my room. Turning my head works, the movement free and unrestrained, my head lifting easily as I crane my neck to see the bald man move closer, his features coming into focus, the cloud of my mind recognizing everything about him in a second. "Dr. F." I let my head fall back as he moves closer, his hand resting with reassurance on my chest, his face looking down on me with concern. "Where am I?"

"You're at Jillian's home. She thought this would be a better place to keep you, away from the press or public eye."

"Untie me." I try to ask with as much civility as possible, but am certain he hears the expletives behind my tones.

"Not yet. Jillian told me what happened ... for our own safety we need to keep you restrained a little longer." His hand pats my arm as if he is turning down my request for a popsicle, not my God-given right to freedom.

"Let me the fuck up. I'm not going to hurt you. I've done nothing to allow you to restraint me like an animal." I spat out the words, yanking with all my might at the restraints, feeling claustrophobia swell through me.

"Brant, forget the restraints for a moment. We need to talk." He returns to his seat, ignoring my personal alarm, pulling a pen out and clicking it open.

I close my eyes and will my muscles to relax, to cease the press of skin against restraint. Envision the motherboard of Laya. The components that connect to make it run. The pieces of nonsense that communicate to breathe life into an inanimate object. *Peace.* I open my eyes. "Talk."

"What happened when you blacked out?"

"When?"

"Yesterday. Here. You blacked out in Jillian's den."

"It's not a fucking den. It's a formal room designed for uninteresting chitchat. And it couldn't have been yesterday. Had to be today ... I—" I notice the light streaming through the windows. It *was* yesterday. "Where is Lana? I want to see her." *I need to explain the things I don't yet know.*

"We don't think you should have any visitors until we figure this out."

"Excuse me?"

"We don't think—"

"I heard you. I just can't believe you would speak to me as if I am a child. I am an adult. I don't care what you *think*."

"Mr. Brant, you've been declared incompetent. For the moment, I am your personal physician, unless Jillian appoints another one. And Jillian is your personal representative."

Oh my God. I'm going to break again. I can feel the creep, can see dots in my vision ... "I can't have been declared incompetent. There is a process involved. Probate court. A psychological examination by a medical practitioner."

"I am a medical practitioner, Brant. And Jillian had some strings pulled. We have a provisional application in process, which has been approved by a local judge. It will stand until the courts open on Monday. Please relax and let us treat you."

My brain tries to grab at straws it can't reach. "I need my medicine," I gasp. "Please."

"We are going to hold off on any medication until we see the frequency of your switches."

"My switches?" My chest hurts. Stress leaning on my chest until I fear it will break.

"Your switches into other personalities. We can't understand them until we observe them."

"Other personalities?" *So it is true*. I need Layana. Need to explain...

BLACK.

Chapter 58

I've woken up in fucking old lady luxury. Lee shifts in the bed, his gaze moving over ornate wallpaper, his mind trying to place where he is. How drunk he got to take home a senior citizen and end up in her bed. Moving his head slowly to the left, he comes face to face with an old bald man. He blinks, the man staring at him like dissection is planned. He tries to sit up and realizes that his hands won't move, a hard jerk of wrist doing nothing but alerting him to the fact that his arms are sore, like he has struggled for hours.

"Who the fuck are you?" he snarls.

The man smiles, a patient gesture. "Let's get your name first. Then I'll tell you mine."

"Lee."

"Lee what?"

Lee frowns, not sure what he is getting at. "Lee Let-Me-The-Fuck-Up-Before-I-Kick-Your-Fucking-Ass."

Baldy has the guts to laugh. "Oh, *that* Lee. Nice to meet you. I'm Dr. Finzlesk."

"Am I under arrest?" Wouldn't be the first time he's woken up in a jail cell. Though most jail cells don't have hardwood floors, twelve-foot ceilings, and framed art.

"No. I'd just like to ask you some questions."

"How'd I get here?"

"Is that a question you often ask yourself?"

He stares at him. "Answer the fucking question."

"You grew violent; you were sedated. We restrained you so that you wouldn't hurt anyone else."

"I hurt someone?"

"Not too badly." The man smiles at a time when a smile seems off. Looking through his answer, Lee tries to figure it out. His head hurts. He closes his eyes.

"Whose house is this?"

"A woman named Jillian Sharp. Do you recognize that name?"

"No." *Sharp.* "Is she related to Brant Sharp?"

"Yes."

Yes. So helpful. Baldy's bedside manner sucks. So he had hurt someone in the house of someone related to Brant Sharp. Maybe he'd finally snapped. Tracked down that rich fuck and kicked his ass. Fought for the woman he doesn't really deserve the likes of.

"What's the last thing you remember?"

Screw this asshole. Who ties someone down, wants to examine their head, and won't provide any information of their own? He stares at the ceiling.

"Lee? What's the last thing you remember?"

"Fuck you. Give me my phone call."

It is the last thing he says. Hours come and go, Baldy sticks by his bedside, and Lee keeps his mouth closed. Ignores every question that comes. At some point, the windows dark, the hour unknown, the man stands with a sigh. Setting down the blank notepad, he opens his bag, removes an item, and approaches the bed.

Lee jerks at the hot prick of metal, turning a furious face to the doctor, his arms jerking, muscles pulling at the unforgiving restraints. "What was that, you fuck—"

BLACK.

Chapter 59

It has been two days. Brant won't answer his cell, neither will Lee. Funny how, even now, I still think of them as separate individuals. I drove to Jillian's yesterday. Stood on her front step and stared into her eyes. Her pupils red, her face as strained as my own. We both love him; I understand that. Understand that she has dealt with this for decades longer than me. I understand that she is upset with me for breaking the balance, for shoving the truth into his face despite the consequences. I may be responsible for losing him. I may have tipped the scale and caused his psyche to crash. Fall to a depth that it is unable to rise from. I could have, in my moment of confession, lost the man I love.

It is an unthinkable thought, but one I must consider.

She didn't know where he was either. He hasn't called her, hasn't responded to her texts. She didn't say it, but I could feel the blame. This was what she warned me of, and her face clearly stated her opinion of me. For the first time, I feel I deserved her scorn.

We agreed not to call the police. To wait and hope for him to surface. She is monitoring his credit cards and bank accounts. Sooner or later, he should use one.

I returned home afterwards. Paced every floor of our home and prayed into the wee hours of morning.

***

At 4 AM, I wake with an idea. Toss and turn over it before my brain functions enough to iron out a plan. I consider and discard Don, then call Marcus. "Where are you?"

"In bed. It's the middle of the night."

"I'm coming to you. Text me your address."

"Is this about Molly?"

I hang up the phone without answering, shove my feet into Uggs and grab my keys. Take the elevator down and step into the garage. My phone dings with Marcus's address at the same time that the garage bay doors open.

Marcus had gotten rid of Molly. Hopefully he would help me find Brant.

***

Marcus answers the door in nothing but pajama bottoms, the view of chiseled abs doing absolutely nothing for me. I move into his house, beelining for the kitchen and slap a piece of paper on the counter.

"This is what I need." I explain the plan, then push my cell toward him. "Call them."

He looks at me with speculation. "A phone call? That's it? For a thousand bucks?"

I shrug. "It's five am. I figure I'm paying graveyard rates. Sell it."

He lets out a rumble of a sigh, pulls the paper closer, and dials the number.

"Put it on speaker," I whisper.

He obliges, giving me a look that many would classify as disrespectful.

"Eurowatch Assistance, how may I help you?"

Marcus glances at me. "This is Brant Sharp. I need help in locating my car."

"Certainly, Mr. Sharp. I will need to ask you a series of security questions to first verify your identity."

"Go ahead," Marcus says with a wary glance in my direction. I nod at him.

"What is the VIN number of the car you would like to track?"

"J2R43L2KS14JD799F" he recites, reading the line of numbers off the paper.

"Excellent. Please hold while I pull up your profile." There is a series of keystrokes before the interrogation continues. I cross my fingers and hope that I have enough information. I had cleared the safe of as many files of importance as I could grab, getting the file on the car as well as the personal file that holds copies of all of his identification documents. I can't imagine that Aston Martin knows much more than what was presented at the time of purchase.

"Mr. Sharp, may I have your address please?"

"23 Ocean's Bluff Drive."

"And your driver's license number?"

There are three more questions that Marcus passes with flying colors, us both breathing easier when the representative moves on.

"Please hold while we locate the vehicle. Would you like us to also notify local police?"

"No," Marcus said with an easy laugh. "My nephew was due home two hours ago. Borrowed it for a date. We're thinking he's sleeping off a party somewhere. I'll just breathe easier knowing where it's at."

"Excellent, sir. One more minute on the location."

I give him a thumbs up and he rubs his fingers together. Digging in my pocket, I come up with and toss his cash across the counter. Pulling the paper closer, I grab a pen. Wait for the voice to tell me my soulmate's location. Cross my fingers and pray he has stayed with his car.

"Mr.Sharp, if you have a pen, I have the location."

"Go ahead."

I pose over the paper.

"8912 Evergreen Trail, San Francisco, California. Please know that, if you wish, we can remotely disable the engine."

Marcus glances at me, and I shake my head in response. "That won't be necessary. Thank you for your help."

"Thank you for calling Eurowatch, Mr. Brant. And thank you for being a member of the Aston Martin family."

Marcus reaches out and ends the call. "That help?"

"Yes, thank you." I key the address into my phone, grabbing the papers, my mind mentally walking through the next steps. I should call Jillian. Get her involved, or at least in the loop before I head to wherever Brant is.

I come to a sudden stop before the door, his body hitting me from behind. "What?" he says, stepping back. "Everything okay?"

I stared at my phone, at the first search engine result: the property appraiser site for San Francisco County. 8912 Evergreen Trail is a home. A large one, purchased for $6.5 million seven years ago by one Jillian Sharp.

I lock my phone and yank at the front door, fury propelling me forward.

"What's wrong?" Marcus calls after me, my backward glance catching him in the door, his hands braced on either side of the frame.

I take a step back, rip a page from the folder and scribble down the few items that the Aston Martin representative had asked for. Thrust the paper at him. "Call them back. Invent a new story, but find out how long his car has been there. Then text me it."

"For free?" The incredulity in his voice has my eyes snapping back, his hands raising up when he sees the fire in my glare. "Okay. Just joking. I'll call them."

"Now!" I call out, turning and jogging down the hill of his driveway, my car chirping as I plow toward it.

My suspicions are confirmed when the text from Marcus comes through.

SINCE FRIDAY NIGHT.

Bitch. That woman had stood on her front porch and lied to me, his car no doubt tucked away in one of her garages. Let me stand there guilt-stricken and led me to believe that Brant was wandering around lost. Unsure of who he was, in the middle of a psychological break because of my actions. Had stood there with her judgmental Iwasright glare. When he had been inside her house the whole time. Had he stood by the window and watched me? Is he mad at me? Is she using this time to turn him against me? I need to know what is being said, where his mind is. If he is in a strong place or a weak one.

5:24 AM. I take the exit for her home and kick myself for not instantly recognizing the address the moment it had been announced by the helpful customer service representative with the mandatory British accent. Brant and I have driven by her home so often that I know it by sight, not address. Still. I bite my lip and try to organize my thoughts. Soon, I will see Brant. He is safe, not lost. His mind is intact if he is at Jillian's. I need to talk to him. Without him, I am lost.

Chapter 60

Jillian lives in Nobb Hill, the snooty area of San Francisco, if I have any right whatsoever to call anything snooty. I pull into her drive and park, shutting off the engine and staring at the house. There is a late model BMW parked on the pavers beside me. I look at it with new interest, trying to remember if it had been there yesterday. Coming up blank, I step toward the front door. Pause and consider the fact that it is five thirty in the morning.

Extremely rude to knock at this hour. My manners stop my reach toward the door. I step back. Think. Step forward and try the knob. Locked. Big surprise. I wince, then reach up and pound the shit out of the door.

My trepidation disappears the moment Jillian answers the door, fully dressed, makeup on. Her puzzled look turns to an impressive show of alarm upon seeing me. "What's wrong? Is it Brant? Did you find him?"

I stare at her, slack jawed, my mind furiously working, something it should have done during the drive here. *She's continuing the façade*. I had expected, upon my early morning arrival at Casa Jillian, for her to be contrite and honest.

"No…" I say slowly. "I haven't. May I come in?"

Her mouth closes and a regretful look passes over her face. "It's awfully early, Lana. The staff isn't even up yet."

I can call bullshit on that. Jillian demands secretaries at BSX arrive by 6:30 AM. I'm pretty sure her house staff starts their day before the sun rises. I also notice her use of 'Lana' — an endearment never extended before. If she thinks I'm that pliable, I'm going to dissuade her right now. I step forward, pressing a firm hand on the door and squeeze by her, a huff of annoyance heralding my entrance. "I just need a minute, Jillian. I'm going crazy with worry." I allow my voice to wobble, hoping that it passes as hysterical.

"Well, please keep your voice down," she says stiffly. "This needs to be a short visit, Lana."

Short visit, my ass. I wait for her to shut the door. Watch her turn to me and gesture toward the closest chair.

***

I have underestimated this woman. Faced opposite her for three years but I haven't known the level of her deceptive abilities until now. Now, in a situation where I know the truth yet am almost persuaded by her acting. I sit in her home, listen to her lie, and feed her rope. I feed her foot after foot of rope and watch as she, seated in a plush red upright chair, tie a complicated noose around her neck and hang herself.

It is a masterful act. One that goes through irritation, then sympathy, then a full-breakdown of tears over 'where our boy may be'. Her worry for him. Her terrified portrayal of a loving aunt. Played to perfection. I watch her performance with dead eyes, horrified by the ability of this woman, one who has orchestrated Brant's life for two decades. Ran BSX during that time. Protected secrets while spinning lies of her own. I sit before her, grip the arm of a chair, and wonder where in the home Brant is.

Once the noose is tied.

Once I know her selfish loyalties.

Once I understand my enemy.

I stand.

Throw back my head and scream Brant's name as loud as humanly possible.

Chapter 61

Jillian shoots to her feet, confusion in her eyes, her gaze darting to the right, and I take off running, up the staircase, my Uggs taking me faster than a high-heeled senior citizen can even think about moving. I scream for him, scream his name over and over as I tear down a marble hallway, my feet slamming to a halt when I hear my name, called from a few doorways back, and I whip around, bursting into a bedroom as my eyes catch sight of Jillian's entry from the top of the stairs.

I don't at first understand the scene. A man I've never seen, standing at the edge of a bed, the thrashing figure before him a tangle of sheets and movement. I come to a stop, the stranger and I staring at each other for a brief moment, then my eyes are on Brant and he smiles and it feels as if my heart will explode. "Lana," he gasps. "Get me out of here." Then he jerks his hands and I see restraints and my entire world goes red.

"WHAT THE FUCK IS WRONG WITH YOU?!" I whirl, Jillian's entrance into the room skirted by two employees, three flushed faces who stare at me as if preparing for battle.

"Layana," Jillian starts, her hands patting the air in a calming fashion.

"WHO THE FUCK HAS THE KEYS TO GET HIM OUT OF THOSE?" I point to the shackles *ohmygod* that hold Brant down. *Hold him down*, as if he is fucking dangerous. Or insane. Or anything other than Brant, my gorgeous brilliant man, currently tied down like an animal.

"We had to restrain him. He was violent."

"No I wasn't," Brant speaks from behind me.

"You don't know what you were!" Jillian snaps.

"You," I snarl. "You don't have the right to fucking talk to him anymore. I'm taking him with me right now."

"Language," Jillian clicks her tongue disapprovingly. "It's nice to see the trash that lies beneath that blue blood smile, Layana."

I look at her in disbelief. "My *language*? That's what you want to discuss right now? While you have Brant *tied down*?" I look from the strangers face to her employees, all who look unsure. "WHO THE FUCK HAS THE KEYS?" I scream, my own hold on rationality questionable.

"I do." The man in the room steps forward. Pulls a key chain from his pocket and looks to Jillian. I move in between them, blocking his view, and point to the bed.

"Untie him."

"Don't move, George," Jillian's voice rings out.

I step forward, snatching the key ring from the man and move to the bed. Meet Brant's eyes while freeing his right hand. "I love you," I breathe.

"I'm sorry," he responded.

"Shut up baby." I turn to his leg strap and come chest to chest with Jillian, her fingers wrapping around my wrist with an iron grip.

"Please call Duane and Jim," she says crisply to the women behind her. "I need them to get over here immediately."

I jerk my hand back, twisting it until her fingers lose their grip. I place both hands on her chest and shove, the woman letting out a cry as she stumbles back, her legs giving out and falling to the floor. "Stop!" I cry at the uniformed women, their exit paused as two pinched faces turn to me. "Right now," I gasp. "You have a decision to make. You are, I assume, both BSX employees. If you have any interest in future job security, I'd get over here and help me free the owner of your company."

***

My car burns rubber on its Nobb Hill exit, Brant's groan from the passenger side causing my foot to ease slightly, my eyes leaving the road for a moment to assess his condition. "What's wrong?"

"Nothing. Just get us away from her."

I press a button on my steering wheel, speaking when the tone sounds. "Call Home."

I reach over and grip Brant's hand, my fingers looping through his. An interlocking squeeze that I don't want to ever lose.

The ringing through the speakers ends, replaced by the efficient voice of one of our security personnel. "Sharp residence, this is Len Rincon. Good morning, Ms. Fairmont."

"Len, I'm with Brant. We'll be arriving home in about ten minutes. I want the house on lockdown. No one coming in or out unless you talk to me. Especially not Jillian Sharp."

"Is Mr. Sharp also available, Ms. Fairmont?"

"I'm here, Len. And I agree with everything Lana just said." Brant leans forward to make sure the speaker catches his voice.

"I'll need you both to provide your security passcodes." Any comradery I've shared with this man over the last six months is gone. Suddenly, I see the ex-Special Forces asset we had hired.

"4497," Brant mutters, sinking his head back against the headrest.

"1552," I say.

"Thank you. We will be ready when you arrive. Would you like me to alert the police?"

I glance at Brant, speaking when he shakes his head. "No, thank you. Just make sure Windere is secure."

"Will do, Ms. F."

"And please connect me to Anna.."

"Certainly."

The house manager answers promptly and with more perkiness than any individual should contain before 7 AM. I speak quickly, wanting to get off of the phone and talk to Brant. "Can you have Christine prepare breakfast? A full spread of everything Brant likes. Also, please prepare the bedroom. Draw a hot bath. And light the fireplace. I also need you to bring a physician in. He needs a full tox screen done, so have them bring whatever they need for that." I had a sudden thought. "Actually, call Dr. Susan Renhart. She's at Homeless Youths of America. Tell her it is urgent, and that discretion is important."

She repeats the instructions back to me, then I end the call and glance over at Brant, his eyes closed. "Stay with me, babe," I say softly, the sun rising spectacularly as my car whips around a curve.

"I'll never leave you," he says. "Not willingly." He sits up, pulls on my hand slightly. "I'm so sorry, Lana. For everything I must have put you through."

"We have the rest of our lives to talk about it." I squeeze his hand. "Right now I'm more concerned with Jillian. Brant ... she's..."

"Crazy," he finishes with a growl. "Crazier than me," he adds with a wry laugh.

"Should you call your parents? I'm trying to think through her next course of action. It might be best for you to speak to them before she does." I reluctantly pull my hand from his, put both on the steering wheel before he feels the shake in my palms. I was literally *shaking* with anger, at myself, at Brant, at the manipulation this woman has had in our lives. "I mean ... Brant, she *tied you down*. What kind of sick person does that?"

"What if I'm dangerous, Lana?" His voice is quiet but walks the steps of giants.

I slow the car, jerking my gaze to him. "You're not dangerous, Brant."

"Brant isn't dangerous. But you said yourself I have other personalities, what if one of them..." He suddenly leans forward, gripping the sides of his head. "Oh my God."

"What?" I reach a frantic right hand out as my left pulls the wheel hard enough to turn through our gates. Tugs at his knee as I careen down our driveway. Pull at his shirt as I shift into park. Try to break through, but he ignores me, gripping his head as he shakes it from side to side.

"October 12th," he whispers. "Oh my God. October 12th."

I say nothing, wait, as he repeats a date that means nothing to me. Then, he stills. His head stops moving, he slows his frantic rock, and drops his hands, a calm settling over him as he raises his head and looks at me.

"I remember." He says softly. "I remember October 12th."

Chapter 62

There is not a moment when I feel the switch, when it bubbles through me and replaces one person with another. There is nothing to fight. Nothing to struggle against. I simply open my eyes to a place I don't recognize. Stare around, take in my surroundings, and then continue.

Our minds are unique in that they are like infants in their acceptance of what is shown. I don't wonder that I don't remember yesterday, because I have always had no yesterday. It, to me, is normal. That personality has never lived another way. I don't find it strange to be suddenly awake and at a restaurant and midway through a meal because that is what I know. How I know life to be. The regular world, as a species, doesn't question the fact that they close our eyes and—for eight hours—time passes in literally the blink of an eye. Doesn't question the fact that they may have said things in our sleep, held a brief conversation in the middle of the night with a spouse—a conversation that they remember nothing about. And just as they don't question that, I never questioned the two decades in where things didn't always make sense. Blamed any gaps in memory or sudden changes in location on my medication's side effects.

But now, suddenly, I remember something. One glimpse into a day I have wondered about for twenty-seven years.

I didn't know much about my world when I opened my eyes on October 12th, other than a few simple facts. I was Jenner. I was eleven. There was a girl down the street named Trish who had a pet mouse and wouldn't let me play with it. She'd shown me the tiny, trembling figure a few weeks earlier and I had touched it. Pale white with red eyes, and I had poked it too roughly and she had pushed me away. Pulled it close to her chest and screamed that I'd never touch it again.

I digress. I was Jenner. I did not know who this woman before me was and had no interest in her brand of authority. I wanted my mom. I wanted my blue house with the broken porch rail and the iced tea pitcher that collected condensation in the fridge. I didn't want to be in a basement with a woman whose mouth was tight and eyes were black, who smelled of vinegar and coffee and whose finger wouldn't stop jabbing the paper before me.

"Focus, Brant. Multiply the fractions. We don't have all day."

I'd never seen this pile of crap before. Numbers above and below lines. The crooked cross, which I knew *meant* to multiply but I didn't know *how* to multiply. I pushed the paper away and looked at her. Said the only truth that didn't make me sound stupid. "I'm not Brant."

"You certainly are Brant. And you did three pages of these yesterday in the time it took me to use the restroom. So don't tell me you don't know how to do it."

I don't know how to do it. I said nothing, only stared in her face. "I want my mom." It wasn't so much as wanting my mother as wanting to get away from this woman.

She looked at me. "Your mother is at work, Brant. You know that. She'll be home at six. Until then, you're stuck with me."

She was a liar. This ugly woman opened her mouth and all that spewed was a lie. My mother didn't even have a job. She stayed home all day. Spent time with me. Let me watch TV and slipped me Hershey's kisses and glasses of milk during commercial breaks. I closed my mouth and stared at the paper. Hated this stranger.

"Do you want to work on your computer for a bit, and then return to this?"

"I want to watch TV." The clock above the shelves showed that it was almost four. My mom would let me watch TV anytime after three.

The stranger frowned. "You don't like TV anymore, Brant. It hurts your head, remember? Why don't you work on your computer." She pulled at my arm and I snatched away, her grip slipping off, the return of her hand harder, her nails digging into the soft skin in a way that *hurt*.

I didn't know what she expected me to do with a pile of junk stretched out, a computer screen hooked to a chain of pieces. There was no computer there, just a jumbled mess of wires. The only computer I'd used was my father's, which was simple, the first step being the large and easy-to-find power button. There was no power button there, and that only served to make me feel more stupid. I shook my head.

"Then we're back to fractions," she sighed. "Do these four pages now, no excuses, Brant."

I looked up, away from the worn page that had been pushed and pulled between us until it had a small rip in the right corner. "I'm not BRANT!" I screamed, the anger pushing out of my throat like it had legs and arms and would fight to be heard.

The woman started, her head jerking back, and I saw a change in her eyes, a hesitation of sorts. A look I liked. I pushed away from the desk, standing, almost as tall as her, a growth spurt already putting me a head taller than my classmates. Giving me strength over others. Over this woman.

"Shush, Brant!" she scolded, regaining her footing and putting a hand on my shoulder, digging in her nails and trying to push me down, into the chair, the muscles in my legs fighting her attempt without struggles.

"I'M NOT BRANT!" I screamed and reached out. Shoved both hands into her chest, having a moment of adolescent pleasure at the forbidden feel of female breasts, even if they were attached to an old woman. She fell, stumbling, her hand leaving my shoulder and waving wildly on its way down.

I moved closer, sitting on her stomach, like how Rowdy Roddy Piper had done to Hogan on TV a few weeks earlier. The move worked well, she struggled and yelled but went nowhere. Hulk had done an athletic spring jump that had thrown Roddy off and across the ring, but she only squirmed underneath me like an overanxious dog.

"Brant!" she yelled, hitting my chest and using the voice that my mother did when she was really serious about something.

"I'M NOT BRANT!" I swung with a fist, the way my father taught me, in our garage, against his baseball glove, my thumb safe, my wrist strong. Saw her head snap, her yells stopping as her hands flew up to protect her face, swing after swing breaking easily through the fluttering of her hands, her voice becoming a river of sobs, finally quieting by the time my hands tired.

My father had been clear in his teachings. You only allowed someone to push you to a certain point, then you pushed back. Stood up for yourself, first with your words, then your fists if the words weren't effective. I had used his words against this liar. Asserted myself clearly before using violence.

The fists. I had enjoyed using the fists. I looked at the still woman beneath me and almost hoped she called me Brant again. Crawling off of her, I looked at my hands, ignoring the moan from behind me. *I have blood on my hands.* Someone else's blood. A first for me. I brushed them off on my pants, realizing too late, that my mother would be upset by the streaks of red against the tan fabric. Then I head for the door, certain that somewhere nearby there will be a TV. And I had almost two hours to watch before my mother would be here to pick me up.

I climbed the unfamiliar set of stairs and smiled, certain my father would be proud.

Chapter 63

Brant finishes the story, torment ripping vulnerability through his eyes and for a moment I think he's going to cry. Break in front of me. I grip his hand, bring it to my mouth. "Brant, it wasn't you. You know that."

"What I just saw ... where I just went ... that was me. Me peering into another world that makes no rhyme or reason. *I did that*. I hit her over and over, like she was an object, a game. My mother..." His voice dropped and his hand came up, pinched the skin between his eyes. "My mother came home and found me on the couch, watching television, eating popcorn, with fuckin' blood on my hands." He lets out a hiss. "I remember that. Like it was me, even though it wasn't. Why am I suddenly remembering that? After twenty-seven years of nothing."

"Do you know Lee? Remember anything of his?" I am almost scared of the answer. Of Brant's reaction to Lee's memories.

He shakes his head. "No. I have ... nothing, Lana. One memory, that's it. That's enough. After that, I don't want any more."

I squeeze his hand and release it. "Let's go inside. Stop thinking for a bit and let me baby you."

***

Anna has earned every bit of her salary. We walk into a house that smells of food and home, the staff fading into unobtrusive corners upon our arrival. Brant sits down at the kitchen table, silence falling over the room as he puts away a crabmeat omelet and two waffles. He avoids my eyes, his stare on the food before him. When he finishes, he stands with a quiet cough, wiping his mouth with a linen napkin. "Please tell Christine thank you for the breakfast."

"I will. Anna drew a bath if you'd like one."

"I think I'll take a shower instead."

Any thought I have of settling into hot bubbles with him disappears. I nod, smile. "Of course."

Suddenly strangers, two lovers awkward in their own home. I don't know what to say to him and he seems embarrassed, all over a fact I have known for two years. I want to hug him. I want to pull out his fears and lay them to rest. Kiss him and tell him I will always love him. But he steps, moves, speaks — all with a cloud around him, one that screams 'Don't touch!'. I stay in place and watch him head for the bedroom.

As I reach for his plate, Anna scurries around the corner. "Let me get those, Ms. Fairmont."

"Thank you." I drop my hand. "Did you reach the doctor?"

"Yes, she'll be here within the hour."

"Can you show her to the master suite when she arrives?"

"Certainly."

"Thank you." Having no more purpose in the kitchen, I walk to the bedroom, easing open the door quietly before stepping inside. The lights are off, the only illumination the dawn, dim over the Pacific. Behind me, the crackle of the fire takes the chill out of the air. I enter the bathroom, check to see that towels are heating, my eyes pulling to the fogged glass of the shower.

I stare at the glass, trying to guess what this man wants. Coming up blank, I pull off my clothes, leaving them on the marble floors, and step into the shower.

The shower is a cloud of fog, the hand before me hidden by a mist of white. I stumble through the steam, my feet feeling their way across the stone floor until I hit the warm body of Brant, his skin jumping underneath my touch. I say nothing, only step closer, into the hot spray, my arms wrapping around his body, my head resting on his wet chest.

"I'm not very good company right now," he mutters, his hands sliding down and around me, a hard hug squeezing me into his chest.

"You're always good company." I stand on my tiptoes, pressing a soft kiss on his lips, my first attempt missing as our movement clashes.

"I'm so lost right now, Lana," he whispers.

"You have me. Together, we'll never be lost."

"I have you for how long? You aren't going to want to put up with this."

I run my hands up his arms and across his shoulders, my hands ending up where I wanted them: cupping his face. "Forever. I've been telling you that for years, Brant. Years in which I knew about your condition. Years I've loved you through. I don't love you *despite* this. I love you, *including* this. Every part of you, even parts you don't know."

He growls, his chest vibrating against me. "That drives me crazy. I'm jealous of him, you know that?" His gruff tone holds an edge of possession, and I smile, glad he can't see me.

"Who, Lee?"

"Yes, *Lee*." He says the name like it is dirty.

"It's a mutual dislike. He's extremely jealous of you."

"He is?" The shock in Brant's voice makes me chuckle.

"Are you kidding? The billionaire who spends his nights with my sexy ass? Of course he's jealous. He knows how much I love you, even if you are blind to it."

He lowers his mouth to me and I feel our connection return, a righting of the balance between our souls. "This is why, right? Why you won't marry me?"

I swallow. Run my hands down his chest and around his back, bringing my mouth to his skin and kissing the line of his collarbone. "It was why I *wouldn't* marry you. Because of my lies, the secrets I kept from you because of it. I didn't think you deserved a wife with a secret."

He lowers a hand until it cups my ass. Squeezes it lovingly. "And now?"

I pull away enough to look up, into the steam where I can barely make out the features of his face. "And now ... there are no more lies. Not from me."

His entire body freezes in that moment, skin tightening, rigidity forming, my hands and body feeling the change. When he speaks, it is only his lips that move. "Are you saying ... that now..." his voice drops, vulnerability carrying through the whisper of his words... "that you'll marry me? With me like this?"

I step forward, pressing every piece of me against him, wanting to crawl into and hug his broken, terrified heart. "I'm saying nothing would make me happier."

He groans, pressing his lips against mine so hard, so strong, that it almost hurts, his hands grabbing at my skin with long, possessive grasps, pulling me against him as if he will never have the chance to touch me again. "That's a yes?" he asks abruptly, pulling off my mouth, as if the last-minute verification is needed.

I smile, finding his eyes. "That's a yes, Brant Sharp. I will marry you and be your wife whenever you want to have me."

"Yesterday," he blurts, returning to my mouth. "Now." He presses forward and pulls me tighter, my body made aware of the size of his need. "Forever."

Then my future husband makes love to me in the shower of our home. And I make sure, for the next fifteen minutes, that no one else crosses his mind. Literally or figuratively.

Chapter 64

"When will the doctor be here?" Wearing boxer briefs, Brant pulls on a T-shirt, his hands reaching for jeans when I'd really rather him be in pajamas, in bed, behaving as my patient.

"In the next half hour."

He opens a drawer and reaches inside, grabbing a bottle of Aciphex and tossing it to me. "Ask her what this is, and what it's meant to treat."

I examine the bottle, twisting open the lid to see it stocked with white tablets. "These aren't Aciphex?"

"No." He looks, for a brief moment, sheepish. "Jillian told me they were to control my blackouts."

"Your what?" I hold up a hand. "Wait. We have so much to discuss it's crazy. The majority of it concerning Jillian. Can you tell me everything in fifteen minutes?"

He shrugs. "I can do it in five."

I pocket the bottle of pills. "Let's sit on the deck and talk."

***

"When I was eleven, everything in my life started to change. It came with the onset of my family's purchase of a computer, the introduction to advance technology affecting more than just my interests. It was as if my brain turned on full force, in a hundred ways at once, an unlocking of a door that I had shut. I was always intelligent, but I was suddenly gifted. I began to apply the simple facts, concepts, mathematics that I knew, and used them in the way that the computer did – as simple rules that can work with each other to conclude an output. My brain was reborn and it was obsessed with discovery. I could think, could process more, do a hundred calculations in a minute, but I also was bombarded with colors, images, thoughts ... more than I could handle at one time. I'd want to build three things at once. Or have two different opinions on the same subject, at the same time. I'd argue with myself, presenting both sides of an argument, my mind understanding the nuances and opinions of either side and feeling strongly on both points." He collects his thoughts, then continues.

"Everything became, in a series of months, maddening. My brain worked in overtime, and I was exhausted over it. At some point during that time, during that summer ... That was when the blackouts started. My brain would go a hundred miles and hour then ... nothing. There would be hours of time where I would black out. Say and do things I had no recollection of."

He pauses and I wait for him to continue.

"Then, on October 12th ... I woke up from a blackout in a child's psych ward. Jillian was in the hospital. That was when the doctors and medical tests started. I don't remember a lot of that time, but when I got out, Jillian moved into our house. I never went back to school, didn't see my friends again, everything was focused on keeping me home, keeping my brain busy. We discovered I did better if I had a problem and focused on it. Complex math problems, or unraveling code to debug a virus ... anything that involved complex thought quieted the madness. This was before commercial use of the internet, back when computers were basic input output computation tools. Data processors. That was about it. I had already learned to build a computer. When I was in the basement full-time, I began the focus of improving the machine, its performance, then—once that was solved—its capabilities." He takes a sip of coffee, glances at me.

"But the blackouts continued. My parents ... they were worried. Worried I would have another occurrence of whatever had happened in October. So I was put on a sedative, something to keep me calm. It stopped the blackouts, but I couldn't think on it. It dulled everything, including my ability to process intelligent thought — at least not on the same level as before. I grew increasingly quiet, lost interest in computers, in everything. So..." He shifts, lifting a foot and placing it against the stone wall. "Jillian and I made a deal."

My mouth dries out as I forget to swallow. "A deal?"

"I stopped taking the medication, and she covered for any blackouts I had. At that point in time, close to the completion of Sheila, I was in the basement 90% of the time, with her for the majority of that. My parents — I was only seeing them at meals and before bed. Any blackouts I had, Jillian concealed. In exchange, I focused on getting Sheila finished and ready for our meetings with investors."

"You were, what? Twelve at this point?"

"Yes, had just turned twelve."

"Not old enough to make that deal."

"I wasn't a typical twelve-year-old. I was intelligent enough to make a quantified decision of risk versus reward. And since Jillian was the one most at risk, and since she was the one spending time with me ... I made the decision."

"No. *She* made the decision. How much did she make in your initial sale?"

"A few million dollars. Ten percent of the deal."

I keep quiet, allow him to pull his own conclusions of my thoughts on the matter. After a moment, he resumes.

"When I was around twenty, we started BSX. Stopped selling off my developments and instead moved them in-house. Our income increased tenfold and I decided I had enough. Enough money to live the rest of my life in wealth. Enough residual income that my children wouldn't ever have to work. I went to Jillian and told her I wanted a change. Told her I wanted to resume the medicine."

"Why?"

He sighs. "Not knowing about my blackouts ... it was a constant fear in my life. I'd have them without even knowing it. Jillian would wear a longsleeve shirt, and I'd wonder if she was covering up bruises from my touch. We were still, for the most part, sequestered from the outside world. And I wanted to live, to have a life, to work in an environment where I could collaborate with others, have relationships, friendships. I wanted normality, and I was willing to sacrifice my career for it. Willing to set aside computers and live a muted intellectual life if it meant security in knowing and controlling my actions. In knowing, more importantly, my lack of unknown actions."

"What'd she say?"

He snorts. "She didn't take it well. Thought it was a horrible idea. Brought up the projects we had ongoing. Printed out our ten-year plan. Cursed me for wasting my talent. But she came around. Tracked down my old doctor, the man you met this morning at Jillian's. Put him on salary for BSX."

Some sort of a growl comes from my mouth. He laughs, holding out his arms. "Come here." I move, from my chair to his, the chaise lounger not big enough to allow anything other than my curl on his lap, his arms coming around and hugging me to his chest. "Dr. F tried me on a different medication, whatever's in that bottle. It was supposed to be a downer with caffeine, something to calm me while keeping me alert, focused. It worked immediately. My brain processes were as strong as ever, my blackouts stopping."

I wait for more, the moment stretching out until my curiosity can't hold it in any longer. "And?"

"That was it. I've been on that medication for almost two decades. Haven't had a blackout since." I lean back and look up at him. His mouth is tight, eyes distracted. Working out the problem before him.

I lead his horse to water. "So ... you believe that? Or do you think that she's been lying to you? Hiding blackouts from you?"

He drops his eyes to me and I see the pain in the lines around his eyes, the tightening of his jaw when he swallows. "She's... been like a mother to me. I've depended on her for so long. I can't image -- I don't know why she'd do that."

Bullshit. He knew exactly why she'd do that. But I wasn't going to insult his intelligence by spelling it out. Knowing him he probably had half of a Venn diagram already completed in his head.

"There's another issue." He looks away, sighs, readjusting me on his lap. "Jillian says she's had me declared incompetent, with herself appointed as my conservator."

"Conservator? Meaning she'd be in control of your business, your finances?" I frown. "Can she do that?"

"The question of my competency could certainly be challenged. I can see a valid argument for the possibility that another one of my personalities was making choices that negatively affected my life, and that that decision-making ability should be removed from my person all together."

"But ... you're brilliant. You've been in control of your decisions for twenty years!"

"And did I ever risk what I had? Did you ever see me take actions as Lee that might have endangered myself or our lifestyle?" He turns me in his lap so that we have direct eye contact. Eye contact that I avoid as I think through the last two years.

Lee: seeing multiple women. *Endangering our relationship, his possible exposure to STDs.* Lee: drunk, in fights, bloody and bruised. *A liability nightmare as well as danger to himself and others.* Lee: a heavy drinker, prone to tempers and driving under the influence. *More liability. More risk.*

"Did I?" Brant pushes the question, his hand pulling my face back to him.

"In ways," I answer carefully. "Lee is a loose cannon. He doesn't have your level of control, nor intelligence. Doesn't think things through, but acts first. But he also isn't going to walk into your bank and withdraw your money. He has no idea that he is you; he isn't going to mess with your business or finances. The risk he posed to you was more one of liability. That he might do something that Brant Sharp is then sued for. He is not a dangerous man by intent, he is just a reckless one."

Brant groans, dropping his head back. "That sounds disastrous."

"When is this happening? The competency thing."

"My days are a little confused due to the medication, but I believe it's happening this morning."

Behind us, the sliding door moves, Anna's head tentatively sticking out. "Mr. Sharp? Ms. Fairmont? The doctor is here whenever you're ready."

"Thank you." I smile at her, waiting for the door to close behind her, then I meet his eyes. "Let me call my family's attorney. Have him stop Jillian. I don't want to trust BSX legal—"

"I don't either," he interrupts. "I agree. Use an outside attorney. Your father's will work until we can find permanent counsel."

"You should call your parents."

He frowns. "I know. It's not a conversation I'm looking forward to having."

"Do you think they'll side with Jillian?"

He shakes his head slightly, his gaze fixed unseeing on the water. "I don't know," he says slowly. "We've all let her run things for so long, without question. I don't know if I would have believed it had she not chained me to a bed."

I watch his hands tighten, the first hint I've seen at anger. I curl into his chest. "I love you," I whisper.

"I love you too, Lana. Thank you ... for sticking with me through this."

I grin. "Thanks for not giving up when I turned down your other proposals."

He tugs at my hand, running his fingers over the bare digits. "The ring is at the office. Let's get it today. I don't want to go another night without seeing it on your finger."

"Deal." I untangle from his lap and stand. "Ready to see the doc?"

"Absolutely."

Chapter 65

I've previously met Dr. Susan Renhart several times. Almost as tall as Brant, she greets us both with a tight smile, showing none of the bright grins she showers on the HYA children. I introduce the two of them, then Brant explains what he best remembers.

"I've been on these pills for almost twenty years," he pushes the bottle over, her eyebrows rising at the name on the bottle, her hands opening it with a practiced efficiency and sprinkling the white pills along her brown palm.

"What were you told that they were?"

"A depressant of sorts, once that had a caffeine agent. Something to keep me productive while keeping me calm enough to avoid a blackout. Whenever I get stressed, I take one. I also take two a day, in the mornings."

I listen with half an ear, interested in his words, but needing to call the attorney. I scroll down, to John Forsyth's number, a man I haven't spoken to in years, and pressed Send.

The doctor rolls the pills in her hand before keeping one and dumping the rest back. "When's the last time you took one?"

"It's been about two days. The morning before last. And ... having not taken them, I may have had blackouts in the time during which I was at Jillian's. I'm not sure."

"Blackouts?" she frowns. "I thought the issue was DID."

"It is." He stops, glances at me. "I'm sorry. I'm so used to thinking of them as blackouts, that's what I know them to be."

She shrugs. Dismisses the thought. "Did you take any medication at Jillian's?"

"Not willingly. But the doctor there injected me with something. Maybe twice, I'm not sure. I want to know what's in my system now. And have documentation of that, should we need it."

She nods, pulling items from her bag. "Let's pull some blood and get a urine sample."

"Layana," the attorney's voice, a booming bass of a sound, crackles through my cell, and I step away, into the hall.

"Hey John. I need your help."

***

Team Jillian shows up before Dr. Renhart has finished, the guard shack calling the house to alert us of their presence. It takes less than four minutes for her brigade to leave, the three Escalades doing a quick roundabout through the cul-de-sac outside our gates. I guess the sight of three armed guards blocking our gate changed Jillian's mind. I watch from an upstairs balcony, and try to understand the woman below me. A woman who seems staunch in her belief that she is in the right, justified. Even in her lies, her deceit. For what? The good of Brant? The good of BSX? Or the good of herself? I step away from the window and walk downstairs, Brant's form by the door, his hand clasped by the doctor's, goodbyes in full force.

"The results of the blood tests won't be available until tomorrow. I'll email you the findings as soon as they are processed. But I would guess, speaking to you about your experience ... anything you were injected with will pass through your system in the next twenty-four hours." She fishes a card from her pocket. "This is Dr. Henry Terra. He's, as best I could tell from my connections, the foremost authority on DID. I would suggest you call him immediately, if not for your own psychological therapy, then to get his legal advice and support for whatever battle you end up fighting. I have to assume treatment of DID has progressed since you were a child." She turns to me and reaches out, wrapping me into a firm hug. "Once you sort this out, I expect to see you at HYA."

"You know me, I can't stay away." I grin at her, and there is a moment of sad connection, when I see the pity in her eyes and want to brush it away. Brant and I are fine. We are strong. I pulled back the roof of lies and we survived, are fighting, our anger focused on Jillian. We have love, the rest will get better or worse, and I would rather have worse than have any more lies. I hold the door and watch her leave, Brant's arm wrapping around and pulling me close, his mouth soft against my neck as he bends down to kiss me.

It is horrible for me to think, to wish for, but in that one moment of peace, of unity, the two of us against the world? A part of me really wants

Lee to show up, to take me against the wall and fuck my brains out. No thinking, no analysis, just raw need fulfilled by both. I roll in Brant's arms. Try to press against him and light the fire of my body, but there is nothing there. Not in this moment when he is broken and I am exhausted and the white hat is so heavy on my head.

I would rather have worse than have any more lies. I just told myself that. I had loved Brant, had only gone after Lee for the purpose of keeping both halves of my man loyal, keeping him close. If he leaves, if the doctor has a cure, if he weeds out Lee and I am left with only Brant, that should be perfect, right?

Right?

I avoid the answers my heart pushes forward. The admittance, in my bones, that a part of me loves Lee. Needs him.

Chapter 66

Tuesday morning.

Jillian's injunction to push Brant's custodial motion through is stopped, courtesy of our new team of legal representation: six attorneys rigorously opposing any and all attacks on Brant Sharp's character for an enthusiastic eight hundred dollars an hour. Jillian has funds, so she can fight us tooth and nail, but I don't think she will. Not when an end result will require months of broadcasted legal battles that will only hurt the public image of BSX, as well as any chance of a family reunion between she and Brant. Not when the test results showed that she had injected Brant with a cocktail of illegal drugs while keeping him prisoner. We haven't heard from her since her arrival at our home yesterday. I am assuming she is licking her wounds while removing any trace of the imprisonment that occurred in her home.

The hum of the highway rolls with a muted sound through the car as we head back from the office, my ring finger heavy with the weight of my new acquisition. I finally feel worthy of it, allowed Brant to drop to one knee on the carpet outside of his safe and repeat the question he has spent years perfecting. We had decided to wait until today, for any legal issues to be handled before showing up at the office, not wanting police awaiting our arrival, or some similar scene orchestrated by the control freak that is Jillian.

"What are you going to do about her?" I look away from the window, my eyes catching the quick glance from Brant as he takes his eyes from the road to visit mine for a moment. His jaw tightens, his grip on the steering wheel working the leather as he flexes his hands.

"I don't know. I want to talk to the DID expert, find out my ability to run the company. Regardless, I don't think I have a choice about Jillian. She has to be removed from any role of power."

I sigh. "The company's her life. Has been for twenty years." He won't want to run a company. At least not old Brant. Financial sheets bore him, meetings drive him insane, and he can't name ten employees off the top of his head. He likes to be in a room, alone. Working, fixing, creating. Jillian has done a great job in her role, even if she had been psychotic in her treatment of Brant. I have no desire to reward the woman but hate the waste of the situation.

Brant's hands move on the steering wheel and I glance over, see his fingers pull up the phone prompt and dial the number for BSX.

A perky voice answers moments later.

Brant clears his throat. "Hank Michen in Security, please." I blink, surprised that he knows a name in security. Maybe he *can* name ten employees without pause.

The next voice is deeper. More intimidating in its greeting.

"Hank, this is Brant Sharp. I need to lock Jillian Sharp out of everything."

There is a long pause. Finally, the voice drawls back through the receiver. "At the risk of losing my job ... is this a joke?"

"I assume you have caller ID. Verify it against the internal corporate directory. I can also verify my driver's license number or social security number, both of which I assume you have on file in some location."

"That won't be necessary, Mr. Sharp. When you say *everything*, do you mean—"

"Her office, her email, her remote ability. Anything that could give her an iota of access. Turn off her campus gate codes and transponder. I don't want her to step on BSX's campus without being flagged and stopped by a member of your staff."

Another long pause. "Is this a temporary or permanent situation?"

"I'm not sure yet. For now, it is indefinite, unless you hear otherwise."

The man clears his throat. "You should know, Mr. Sharp, that we received a similar call from Ms. Sharp yesterday with the same instructions for you."

"And?"

"And I refused. I attempted to call you at that point but you did not answer your cell. I left a voicemail for you."

"You did the right thing. How long will it take before her access is stopped?"

There is the muffled sound of a receiver being covered, then he returns to the line. "Less than a half hour. We'll have remote access cut before the end of this call, sir."

"Thank you. I'll call you directly if there are any changes. Don't accept orders from anyone other than me. And text me your cell phone number."

"Yes sir."

Brant glances at me. Appears to weigh something in his mind. "Hank, if I do call, or if someone else calls pretending to be me, don't listen to my directives unless I verify my identity with a code word. I don't care if I'm standing in front of you, don't do what I say unless I verify it with the word."

"Which is what, sir?" The man seems unaffected by the strange demand.

"Sheila."

"Got it."

"Also, you may take instructions from Layana Fairmont, should I be incapacitated for any reason."

"I don't really feel comfortable taking orders from someone who is not a BSX employee, Mr. Sharp."

"This is a unique situation. Just until we get this sorted out."

The man sighs, a sound thick with his feelings on the subject. "Does she have a code word also?"

I spoke up, my voice caught easily by the Bluetooth. "I'll use the same word, just to keep things simple."

"Okay. Anything else, Mr. Sharp?" The emphasis on the Sharp name made it clear his level of acceptance of me. I grinned at the snub, reaching over and running a hand over the back of Brant's neck.

"That's it. Thanks Hank." He ends the call and leans into my hand. Says nothing as the car screams down the 280.

***

That night, in bed, the television turned down, his arms wrapped around me, I feel his worry. Feel the moment when his brain works through all of the possibilities the last three years has brought.

"Have I cheated on you?" His voice is low against my neck, a thread of hope in it that I am asleep. I roll, staying close, looking up into his face.

"Never."

"But ... as Lee ... I never had..."

I lean forward and kiss him. "You did, but it wasn't cheating."

"Don't justify it, Lana. If I kissed ... touched other women ... I was unfaithful to you."

"I did some pretty despicable things to win you over," I say. "Things I'm not proud of."

He frowns. "With men?"

I slap his chest. "No!" The dark leaves his eyes and it is his turn to steal a kiss, this one deeper, his hands pulling me atop him as he rolls us over. "God," he whispers, his hands sliding down my back and cupping the meat of my ass, squeezing it so hard it hurts. "There were so many nights I watched you sleep and wondered if you were cheating. Wondered what you were keeping from me."

I pull back, sat up on him, the flickering light from the television illuminating the torture of his face. "What? You never said anything to me."

"What would I have said? Accused you of cheating?"

"Yeah. That's exactly what you should have done. I can't believe you didn't confront me." I frown, unsure why exactly my feelings are a little hurt over the omission. We have always been so forthright. So honest. At least about everything except the previous giant hole of deception.

"I didn't want to lose you, Lana." He reaches up, running the fingers of one hand up into my hair, his brow furrowed as he pulls me almost to his lips, his other hand pulling me tightly to him, his need hard against me. "I was worried," he whispers, "that you might—"

"Never be worried." I breathe, taking his kiss when he forces it on me, the crush of his lips as his hand grounds me hard, my hips moving underneath his push, rocking me back and forth against the heat of his cock, my panties sticking to me, the extra friction maddening in its delicious rub. I pant against his mouth. "You will have me forever. You always have."

He rolls us as a unit, his hand rough between our bodies, pulling my panties aside and the top of his underwear down, until the barriers between us are removed and the push of him is suddenly inside me. Oh my God. It is a first, Brant giving me himself bare. Even though I'd had it with Lee, it is different. Everything has always been different between them. Their kiss, their touch, their fuck. Brant shoves inside, I open my legs, pull him into me with greedy hands, and cry out his name as he thrusts in every bit of his possession with strokes that reprint his name on my soul.

Without the lies, without the secrets ... it is better than it has ever been. I break beneath his body and sign away the last bit of my heart to this man. This complicated, layered, brilliant man. Owner of my soul.

Chapter 67

Wednesday. Dr. Terra, the specialist, flies in to San Francisco from Dallas, arriving in the afternoon. Brant had spoken to him yesterday, stressing the need for an immediate meeting. The man has cleared his schedule for the entire week upon Brant's mention of generous compensation. I guess DID billionaires are few and far between.

We are waiting at the private airport when Dr. Terra lands, Brant's frame rising at the sight of the jet. I can feel his nerves, the jump on his skin when touched, the shake of his knees that indicates an abundance of jitters. He is different off the medication. Reacts in new, unexpected ways. Talks more. Smiles more. Even on a day when we've had little to smile about. I loop my hand through his and we wait, watching a short black man limp toward us, his mouth curving into a smile as we make eye contact.

"Good afternoon." He beams. "Brant Sharp, I presume?"

"Yes. This is my fiancée, Layana Fairmont."

"Pleasure to meet you. Thank you for coming out on such short notice."

He nods quickly, rubbing his hands together. "I'm anxious to speak to you both."

"My car's out front," Brant said. "Let's head to the house. We can dive into everything on the way."

***

"My primary concern is fixing this," Brant says the moment the car doors close and privacy is established. He yanks the car into drive, the Aston jumping to attention, the doctor quickly reaching for his seat belt.

"Fixing ... by fixing you mean removing excess personalities?"

I stifle a grin, biting the inside of my cheek as Brant comes to a rough stop at the exit of the airport, waiting impatiently as the gate slowly opens. Patience is Brant's weak point, in all areas of study. He will be frustrated with the need to catch this man up on the clusterfuck of our situation. He will be frustrated with gates and traffic and the inconveniences of taking care of things Jillian previously handled. Money will help. It always does. More employees can be hired; the situation will iron itself out. But money can't walk Dr. Terra through Brant's past. Money can't massage the fact that, right now, my man feels broken.

***

"Dissociative Identity Disorder is not an easily fixed affliction. While other psychiatric disorders can be controlled by medication, DID is not a 'curable' disease. The original medication you were given as a child, I have to assume, was depressants, given to a level that would have dulled any personalities to a point where they were undistinguishable. Obviously, that is not a solution worth exploring."

Brant's hand tightens around the pen in his fist, the flex of his forearm distracting. I place a hand on his arm, squeeze the muscle there. "So what solution *is* worth exploring?" he asks quietly.

"Therapy. It's not sexy, and it takes time, but it has the highest probability of success. I'll set you up with a local doctor and you'll have to come in a few times a week. Go through a lot of hypnosis. The doctor will speak to you and Lee. Counsel you both through the process. Eventually, Lee will either fade away, or parts of his personality will merge with yours."

I see signs no one would ever recognize. The slight pull of the skin around his eyes. The whitening of the back of his hand as his fist tightens. "It just doesn't feel like someone else in inside of me. Could she be wrong?" He doesn't look at me. We sit next to each other, our legs touching on the couch of this temporary office, yet are a hundred miles apart. *Could she be wrong?* A question that really means 'Is she lying?'

The man smiles a smile that dips itself in sadness and comes out with understanding. "You may not know Lee yet, but you will before this process is over. Assuming you participate in my suggested therapy program."

"I'll participate. I want to do whatever I can to get it out." The bite in his voice puts me on edge. As does the word 'it' in regards to Lee.

"It'll take both of you. I'll need Layana's help to speak to Lee. Convince him to leave."

I look up. "Convince him to leave?" I have never convinced Lee, in two years, to do anything. Every interaction was a struggle, my only success the manipulation of him in regards to the Molly breakup.

"Yes. We can't force him out of Brant's life. It will only be successful if Lee is willing."

I nod though it contradicts my inner thoughts. "I'll do whatever I can to help." The words are expected, so I say them. Inside, I try to figure out how I feel about Lee leaving me forever.

Brant speaks, "And I don't want you to refer me to a specialist. I want you, here. For the next few months at least."

I smile politely, the false paint of a face I thought I had abandoned. Smile and search through the dark recesses of my soul in an attempt to unravel the thoughts that are clouding my brain. Try to understand how I feel about this.

Stop. I force the action, force the turn of my mental gears to skid to a halt. It doesn't matter what I want. Who I love. My happiness is sacrificial in order to save Brant. I watch the doctor's mouth. Try to decipher its movement and catch up to the current place in the conversation.

Chapter 68

TWO MONTHS LATER

"You're breaking up with me?" Lee stares at me, his hands tight on the chair before him, his face hollowing as he bites the inside of his cheek, a nervous gesture I suddenly miss. I will miss that tic. Miss the way he sometimes drops his eyes when he asks a question, as if he is afraid of the answer. Miss the way his smile pours through his eyes, like the sex that comes off his body. Miss the way that he is the sexiest, most confident man I have ever met, yet insecure in a way that hurts. He has been terrified of rejection since the day I met him. And now, in a room he doesn't recognize, the psychiatrist's new office cold and impersonal, his fears are becoming a reality.

"Lee, try and relax," Dr. Terra says, speaking from behind us.

I close my eyes at the sound of the doctor's voice. He needs to shut up. He shouldn't be here. I told him that. Told him that this is a private moment. That it will go over better if there isn't a party to Lee's rejection. Especially not a party who feels the need to interject. But they — the doctor and Brant — worried about my safety. Thought the doctor and his sedative should be present, in case it needs to be used. In case Lee gets violent. He won't. I know he won't, not to me. But they wouldn't listen. So now it is Lee and I ... and the doctor. A doctor Lee just turned his full attention to.

"I'm sorry, who the *fuck* are you?" In three steps Lee has his throat in his hand, the doctor on his feet and backed against the wall. His face close to the doctor's, his entire body trembles as he glances over at me, unmindful of the delicate throat grasped by his hand. "Are you fucking serious, Lana? You're breaking up with me? For that rich dick?"

I stare into Lee's eyes the whole time. During the fumbling moment when the doc reaches into his pocket. The instance when his hand withdraws and the syringe stabs through the thin cotton of Lee's shirt. I hold the stare when Lee's eyes flinch. When betrayal seeps through them and he glares at me like he hates me and loves me and misses me, all at the same time. I stare at him and watch as his eyes close and he slumps to the floor.

Chapter 69

BRANT

Ever since finding out my condition, I have read everything I can find on Dissociative Identity Disorder, my reading slowed by the fact that there is little available on the subject. But what I have read is troubling, made more so by the apparent omission that my mind will not reveal.

DID is typically caused by emotional trauma of some sort. Abuse, or a significant event, one the brain tries to hide, initially creating the first sub-personality as sort of a protective defense against the knowledge it doesn't want the brain to have. The rare DID exceptions are brain damage, physical impairments that cause a shorting out of the cranial lobe from which idiosyncrasies result.

I haven't had any physical damage, no hard blows to the head, no horrific accidents that would have caused multiple Brants to emerge. I also, with the exception of October 12th , haven't had any traumatic events. And October 12th happened after – was a result of – my development of DID.

The obvious answer is that I must have had a traumatic experience and have psychologically hidden it. I've asked my parents and believe them when they claim ignorance of any triggering events. My curiosity isn't worth contacting Jillian, my anger building into a grudge that won't soon fade.

Dr. Terra has tried, in a roundabout way, to unearth this possibility. He forgets the man he is dealing with. I am an intelligent enough individual to attack a problem head on. I don't need subtle pecks at the corners of my brain. I need to split my psyche open and dig at the root of my problem.

I can feel the incident. It nags at a part of me, like that errand you walked into a room to do and then forgot. It lies, just out of reach but at the corner of my mind, occasionally tapping at my brain matter when it wants to drive me bat-shit crazy. I need to unearth it. Need to open my past and find the key.

Now, for the 32nd evening in a row, I try. The chair beneath me creaks as I sit on the back veranda, my feet propped against the railing, the skies dark as a storm approaches. I can feel the air thicken, thunder clapping as lightening streaks the sky. I contemplate going inside, avoiding the rain, but the overhang will keep me dry. As the skies open up, rain tapping a staccato beat on the roof above me, I close my eyes and try to remember the past. Try to remember a summer twenty-seven years ago.

And then, listening to the familiar sound of rain against a roof, it comes to me.

Chapter 70

Sheila Anderson had been beautiful. Half Cuban, she had tan skin, dark hair and eyes that gleamed when she laughed. I had never spoken to her. Only sat three seats behind and one seat over, and stared. I was nervous; I was awkward. She was untouchable.

When she left school, I followed. Always had. I had an excuse. She lived a street over; our paths home followed a logical route. So I followed, and I watched her hair bounce, and I stared some more. She was always with friends, she giggled, she whispered, she hummed, and I listened. Until the day that she cried, and my world broke in two.

A Wednesday. It rained. A big sloppy downpour, where one foot outside meant a plaster of clothing to skin, no 'quick dash' possible to keep yourself dry. I saw her standing, out front of the school, her steps tentative as she contemplated the initial step into the torrent. I stood beside her, offered a small smile to her friendly beam. We waited, together, till the moment that she ducked her head and ran, squealing, her hands covering her head.

So I followed. And it was just the two of us running across the parking lot. Through the church. Down the road with the fence. Past the house with the dog. We ran, and it poured unrelenting rain. Then she slowed, and I slowed and it came time for me to turn. I stopped. She continued on. Smiled. Waved through falling rain. I watched her until I could barely see her pink shirt. Then I glanced left, the sight of my mailbox barely visible through the rain, ducked my head against wet needles, and ran after her.

The man's arm is one I have seen in a hundred nightmares and never understood its place. Thick and dark, not from the color of his birth, but from the tattoos. A sleeve of evil, skulls and snakes, the muscles of his arm jumping with the action of his ink. I was one house back when his arm shot out, grabbing the back of her as easily as one would pluck up a cat, the rain obscuring my view as I saw a blur of arms and legs, the heavy patter of rain muffling the cries. I slowed, unsure of what was happening as he pulled her against his chest and stepped away from the sidewalk, into the heavy shade of trees, ducking into the yard he had come from. I wiped at my face and moved closer, my chest heaving from exertion and something else – the tight feeling that something was wrong. The yard showed no sign of them, but I heard her. Screams muffled by something other than rain. I looked right and left, tried to see, find, something other than rain. An adult. I needed an adult.

Then I moved. Closer to the house. Picked my way over its stepping stones, one slick enough to put me in the grass, my hands skittering over the ground and coming up dirty as I pushed myself to my feet. I couldn't hear her anymore and that scared me more than the screams. I hitched my backpack higher and wiped my hands on the front of my jeans. Looked at the front step of the house's porch. Took a step up and left the rain behind.

It was strange to be covered. Quieter. Quiet enough that I heard something. I took the next two steps carefully and moved to the front door. Stared at it. The doorbell. It. The doorbell.

There was a noise from inside, and I bolted to the corner of the porch. Ducked into a ball behind a swing that creaked, bumped, gave away my position with the reaction of its body. I moved away from it, against the house, and was brave enough, for a brief moment, to kneel and peer into the window. Saw through the bare slit between two blue curtains. Saw a television. A rug. A beer can, on its side, a few feet from the trash. Then my eyes lifted, to the room beyond the can, and I saw Sheila Anderson.

I won't share the horrors of what I saw, on my knees, on that porch. I know I closed my eyes too late. I know my hands fisted on either side of my head as I tried to drown out the soft sounds of her screams. I now know why I hate the sound of rain. I now know why, that afternoon in August, my mind broke into smaller pieces and locked that afternoon into a place where I was never to find it.

My foot falls off the railing as I push away, struggling to my feet, the image of that day imprinted on my mind. I stumble to the door wanting, at minimum, to escape the sound of rain. Opening the slider, I see Lana stand from her place on the couch, her eyes on me. "Did you remember?" she asks.

I nod, unable to say more, and open my arms to her as she steps forward and wraps me in a hug.

Chapter 71

Round 2: It's the second time I'm attempting to break up with Lee, and this time the doctor has agreed to stay quiet. To stay behind the one-way glass in the adjoining room. Brant hates it; he cursed us both until he lost control and left the room, but we all eventually agreed, and now I am alone, repeating the lines I have been coached through, the lines that will bring Lee out of Brant's hypnosis.

My initial breakup attempt had been done without clueing Lee in to his condition. With the massive failure of that experiment, we regrouped. Decided to share the condition and hope for better results.

Two weeks ago, Dr. Terra told Lee about the DID. Lee refused to believe it, wanted to talk to Brant, then trashed the room when that option was refused. Dr. Terra stayed calm, citing facts that laid the truth out in big, fat letters that a child would understand and believe. Lee resisted, vocalizing his hatred for Brant in every four-letter word known to man. It was disastrous. I fled the room halfway through the outburst, unable to watch the systematic breakdown of a man who a part of me dearly loves.

Since then, Dr. Terra has spoken with him four more times, Lee getting less aggressive and more unresponsive with each session. The last meeting he spoke but didn't stand, didn't even open his eyes. Just laid on the couch and cherry-picked the questions he felt like answering. Today, I just hope he is open. I hope he listens. I hope he doesn't break my heart any further.

"Lucky." His eyes open and he sits up. Looks around. I wait for his body to tighten, for him to spring to his feet with clenched fists, but he doesn't. Only rubs his neck and shoots me a sad grin. "Still stuck in crazy town, huh?"

"Yeah."

He holds out his arms. "Come here. I need to smell you. Touch you."

Such a basic request. I walk forward, breaking our plan already, but I need him. Miss him. I sit sideways on his lap and lean into his chest as he inhales against my neck, his chest rising as he sniffs me, his mouth grazing my neck, his teeth scraping and then gently biting the skin right below my ear. I lean further, feel every single bit of his hands as he runs them down and along the lines of my body, his mouth letting go of my name as he kisses a line from my ear to my collarbone. "Don't do it," he whispers. "I know what you're going to say and you can't say it."

"I have to," I breathe, his hand running over the top of my bare thigh and sliding down, in between my legs, his fingers pushing roughly against any attempt of mine to keep them together. I think of the man on the other side of the glass. Of the video filming this instance for Brant's eyes later. Of the script that I am supposed to stick to. The one in which I tell this beautiful man that I never loved him. That I only dated him to keep tabs on Brant. That I want him to leave so that I can be with Brant. *Lies*. Black, dirty lies. I feel the push of his fingers as he slides his hand higher up my thigh, underneath the skirt that is doing nothing but helping his cause. I picked out this skirt. Pulled it on this morning when I could have worn a hundred more restrictive outfits. Did I know? Did I pick it intentionally? Am I really that cruel? To myself? To Brant? I fear asking the question when part of me already knows the answer.

"You don't have to," he says, his hand traveling higher as his other hand pries my legs apart, his mouth hot against my neck, stealing kisses in between his words. Kisses that claw at my skin and leave marks that won't wash off.

"I do, Lee." I fully abandon the script the moment my legs lose the battle and part further, the fingers of his hand at the silk of my panties, rubbing hot lines over my barely covered sex, teasing me through the fabric, his mouth moaning my name against my neck. "I can't keep dragging Brant through this. The only way it will work is if you leave."

He tugs my panties aside and pushes two fingers inside, the sudden invasion causing me to gasp, his mouth taking advantage of the opening and closing hard on my lips. He kisses me as he pushes and curves his fingers. Finger-fucks me there on the couch, my legs falling fully open as we create an image that I flush over. But I can't stop. Not when I have needed this every night I have lain next to Brant. Felt the cold distance as he tried to sort his way through this. I open up my legs and let his fingers slide inside, feel the level of my need. Take me to the edge that I want to fall over.

"I don't give a damn about that man," he growls, lifting off my mouth and bucking underneath me, dumping me off his lap and catching me with his hands before I hit the floor, his rough pull of me more out of need than chivalry. "Bend over," he orders, yanking at the zipper of his jeans. "Lucky, I will never leave you. I will never let you fuck him without my name on the edge of your lips." He pushes hard on my back, shoving me over, his other hand jerking at my skirt. "Tell me you still love me." My back arches without control on his first thrust, a full-fledge push of hard, angry man that shoves through any remaining control on its way in. I gasp, clawing at the back of the couch as he withdraws and then shoves back in. I see stars when he pushes in and feel the delicious want when he withdraws. I cry when he stops, when he pauses with only his head inside, the gentle push so different, the stop of him so jarring. "Please," I beg, reaching for him, my moment of need never as strong as it is in this one moment.

"Tell me you still love me."

I fight it, close my eyes so tight the tears fall, my feet straining on their tiptoes as he rocks a tiny bit inside and breaks every last dam around my heart. "I love you," I whisper, and earn an inch or two of push.

"Tell me you need me."

"I need you," I weep. "Please."

He sweeps a hand down my back and grabs the meat of my ass, squeezing the material of my skirt as he pushes fully in and then drags out.

Over.

And Over.

Over.

And over. He fucks me as if I am dirty and his slut and his to do whatever he wishes with. He fucks me as if he can give an order and I will drop to my knees to worship him. He fucks me as if his cock is my lifeblood and every stroke of it ties me to his will. I cry his name and close my eyes to the tears as he fucks me because all of it is true.

"I will never leave you, Lucky," he whispers as he leans forward and wraps a hand around my chest. Pulls my hair until my head is arched back and his mouth covers mine. Rips a kiss from my lips and swallows a bit of my soul in the process. "I will never leave you," he promises as he buries himself in me and comes.

Chapter 72

BRANT

I can't look at her. I can't look at her without picturing her bent over that couch. The look on her face when he thrust. When she cried. When she told him she loved him.

I can't accurately express how it feels. To watch my body, my face, fuck my fiancée. Before Dr. Terra began recording our sessions, there was a part of me that hadn't believed. That thought that maybe *she* was crazy. That she and Jillian were both fucked in the head and I was the only sane one. That somehow my parents had drank the same Kool-Aid. It was an impossible probability, yet my brain held on to it like a lifeline. But then I saw the first hypnosis session and watched myself act in a way I would never act. Smile in a way that doesn't work. Speak in words I've never used. Fuck my woman in a way that I never have.

I don't know what bothers me more. The image of her emotional pain, or the fact that she enjoyed it? I know what arousal looks like on her skin. I know the struggle she had, the fight against an orgasm. I'd like to think I've done that to her before. Made her crave my body in that way. Made her lose all control and sanity with simple thrusts of my cock. I'd like to think I'm not lying to myself, my jealousy justifying away a part of me that she may require.

Now, we drive back home. To the house that we are supposed to have children in. To the house that suddenly feels empty. We are disconnected. I need to find myself so that I can find her again and we can be whole. I need to heal us but I'm too busy healing myself. That man fucking her? He was as close as I've been to her in weeks and I hate him even more for it.

I can't look at her. I can't look at her and see disappointment in her eyes. See her wish that I was Lee.

I look at the road and make the engine roar loud enough to drown out my thoughts.

Chapter 73

I have to do it. Have to stop screwing around and do what needs to be done. Brant's hypnosis is not bringing any other personalities out to play. Lee is it, the only soul between me and Brant and normality. I need to break up with Lee. Ignore him for the next five or ten sessions, long enough for him to give up. Give up and sulk into a corner of Brant's mind where he may never resurface from again. Dr. Terra says a DID mind creates alternative personalities to protect the primary, or to act out in a way that the primary won't allow. If the primary can fill that void by himself, the alternative personality may disappear altogether. *May.* The short word that carries so much weight. Other possibilities ... Dr. Terra won't discuss the other possibilities. He says our awareness of those possibilities increases the likelihood of Brant's mind exploring those paths, playing with the delicate threads for no good reason other than to drive us both bonkers.

So today, I am trying again. To end it in a way that leaves no doubt in Lee's mind. Not like last time, when my pathetic attempt ended with his cock buried inside of me, my head yanked back by his grip, all in full view of the cameras. I am embarrassed by that moment, by the weakness shown to the doctor and to Brant. But Lord help me, I cannot look in that man's face, the same face as my future husband ... and pretend I don't love him. Cannot see anguish — whether it be his eyes or Lee's — and pretend that I don't care. Cannot have the touch of him against my skin and be unaffected. Especially Lee's touch.

I will try my best. And I know, even settling into the chair, with Brant giving me a tight smile, that Lee will see right through me.

I take a deep breath, watch Brant as he lies down on the couch, and begins the hypnosis script.

***

When he comes out this time, it is different. The fight is dimmed in his eyes. He doesn't immediately reach for me, doesn't bound to his feet. He seems, suddenly, an old man in Brant's body.

I don't move from my spot in the chair. I sit there and feel like I am watching him die. When he speaks, his words are weak.

"I'm not smart. Not compared to you and Brant."

I feel tears well and don't know why—don't know where they come from—except that my tear ducts know more about this situation than I do.

"But, I am assuming that you have a plan. You and him. A plan to remove me."

I look down. Break the contact that stretched between us. Feel the drip of a tear as my body betrays me.

"What is it? The plan?" He sighs as if the weight of the question is heavy.

"You already know I mean to break up with you." My voice wobbles when it speaks and I look back up at the man I may never see again.

"And then? When I fight it? When I come out of Brant's body every time his conscience loses control?"

"I'm supposed to ignore you. Snub you. Make it clear how I feel."

He laughs softly and sadly, a chuckle that runs fingers up my inner thigh and breaks my heart, all at the same time. "Your feelings for me show every time you look into my eyes. I used to think it was love for me. Now, I think it is your love for him." He rubs a rough hand over the front of his pants. "I spoke to the doc, sometime after you and I fucked in here." I flinch at the words, spoken carelessly, as if the act had been nothing. As if it hadn't ripped out my heart and left it on the carpet that now lay between us.

"You talked to Dr. Terra?" I frown, irritated by the fact that Brant and Dr. Terra have kept this from me.

"Yeah." He leans forward, resting his elbows on his knees and looks at me, the slight distance closer making my heart beat a little faster. "He explained to me how you were dating me, fucking me, just to keep Brant closer." He stands, holding my eyes, and walks closer. "How every time you kissed me. Spread your legs for me. Got on your knees and sucked my cock, it was *for him*. Do you understand how that makes me feel?" He leans forward, places a hand on each arm of my chair and bends over me, my back stiffening as he lowers his face to my neck and inhales my scent. Buries his face in my hair and whispers my name as he smells me. "God, I'm gonna miss your smell."

The tears flow down my cheeks, my control breaking into a thousand pieces as I clench my eyes shut and stay still, my fingers digging into the leather of the seat so hard that my hands cramp. I take a shaky breath, the action a sob, his head pulling back enough to place a soft kiss on my cheek, gentle imprints of lips along my cheekbones and chin, taking my tears before he takes a brush over my mouth. I open my lips but he withdraws, pushing off the chair arms. I feel his absence before I open my eyes, my vision clearing to see him standing before me, his hands tucked in his pockets, his face tight in a mixture of anguish and anger.

Anger. I understand it but I hate it. Understand, looking into his eyes, that he thinks I used him. Hell, maybe I did. I didn't love him fairly and completely. I loved *Brant*. I loved fucking Lee. I loved Lee's imperfections when Brant was so complete, grounded, brilliant. I loved Lee's wild side, my ability to justify that I was *not* my mother, that I had chosen life and a lower class life, even if it was just for long enough to eat wings and fuck a boy and ride in a vehicle that was made in America. Did I use Lee? I stare in his eyes and see hate and love and hurt. I struggle to speak, but can't find anything worthy to say.

"I loved you. I still love you. Even when I hate you, I love you. I always will. I'm not a smart man, but I know that." He bites his lip in a way that tells me he is close to breaking. To crying. That motion alone brings a new wave of tears, my vision blurring and I rub a hard hand over my eyes, wanting to cement every last view of this man before I lose him forever. He blinks and his face tightens. "Tell me what you want. If you want it, I'll leave. Not for him. I'll never do anything for him. But for you, I'll do it. I'll fucking kill myself inside of him."

I want to tell him I love him. I want to tell him but am no longer sure that I mean it. No longer sure that I love *him* and not because he is a part of Brant. The guilt of what I have done is suddenly heavy, enormous. I want to tell him everything I know he wants to hear. I want to tell him the things I do love him for, but will only complicate this situation even more. So I say the right thing. The thing that will help Brant most. I say the words and wonder at the effects they will cause.

"I want you to leave, Lee. Brant and I ... we want a family. A life. But I will never forget you. I will always miss you."

He looks down, a hard swallow moving through his throat as I watch his hands clench, his mouth tightening into a hard line. He looks up, his eyes wet, his face red with emotion, and we stare at each other.

I *do* love him. I must. Otherwise I wouldn't be breaking right now.

He closes his eyes, drops his head. Speaks without looking at me. "Call the doc back, Lucky. Let him take me out."

I swallow. "You're leaving?"

He shrugged his shoulders without looking up. "According to him, I can let go. Go wander in lala-land or disappear into Brant somewhere. Dissolve into fucking nothing. I'll let him walk me through the process. I don't want you here for it."

I want to hug him. I want him to wrap his strong arms around me and kiss me and give me one last moment. I want him to dig his fingers into my skin and pull me into him like he can't get enough. I am selfish. I want it even if it breaks him. Instead, I stand. "I'll look for you in Brant. He could use a little more Lee."

"Yeah. Whatever, Lucky."

Then I stand and walk to the door. Stand there for a moment and wait to see if he'll look up, give me one last contact, but he doesn't. He stares at the floor and I never get a final look at his eyes.

I open the door and leave a part of my heart in the room.

Chapter 74

I wait in the lounge area of the doctor's office for four hours. I pace. Watch TV. Inhale every mini-chocolate that is held in the receptionist's glass dish. I have reached a new level of jittery. Feel like the time in high school, when Dianna Forge's parents were out of town and four of us held an Uppers and Manicures party in their guesthouse. We rolled and giggled and rummaged through her parents' bedroom until we found a dildo and their liquor cabinet. Shared sips of something bitter and expensive. It was all fun and games until everyone passed out and I was the only one awake and the uppers wore off and took me really, really low. I blinked and ground my teeth until 5AM, when the meds finally died down enough to let my body crash.

Today I'm not staring at three bleach-blonde heads, paranoid that we have taken too many pills, or that Dianna's parents might come back from Cabo early. I'm not on a pharmaceutical mix of stupidity. I am, instead, shaking with nerves, waiting alone to see if my future husband comes back as two men or one.

I finally leave. Tell the receptionist I am headed home and to call me when it looks like they are close to wrapping up. I take Brant's car and tear up the highway to Windere. When I arrive, I skip the shower and crawl into bed fully dressed. Pressing the button to close the blinds, the room darkens into pitch black, the hum of the fan my lullaby for sleep. I close my eyes, my legs twitchy and aching from pacing, and wrap a blanket around myself. Willing my mind to stop moving, I say a long prayer for Brant.

Somewhere during the prayer, I fall asleep.

***

My cell wakes me, my body jerking into consciousness, legs kicking the blanket off before my hand finds the phone. I answer it while moving off the bed, my hand groping through the dark for the light switch, my feet finding shoes before my hand finds wall. "Hello."

"Ms. Fairmont, this is Irene from Dr. Terra's office. He wanted me to tell you that he and Mr. Sharp are almost done."

"I'll be there in ten minutes. Thanks Irene." I hang up the cell and step out of the bedroom into the hall, my steps breaking into a jog. Soon, I will have him back. In whatever shape that comes in. I don't even care at this point. I just want him.

***

When he walks out of the office, toward the idling car, the wind buffering his shirt back against his strong frame, I smile. Brant is back. The same Brant who shook my hand three years ago at the HYA Gala. The same Brant who repeatedly proposed to me despite my denials. The weight of his shoulders, the haunted look that had appeared the day I ruined his life, is gone. His confidence is back, the strong pull of his hand around my waist surprising, as is the possessive kiss he plants on my mouth.

"Everything okay?"

He studies me for a quick moment, his hand still gripped around me as if he has no plans of letting me go. Then he smiles. "We're good. Let's go, we can talk in the car." He returns to my mouth without waiting for a response, my breath taken by the force of his kiss, stronger than I am used to from him, the type of kiss that guarantees a long and lengthy fuck the minute we step inside the house. He releases my mouth and my waist but pulls on my hand, heading for the car.

***

"What happened?" I speak the moment the car is in drive, hours of waiting and anxiety spilling out in two words.

"Dr. Terra spoke to Lee. He agreed to leave."

I wait for more. Wait some more. "And?" I finally say.

"And he left."

I glance at my watch. "It's been seven hours."

He frowns, glancing away from the road, his hands sliding effortlessly across the steering wheel as he downshifts, the smooth motion reminding me of his hands across my skin, and the fact that we haven't been together in almost three weeks. "Seven hours?" He checks his watch. "Wow. I..." he glances at his watch again, then at the dash clock to verify. "He must have been in Lee's head longer than I realized."

I look away from him, out the window. "Dr. Terra didn't tell you what was involved in Lee leaving?" *For you, I'll do it. I'll fucking kill myself inside of him.* Lee's words come back to haunt me.

"No. I mean ... other than the fact that Lee had to accept it. The likelihood of success is much more possible if he is a willing participant."

"So, he's gone? Won't ever be back?" My words behave. Come out level and unaffected.

"I'm not cured. He's keeping me on medication ... the same drug I've been taking the last few weeks. My chances of reoccurrence are high, especially if my emotions or stress get out of control. And I'm to avoid alcohol. You know that; you were there when he went through those rules."

I nod. While Brant has been in full-day therapy sessions for the last few weeks, most of my participation has been behind the glass wall, watching the sessions and getting to eavesdrop on some of the instruction. Brant's new life involves lots of rules. Lots of structure. Opposite of the life Jillian had him leading. Brant's subconscious had created additional personalities to take over when his mind felt overwhelmed. When he was young, it was because his brain couldn't handle the constant assault of his intelligence, the nonstop brain functions causing a short of sorts that resulted in another personality, one that was slower and stupider and emotionally unstable. When he was older, it happened when he was under extreme stress, or in strange situations, or anxious over something. It was no coincidence he had switched the night before his initial proposal to me. Or the days before a new product release or company merger. A risk that was only increased by the medications fed to him by Jillian. With the new rules, new structure, and the fact that he now knows of his condition, we are hoping for him to live a relatively un-switching life. One that doesn't include any outside presences, including one troublesome sex machine I already miss.

I watch the ivy-covered walls of Windere move by, the garage coming into view, the slow stop of the car final. I feel his fingers cup the back of my neck, threading through the mess of curls that spill over my shoulders. "You okay?"

I turn and look into his eyes. See the man who I fell in love with before I knew of Lee. The man who, in Belize, I was prepared to marry. "Yes," I whisper. "I'm good."

He puts the car in park. Unbuckles his belt and leans forward. Pulls me forward until we are close. "I will be more," he says gruffly. "I'm going to be everything he was too."

I close my eyes. Try to calm my heart before I open them back. Find his eyes on me as soon as they do. "You are everything I need, Brant."

"I will be," he says, leaning forward until our lips are a breath away. "I promise you, one day I will be."

Then he presses his lips to me and, for a moment, I taste Lee.

Chapter 75

FIVE MONTHS LATER

I stand before a full-length mirror and do not see my mother. It is an odd thought to have on your wedding day, yet it is a happy notation. I turn, expensive hands rushing to adjust the train of my gown, the beaded edges that frame my back. I am beautiful, San Francisco's most elite wedding planner guaranteeing that fact, every detail around me perfectly coordinated to pull off the most immaculate tiny wedding ever had.

There will be none of society's elite here today. No fake smiles of the women I have pretended, for so many years, to like. We will be a small party of nine: Brant's parents and my own, Anna and Christine, Brant and I, plus our flower girl. My relationship with Brant's parents has changed. We aren't close, Brant's own relationship with them stilted from his years of isolation due to Jillian's controlling hand. But the lines between them are mending, his family unit becoming less dysfunctional as time passes and trust grows. I turn, hearing the squeal of our flower girl before she arrives, a bundle of white careening around the corner and coming to a short halt before the mirror.

"Wow," Hannah breathes, her eyes on the mirror. "You look beautiful."

"Thanks sweetheart." I hold out a hand and an attendant helps me down the pedestal stairs, where I crouch before the little girl. "You look equally beautiful." I pick up her small hand and widen my eyes, impressed at her cherry pink nails.

"A lady did them." She plops down on the carpet, unmindful of the mini Dior that christens her body. Gripping a thousand dollar jeweled slipper and ripping it off, she holds up her bare foot, wiggling the toes before me. "Look! My toes match!"

"Very impressive." I smile. "Got your petal tossing technique down?" I pass her shoe back and watch as she pulls it on, a small pink tongue sticking out of the side of her mouth in concentration.

Task complete she looks up with a smile, jumping to her feet and making exaggerated tossing gestures, complete with mini jumps. "Yep!" she beams.

"Awesome." I hold up my fist and she bumps a mini version with it, giggling when we 'blow it up.'

"Where's Mister Brant?" she suddenly asks, looking around.

I shrug, rising to my feet. "Not sure. Why don't you go track him down and escort him to the garden? We don't want him to be late for the ceremony."

She nods solemnly, the importance of her task taken very seriously. "I'll find him right now," she promises, before turning and, with a peal of laughter, taking off through the open doorway.

I turn back to the mirror, straightening the line of the dress.

"She's an adorable little girl," the woman behind me says, her eyes meeting mine in the mirror.

I nod, smiling at the memory of Hannah aboard our jet, her hands touching every surface twice before the plane even took off. "She is. Always has been. Adorable with a side of demon," I warn her. "Keep an eye on her; she finds trouble as quickly as hugs." A timely crash sounds from the direction of the kitchen, sending the woman before me fleeing. I laugh, stepping toward the vanity and grabbing the final piece of today, the diamond studs that Brant gave me our first Christmas together, putting them on as I stare in the mirror.

My wedding day — a big moment about to occur — the forever joining of my and Brant's lives. I search my eyes for trepidation, but find none. I'm not surprised. I can mark the leaving of Lee as clearly as my birth, the change in our relationship greater than I would ever have expected. Looking back, it was as if our relationship began anew that day.

Chapter 76

I walk down a short aisle lined with hibiscus, our Hawaii home behind me, Brant and a pastor alone before me, the ocean the background to this moment of our love.

Each step closer is like a page turning in our lives.

Step. The night of Brant's return from the doctor's, Lee having finally left our lives. His hands on me the moment we stepped inside, a tumble of us both onto the couch, his hands frantic, needy as they yanked the clothes from my body until I was bare beneath him. He fucked me as he never had, as Lee used to, as if he was marking me, making me his. He gripped my hair when he thrust into me. Moaned my name when he turned me over and took me from behind. He made me come with his cock, then his fingers, then his mouth, before pounding a rhythm into me that I would never forget. Afterward, he took me to the floor in the center of the great room, a fire before us, our chests heaving with satisfied breaths as he rolled me over and took me a second time, slower. More like the Brant I loved. He whispered his love as he mended every fuck he had just broken me with. Then we slept, our limbs intertwined. And when the sun rose through the windows, he was still there. My Brant. And only my Brant.

Step. His abandonment of Jillian, her removal from the Board of Directors, his new place in the company executive in addition to developmental. He doesn't work like he used to, the door to his office now open to employees, two assistants keeping his schedule on track in a way that Jillian never could. He's formed collaborative teams, no longer a solo team of creation. I love seeing him working with others, the awe in the developers' eyes when they see the scope of his intelligence. We were all worried about the possible loss of intellectual ability, the risk discussed and accepted by Brant. But his therapy, while affecting other pieces of his personality, hasn't hampered that in any way.

Step. Lee is still there, pieces of him sprinkled through Brant's personality, sparkling like glitter when it hits the sun. I see it in the smile Brant now carries, a wide grin that squeezes my heart every time it flashes. I see it in the laugh that occasionally bursts, in the cocky wink that I got last week when he stepped from the shower and caught my eyes on his naked body. Sometimes, when he watches me, I swear he is Lee, smiling at me, his eyes staring like he knows a secret I don't, like that secret is the key to my soul and I am all his to do with as he wants. I thought I would be losing Lee but instead I've only gained more sides of Brant.

Step. I see a dart of white and the slip of Hannah's hand into Brant's, her face upturned to his as she smiled. Brant's been joining me on Tuesdays at the HYA compound. He's grown to love Hannah as much as I do. Tonight, after the ceremony, once her belly is fully of cake and toes are white with Hawaiian sand, we'll ask her. See if she will allow us to have her as part of our family. Brant's already had the attorney complete the paperwork. All it needs is her blessing and he'll have them process the adoption. I smile at the two of them, his grin gentle as he pulls his eyes from her and meets mine. There, in the windows to his soul, I see our future. More babies, two or three from our union, maybe more from HYA. Summers in this house, winters back home, giving Windere the family it deserves.

Step. I stop before him and look into his face. Feel my future in his intense stare, in the connection that is now iron strong. We are a team, having jumped hurtles that will make the rest of our life a cakewalk. I have lied for this man, stole for him, cheated on him with him, and sold my soul to his with our first kiss.

I love this man. I repeat, after the pastor, the simple words that interlock our lives, and feel his hand squeeze mine. Leaning forward, I close my eyes and kiss my husband.

Chapter 77

BRANT

I don't know how I got lucky enough to end up with this woman. For my soul to find her, steal her, convince her of love enough to keep her through the rollercoaster of hell that has been our relationship. She is more than my broken self will ever deserve, but I can never let her go, she owns, whether she knows it or not, all parts of me, every inch of my body and soul. Her unconditional love brought me to life. Pulled me from a dry, lonely existence before saving me, quite literally, from myself.

One day, I will deserve her. One day, I will fully fix myself and prove to her that it has been worth it. I will spend every ounce of effort getting to that day. I am moving closer, slowly tying up the loose ends of my sanity.

We went to the police the night I remembered Sheila's death. I told them about the man. His tattoos, the location of his house. We drove by and found it, my memory of that day now painfully clear, as if the decades left it untouched and brand new, in a secret corner of my mind. I had hoped for an arrest, but the officer informed me that the man, one Nick Coppen, died six years after Sheila disappeared. That evidence found in his home had implicated him in multiple unsolved cases. I left that station lighter than I had entered it, Lana's hand tight and strong in mine.

My journey in this relationship hasn't been as difficult as hers, but there were times I struggled. Thank God I didn't walk away when I suspected an affair. Thank God my heart kept an iron grip on her and wouldn't let me move. The frustration, the unknowing, the jealousy… it was grueling, but reinforced one of the first things I said to Lana: 'It was worth it as soon as I saw you'.

And it was. It was more than worth it. It was the start of my life, the day my heart started beating.

I love this woman. I will always love her, as will every part of my soul.

THE END

Epilogue

It is all her fault. I knew she was trouble, should have worked harder, done more, increased Brant's meds until he broke and scared her away. Had she not appeared, wormed her way into his life, then everything would be fine. Going according to plan. BSX strong, Brant and I leading it into the next millennium. Whores keeping him satisfied, the meds keeping him productive. His other personalities weren't hurting anyone; they had been keeping to themselves. Life had been good, all due to my hard work and planning. Nothing in life is given; everything is earned or taken. I earned a great deal. Took the pieces I couldn't earn. And I had reaped the rewards, as had Brant. He would have nothing without me. How could he forget that? How could he let her blind him to that fact?

I need to separate them. Because of Layana, my own brother won't speak to me, won't visit. Because of Layana, I have been kicked out of BSX like a criminal, my titles stripped, any authority I once had revoked. I built that business, slaved over it for two decades. Poured my hopes and dreams into the building's foundation, only to be locked out. If I separate them, I'll have another chance. To speak to him. Get him back to his true potential. The drugs will do that. I can help him do that. Assemble the old team. Put the shadows back on him. Rehire Dr. F. Rehire Molly. Maybe she can dive into Brant's brain and pull Lee back out, even if she did fail horribly the first time. Yes, with proper planning, intelligent design, it can all be made right again. It has to be made right again. I can't continue in this life as it is. I have nothing. I have no one.

And she ... she has everything.

Excerpt, The Journal of Jillian Sharp.

This journal was confiscated from patient's room during a routine search on March 23rd. Also confiscated were three white pills that appear to have been taken from other patients. Due to the content of written matter, as well as the possession of narcotics, patient will continue her involuntary *admittance until such a time that there is no risk of harm to herself or others. As of the date of this report, her next evaluation will be conducted in 86 days.*

Report taken by John Ferguson, Hendu Facility for the Mentally Unstable.

Note from Author

Thank you, dear reader, for sticking with this story until the end. I hope you enjoyed the rollercoaster I just took you on. For me, the writing of this story was one of the most emotional journeys I have made – I left a piece of my heart within these pages. This book intimidated the hell out of me. I can only hope I did it some form of justice.

DISCLAIMER: Before beginning this book and, while writing, I researched DID (Dissociative Identity Disorder). I quickly realized that there were certain characteristics of DID that would make it difficult to write this story in a manner that would be most entertaining to you, the reader. So I have taken some liberties with the telling of this story. Please be aware that, in a real world situation, an individual struggling with this condition might not act in the manner depicted here. If you are interested in learning more about DID, feel free to check out a link of informative resources here: www.alessandratorre.com/DID/

Also, if you enjoyed this book, please consider recommending it to friends, or leaving a review. Also, feel free to check out my website to view the other books that I have available:

www.alessandratorre.com

Want more?
Join my newsletter and get a deleted scene from Black Lies:

www.AlessandraTorre.com/bldeletedscene1

Printed in Great Britain
by Amazon